THE WITNESS
FOR THE DEFENCE

THE WITNESS
FOR THE DEFENCE

BY

A. E. W. MASON

WILDSIDE PRESS

Published by
Wildside Press, LLC
P.O. Box 301
Holicong, PA 18928-0301 USA
www.wildsidepress.com

Wildside Press Edition: MMIII

CONTENTS

v

CONTENTS

THE WITNESS
FOR THE DEFENCE

THE WITNESS
FOR THE DEFENCE

CHAPTER I

HENRY THRESK

The beginning of all this difficult business was a little speech which Mrs. Thresk fell into a habit of making to her son. She spoke it the first time on the spur of the moment without thought or intention. But she saw that it hurt. So she used it again—to keep Henry in his proper place.

"You have no right to talk, Henry," she would say in the hard practical voice which so completed her self-sufficiency. "You are not earning your living. You are still dependent upon us;" and she would add with a note of triumph: "Remember, if anything were to happen to your dear father you would have to shift for yourself, for everything has been left to me."

Mrs. Thresk meant no harm. She was utterly without imagination and had no special delicacy of taste to supply its place—that was all. People and words —she was at pains to interpret neither the one nor the other and she used both at random. She no more contemplated anything happening to her husband, to quote

1

her phrase, than she understood the effect her barbarous little speech would have on a rather reserved schoolboy.

Nor did Henry himself help to enlighten her. He was shrewd enough to recognise the futility of any attempt. No! He just looked at her curiously and held his tongue. But the words were not forgotten. They roused in him a sense of injustice. For in the ordinary well-to-do circle, in which the Thresks lived, boys were expected to be an expense to their parents; and after all, as he argued, he had not asked to be born. And so after much brooding, there sprang up in him an antagonism to his family and a fierce determination to owe to it as little as he could.

There was a full share of vanity no doubt in the boy's resolve, but the antagonism had struck roots deeper than his vanity; and at an age when other lads were vaguely dreaming themselves into Admirals and Field-Marshals and Prime-Ministers Henry Thresk, content with lower ground, was mapping out the stages of a good but perfectly feasible career. When he reached the age of thirty he must be beginning to make money; at thirty-five he must be on the way to distinction—his name must be known beyond the immediate circle of his profession; at forty-five he must be holding public office. Nor was his profession in any doubt. There was but one which offered these rewards to a man starting in life without money to put down —the Bar.

2

HENRY THRESK

So to the Bar in due time Henry Thresk was called; and when something did happen to his father he was trained for the battle. A bank failed and the failure ruined and killed old Mr. Thresk. From the ruins just enough was scraped to keep his widow, and one or two offers of employment were made to Henry Thresk.

But he was tenacious as he was secret. He refused them, and with the help of pupils, journalism and an occasional spell as an election agent, he managed to keep his head above water until briefs began slowly to come in.

So far then Mrs. Thresk's stinging speeches seemed to have been justified. But at the age of twenty-eight he took a holiday. He went down for a month into Sussex, and there the ordered scheme of his life was threatened. It stood the attack; and again it is possible to plead in its favour with a good show of argument. But the attack, nevertheless, brings into light another point of view.

Prudence, for instance, the disputant might urge, is all very well in the ordinary run of life, but when the great moments come conduct wants another inspiration. Such an one would consider that holiday with a thought to spare for Stella Derrick, who during its passage saw much of Henry Thresk. The actual hour when the test came happened on one of the last days of August.

3

CHAPTER II

They were riding along the top of the South Downs between Singleton and Arundel, and when they came to where the old Roman road from Chichester climbs over Bignor Hill, Stella Derrick raised her hand and halted. She was then nineteen and accounted lovely by others besides Henry Thresk, who on this morning rode at her side. She was delicately yet healthfully fashioned, with blue eyes under broad brows, raven hair and a face pale and crystal-clear. But her lips were red and the colour came easily into her cheeks.

She pointed downwards to the track slanting across the turf from the brow of the hill.

"That's Stane Street. I promised to show it you."

"Yes," answered Thresk, taking his eyes slowly from her face. It was a morning rich with sunlight, noisy with blackbirds, and she seemed to him a necessary part of it. She was alive with it and gave rather than took of its gold. For not even that finely chiselled nose of hers could impart to her anything of the look of a statue.

"Yes. They went straight, didn't they, those old centurions?" he said.

4

He moved his horse and stood in the middle of the track, looking across a valley of forest and meadow to Halnaker Down, six miles away in the southwest. Straight in the line of his eyes over a shoulder of the down rose a tall fine spire—the spire of Chichester Cathedral, and farther on he could see the water in Bosham Creek like a silver mirror, and the Channel rippling silver beyond. He turned round. Beneath him lay the blue dark weald of Sussex, and through it he imagined the hidden line of the road driving straight as a ruler to London.

"No going about!" he said. "If a hill was in the way the road climbed over it; if a marsh it was built through it."

They rode on slowly along the great whaleback of grass, winding in and out amongst brambles and patches of yellow-flaming gorse. The day was still even at this height; and when, far away, a field of long grass under a stray wind bent from edge to edge with the swift motion of running water, it took them both by surprise. And they met no one. They seemed to ride in the morning of a new clean world. They rose higher on to Duncton Down, and then the girl spoke.

"So this is your last day here."

He gazed about him out towards the sea, eastwards down the slope to the dark trees of Arundel, backwards over the weald to the high ridge of Blackdown.

"I shall look back upon it."

"Yes," she said. "It's a day to look back upon." She ran over in her mind the days of this last month since he had come to the inn at Great Beeding and friends of her family had written to her parents of his coming. "It's the most perfect of all your days here. I am glad. I want you to carry back with you good memories of our Sussex."

"I shall do that," said he, "but for another reason."

Stella pushed on a foot or two ahead of him.

"Well," she said, "no doubt the Temple will be stuffy."

"Nor was I thinking of the Temple."

"No?"

"No."

She rode on a little way whilst he followed. A great bee buzzed past their heads and settled in the cup of a wild rose. In a copse beside them a thrush shot into the air a quiverful of clear melody.

Stella spoke again, not looking at her companion, and in a low voice and bravely with a sweet confusion of her blood.

"I am very glad to hear you say that, for I was afraid that I had let you see more than I should have cared for you to see—unless you had been anxious to see it too."

She waited for an answer, still keeping her distance just a foot or two ahead, and the answer did not come.

A vague terror began to possess her that things which could never possibly be were actually happening to her. She spoke again with a tremor in her voice and all the confidence gone out of it. Almost it appealed that she should not be put to shame before herself.

"It would have been a little humiliating to remember, if that had been true."

Then upon the ground she saw the shadow of Thresk's horse creep up until the two rode side by side. She looked at him quickly with a doubtful wavering smile and looked down again. What did all the trouble in his face portend? Her heart thumped and she heard him say:

"Stella, I have something very difficult to say to you."

He laid a hand gently upon her arm, but she wrenched herself free. Shame was upon her—shame unendurable. She tingled with it from head to foot. She turned to him suddenly a face grown crimson and eyes which brimmed with tears.

"Oh," she cried aloud, "that I should have been such a fool!" and she swayed forward in her saddle. But before he could reach out an arm to hold her she was upright again, and with a cut of her whip she was off at a gallop.

"Stella," he cried, but she only used her whip the more. She galloped madly and blindly over the grass, not knowing whither, not caring, loathing herself.

7

Thresk galloped after her, but her horse, maddened by her whip and the thud of the hoofs behind, held its advantage. He settled down to the pursuit with a jumble of thoughts in his brain.

"If to-day were only ten years on. . . . As it is it would be madness . . . madness and squalor and the end of everything. . . . Between us we haven't a couple of pennies to rub together. . . . How she rides! . . . She was never meant for Brixton. . . . No, nor I. . . . Why didn't I hold my tongue? . . . Oh what a fool, what a fool! Thank Heaven the horses come out of a livery stable. . . . They can't go on for ever and—oh, my God! there are rabbit-holes on the Downs." And his voice rose to a shout: "Stella! Stella!"

But she never looked over her shoulder. She fled the more desperately, shamed through and through! Along the high ridge, between the bushes and the beech-trees, their shadows flitted over the turf, to a jingle of bits and the thunder of hoofs. Duncton Beacon rose far behind them; they had crossed the road and Charlton forest was slipping past like dark water before the mad race came to an end. Stella became aware that escape was impossible. Her horse was spent, she herself reeling. She let her reins drop loose and the gallop changed to a trot, the trot to a walk. She noticed with gratitude that Thresk was giving her time. He too had fallen to a walk behind her, and quite slowly he came to her side. She turned to him at once.

"This is good country for a gallop, isn't it?"

"Rabbit-holes though," said he. "You were lucky."

He answered absently. There was something which had got to be said now. He could not let this girl to whom he owed—well, the only holiday that he had ever taken, go home shamed by a mistake, which after all she had not made. He was very near indeed to saying yet more. The inclination was strong in him, but not so strong as the methods of his life. Marriage now—that meant to his view the closing of all the avenues of advancement, and a life for both below both their needs.

"Stella, just listen to me. I want you to know that had things been different I should have rejoiced beyond words."

"Oh, don't!" she cried.

"I must," he answered and she was silent. "I want you to know," he repeated, stammering and stumbling, afraid lest each word meant to heal should only pierce the deeper. "Before I came here there was no one. Since I came here there has been—you. Oh, my dear, I would have been very glad. But I am obscure— without means. There are years in front of me before I shall be anything else. I couldn't ask you to share them—or I should have done so before now."

In her mind ran the thought: what queer unimportant things men think about! The early years! Wouldn't their difficulties, their sorrows be the real savour of life and make it worth remembrance, worth treasuring? But men had the right of speech. Not again would she forget that. She bowed her head and he blundered on.

"For you there'll be a better destiny. There's that great house in the Park with its burnt walls. I should like to see that rebuilt and you in your right place, its mistress." And his words ceased as Stella abruptly turned to him. She was breathing quickly and she looked at him with a wonder in her trouble.

"And it hurts you to say this!" she said. "Yes, it actually hurts you."

"What else could I say?"

Her face softened as she looked and heard. It was not that he was cold of blood or did not care. There was more than discomfort in his voice, there was a very real distress. And in his eyes his heart ached for her to see. Something of her pride was restored to her. She fell at once to his tune, but she was conscious that both of them talked treacheries.

"Yes, you are right. It wouldn't have been possible. You have your name and your fortune to make. I too —I shall marry, I suppose, some one"—and she suddenly smiled rather bitterly—"who will give me a Rolls-Royce motor-car." And so they rode on very reasonably.

ON BIGNOR HILL

Noon had passed. A hush had fallen upon that high world of grass and sunlight. The birds were still. They talked of this and that, the latest crisis in Europe and the growth of Socialism, all very wisely and with great indifference like well-bred people at a dinner-party. Not thus had Stella thought to ride home when the message had come that morning that the horses would be at her door before ten. She had ridden out clothed on with dreams of gold. She rode back with her dreams in tatters and a sort of incredulity that to her too, as to other girls, all this pain had come.

They came to a bridle-path which led downwards through a thicket of trees to the weald and so descended upon Great Beeding. They rode through the little town, past the inn where Thresk was staying and the iron gates of a Park where, amidst elm-trees, the blackened ruins of a great house gaped to the sky.

"Some day you will live there again," said Thresk, and Stella's lips twitched with a smile of humour.

"I shall be very glad after to-day to leave the house I am living in," she said quietly, and the words struck him dumb. He had subtlety enough to understand her. The rooms would mock her with memories of vain dreams. Yet he kept silence. It was too late in any case to take back what he had said; and even if she would listen to him marriage wouldn't be fair. He would be hampered, and that, just at this time in

11

his life, would mean failure—failure for her no less than for him. They must be prudent—prudent and methodical, and so the great prizes would be theirs.

A mile beyond, a mile of yellow lanes between high hedges, they came to the village of Little Beeding, one big house and a few thatched cottages clustered amongst roses and great trees on the bank of a small river. Thither old Mr. Derrick and his wife and his daughter had gone after the fire at Hinksey Park had completed the ruin which disastrous speculations had begun; and at the gate of one of the cottages the riders stopped and dismounted.

"I shall not see you again after to-day," said Stella. "Will you come in for a moment?"

Thresk gave the horses to a passing labourer to hold and opened the gate.

"I shall be disturbing your people at their luncheon," he said.

"I don't want you to go in to them," said the girl. "I will say goodbye to them for you."

Thresk followed her up the garden-path, wondering what it was that she had still to say to him. She led him into a small room at the back of the house, looking out upon the lawn. Then she stood in front of him.

"Will you kiss me once, please," she said simply, and she stood with her arms hanging at her side, whilst he kissed her on the lips.

"Thank you," she said. "Now will you go?"

He left her standing in the little room and led the horses back to the inn. That afternoon he took the train to London.

CHAPTER III

It was not until a day late in January eight years afterwards that Thresk saw the face of Stella Derrick again; and then it was only in a portrait. He came upon it too in a most unlikely place. About five o'clock upon that afternoon he drove out of the town of Bombay up to one of the great houses on Malabar Hill and asked for Mrs. Carruthers. He was shown into a drawing-room which looked over Back Bay to the great buildings of the city, and in a moment Mrs. Carruthers came to him with her hands outstretched.

"So you've won. My husband telephoned to me. We do thank you! Victory means so much to us."

The Carruthers were a young couple who, the moment after they had inherited the larger share in the great firm of Templeton & Carruthers, Bombay merchants, had found themselves involved in a partnership suit due to one or two careless phrases in a solicitor's letter. The case had been the great case of the year in Bombay. The issue had been doubtful, the stake enormous and Thresk, who three years before had taken silk, had been fetched by young Carruthers from England to fight it.

14

"Yes. We've won," he said. "Judgment was given in our favour this afternoon."

"You are dining with us to-night, aren't you?"

"Thank you, yes," said Thresk. "At half-past eight."

"Yes."

Mrs. Carruthers gave him some tea and chattered pleasantly while he drank it. She was fair-haired and pretty, a lady of enthusiasms and uplifted hands, quite without observation or knowledge, yet with power to astonish. For every now and then some little shrewd wise saying would gleam out of the placid flow of her trivialities and make whoever heard it wonder for a moment whether it was her own or whether she had heard it from another. But it was her own. For she gave no special importance to it as she would have done had it been a remark she had thought worth remembering. She just uttered it and slipped on, noticing no difference in value between what she now said and what she had said a second ago. To her the whole world was a marvel and all things in it equally amazing. Besides she had no memory.

"I suppose that now you are free," she said, "you will go up into the central Provinces and see something of India."

"But I am not free," replied Thresk. "I must get back immediately to England."

"So soon!" exclaimed Mrs. Carruthers. "Now

isn't that a pity! You ought to see the Taj—oh, you really ought!—by moonlight or in the morning. I don't know which is best, and the Ridge too!—the Ridge at Delhi. You really mustn't leave India without seeing the Ridge. Can't things wait in London?"

"Yes, things can, but people won't," answered Thresk, and Mrs. Carruthers was genuinely distressed that he should depart from India without a single journey in a train.

"I can't help it," he said, smiling back into her mournful eyes. "Apart from my work, Parliament meets early in February."

"Oh, to be sure, you are in Parliament," she exclaimed. "I had forgotten." She shook her fair head in wonder at the industry of her visitor. "I can't think how you manage it all. Oh, you must need a holiday."

Thresk laughed.

"I am thirty-six, so I have a year or two still in front of me before I have the right to break down. I'll save up my holidays for my old age."

"But you are not married," cried Mrs. Carruthers. "You can't do that. You can't grow comfortably old unless you're married. You will want to work then to get through the time. You had better take your holidays now."

"Very well. I shall have twelve days upon the steamer. When does it go?" asked Thresk as he rose from his chair.

16

"On Friday, and this is Monday," said Mrs. Carruthers. "You certainly haven't much time to go anywhere, have you?"

"No," replied Thresk, and Mrs. Carruthers saw his face quicken suddenly to surprise. He actually caught his breath; he stared, no longer aware of her presence in the room. He was looking over her head towards the grand piano which stood behind her chair; and she began to run over in her mind the various ornaments which encumbered it. A piece of Indian drapery covered the top and on the drapery stood a little group of Dresden China figures, a crystal cigarette-box, some knick-knacks and half-a-dozen photographs in silver frames. It must be one of those photographs, she decided, which had caught his eye, which had done more than catch his eye. For she was looking up at Thresk's face all this while, and the surprise had gone from it. It seemed to her that he was moved.

"You have the portrait of a friend of mine there," he said, and he crossed the room to the piano.

Mrs. Carruthers turned round.

"Oh, Stella Ballantyne!" she cried. "Do you know her, Mr. Thresk?"

"Ballantyne?" said Thresk. For a moment or two he was silent. Then he asked: "She is married then?"

"Yes, didn't you know? She has been married for a long time."

"It's a long time since I have heard of her," said Thresk. He looked again at the photograph.

17

"When was this taken?"

"A few months ago. She sent it to me in October. She is beautiful, don't you think?"

"Yes."

But it was not the beauty of the girl who had ridden along the South Downs with him eight years ago. There was more of character in the face now, less, much less, of youth and none of the old gaiety. The open frankness had gone. The big dark eyes which looked out straight at Thresk as he stood before them had, even in that likeness, something of aloofness and reserve. And underneath, in a contrast which seemed to him startling, there was her name signed in the firm running hand in which she had written the few notes which passed between them during that month in Sussex. Thresk looked back again at the photograph and then resumed his seat.

"Tell me about her, Mrs. Carruthers," he said. "You hear from her often?"

"Oh no! Stella doesn't write many letters, and I don't know her very well."

"But you have her photograph," said Thresk, "and signed by her."

"Oh yes. She stayed with me last Christmas, and I simply made her get her portrait taken. Just think! She hadn't been taken for years. Can you understand it? She declared she was bored with it. Isn't that curious? However, I persuaded her and she gave me one. But I had to force her to write on it."

18

"Then she was in Bombay last winter?" said Thresk slowly.

"Yes." And then Mrs. Carruthers had an idea. "Oh," she exclaimed, "if you are really interested in Stella I'll put Mrs. Repton next to you to-night."

"Thank you very much," said Thresk. "But who is Mrs. Repton?"

Mrs. Carruthers sat forward in her chair.

"Well, she's Stella's great friend—very likely her only real friend in India. Stella's so reserved. I simply adore her, but she quite prettily and politely keeps me always at arm's length. If she has ever opened out to anybody it's to Jane Repton. You see Charlie Repton was Collector at Agra before he came into the Bombay Presidency, and so they went up to Mussoorie for the hot weather. The Ballantynes happened actually to have the very next bungalow—now wasn't that strange?—so naturally they became acquainted. I mean the Ballantynes and the Reptons did. . . ."

"But one moment, Mrs. Carruthers," said Thresk, breaking in upon the torrent of words. "Am I right in guessing that Mrs. Ballantyne lives in India?"

"But of course!" cried Mrs. Carruthers.

"She is actually in India now?"

"To be sure she is!"

Thresk was quite taken aback by the news.

"I had no idea of it," he said slowly, and Mrs. Carruthers replied sweetly:

"But lots of people live in India, Mr. Thresk.

19

Didn't you know that? We are not the uttermost ends of the earth."

Thresk set to work to make his peace. He had not heard of Mrs. Ballantyne for so long. It seemed strange to him to find himself suddenly near to her now—that is if he was near. He just avoided that other exasperating trick of treating India as if it was a provincial town and all its inhabitants neighbours. But he only just avoided it. Mrs. Carruthers, however, was easily appeased.

"Yes," she said. "Stella has lived in India for the best part of eight years. She came out with some friends in the winter, made Captain Ballantyne's acquaintance and married him almost at once—in January, I think it was. Of course I only know from what I've been told. I was a schoolgirl in England at the time."

"Of course," Thresk agreed. He was conscious of a sharp little stab of resentment. So very quickly Stella had forgotten that morning on the Downs! It must have been in the autumn of that same year that she had gone out to India, and by February she was married. The resentment was quite unjustified, as no one knew better than himself. But he was a man; and men cannot easily endure so swift an obliteration of their images from the thoughts and the hearts of the ladies who have admitted that they loved them. None the less he pressed for details. Who was Ballantyne?

What was his position? After all he was obviously not the millionaire to whom in a more generous moment he had given Stella. He caught himself on a descent to the meanness of rejoicing upon that. Meanwhile Mrs. Carruthers rippled on.

"Captain Ballantyne? Oh, he's a most remarkable man! Older than Stella, certainly, but a man of great knowledge and insight. People think most highly of him. Languages come as easily to him as crochet-work to a woman."

This paragon had been Resident in the Principality of Bakuta to the north of Bombay when Stella had first arrived. But he had been moved now to Chitipur in Rajputana. It was supposed that he was writing in his leisure moments a work which would be the very last word upon the native Principalities of Central India. Oh, Stella was to be congratulated! And Mrs. Carruthers, in her fine mansion on Malabar Hill, breathed a sigh of envy at the position of the wife of a high official of the British *Raj*.

Thresk looked over again to the portrait on the piano.

"I am very glad," he said cordially as once more he rose.

"But you shall sit next to Mrs. Repton to-night," said Mrs. Carruthers. "And she will tell you more."

"Thank you," answered Thresk. "I only wished to know that things are going well with Mrs. Ballantyne —that was all."

CHAPTER IV

JANE REPTON

Mrs. Carruthers kept her promise. She went in herself with Henry Thresk, as she had always meant to do, but she placed Mrs. Repton upon his left just round the bend of the table. Thresk stole a glance at her now and then as he listened to the rippling laughter of his hostess during the first courses. She was a tall woman and rather stout, with a pleasant face and a direct gaze. Thresk gave her the age of thirty-five and put her down as a cheery soul. Whether she was more he had to wait to learn with what patience he could. He was free to turn to her at last and he began without any preliminaries.

"You know a friend of mine," he said.

"I do?"

"Yes."

"Who is it?"

"Mrs. Ballantyne."

He noticed at once a change in Mrs. Repton. The frankness disappeared from her face; her eyes grew wary.

"I see," she said slowly. "I was wondering why I

was placed next to you, for you are the lion of the evening and there are people here of more importance than myself. I knew it wasn't for my *beaux yeux.*"

She turned again to Thresk.

"So you know my Stella?"

"Yes. I knew her in England before she came out here and married. I have not, of course, seen her since. I want you to tell me about her."

Mrs. Repton looked him over with a careful scrutiny.

"Mrs. Carruthers has no doubt told you that she married very well."

"Yes; and that Ballantyne is a remarkable man," said Thresk.

Mrs. Repton nodded.

"Very well then?" she said, and her voice was a challenge.

"I am not contented," Thresk replied. Mrs. Repton turned her eyes to her plate and said demurely:

"There might be more than one reason for that."

Thresk abandoned all attempt to fence with her. Mrs. Repton was not of those women who would lightly give their women-friends away. Her phrase "my Stella" had, besides, revealed a world of love and championship. Thresk warmed to her because of it. He threw reticence to the winds.

"I am going to give you the real reason, Mrs. Repton. I saw her photograph this afternoon on Mrs. Carruthers' piano, and it left me wondering whether

23

happiness could set so much character in a woman's face."

Mrs. Repton shrugged her shoulders.

"Some of us age quickly here."

"Age was not the new thing which I read in that photograph."

Mrs. Repton did not answer. Only her eyes sounded him. She seemed to be judging the stuff of which he was made.

"And if I doubted her happiness this afternoon I must doubt it still more now," he continued.

"Why?" exclaimed Mrs. Repton.

"Because of your reticence, Mrs. Repton," he answered. "For you have been reticent. You have been on guard. I like you for it," he added with a smile of genuine friendliness. "May I say that? But from the first moment when I mentioned Stella Ballantyne's name you shouldered your musket."

Mrs. Repton neither denied nor accepted his statement. She kept looking at him and away from him as though she were still not sure of him, and at times she drew in her breath sharply, as though she had already taken upon herself some great responsibility and now regretted it. In the end she turned to him abruptly.

"I am puzzled," she cried. "I think it's strange that since you are Stella's friend I knew nothing of that friendship—nothing whatever."

JANE REPTON

Thresk shrugged his shoulders.

"It is years since we met, as I told you. She has new interests."

"They have not destroyed the old ones. We remember home things out here, all of us. Stella like the rest. Why, I thought that I knew her whole life in England, and here's a definite part of it—perhaps a very important part—of which I am utterly ignorant. She has spoken of many friends to me; of you never. I am wondering why."

She spoke obviously without any wish to hurt. Yet the words did hurt. She saw Thresk redden as she uttered them, and a swift wild hope flamed like a rose in her heart: if this man with the brains and the money and the perseverance sitting at her side should turn out to be the Perseus for her beautiful chained Andromeda, far away there in the state of Chitipur! The lines of a poem came into her thoughts.

> "I know; the world proscribes not love,
> Allows my finger to caress
> Your lips' contour and downiness
> Provided it supplies the glove."

Suppose that here at her side was the man who would dispense with the glove! She looked again at Thresk. The lean strong face suggested that he might, if he wanted hard enough. All her life had been passed in the support of authority and law. Authority—that was her husband's profession. But just for this hour, as she thought of Stella Ballantyne, lawlessness shone out to her desirable as a star.

"No, she has never once mentioned your name, Mr. Thresk."

Again Thresk was conscious of the little pulse of resentment beating at his heart.

"She has no doubt forgotten me."

Mrs. Repton shook her head.

"That's one explanation. There might be another."

"What is it?"

"That she remembers you too much."

Mrs. Repton was a little startled by her own audacity, but it provoked nothing but an incredulous laugh from her companion.

"I am afraid that's not very likely," he said. There was no hint of elation in his voice nor any annoyance. If he felt either, why, he was on guard no less than she. Mrs. Repton was inclined to throw up her hands in despair. She was baffled and she was little likely, as she knew, to get any light.

"If you take the man you know best of all," she used to say, "you still know nothing at all of what he's like when he's alone with a woman, especially if it's a woman for whom he cares—unless the woman talks."

Very often the woman does talk and the most intimate and private facts come in a little while to be shouted from the housetops. But Stella Ballantyne

26

did not talk. She had talked once, and once only, under a great stress to Jane Repton; but even then Thresk had nothing to do with her story at all.

Thresk turned quickly towards her.

"In a moment Mrs. Carruthers will get up. Her eyes are collecting the women and the women are collecting their shoes. What have you to tell me?"

Mrs. Repton wanted to speak. Thresk gave her confidence. He seemed to be a man without many illusions, he was no romantic sentimentalist. She went back to the poem of which the lines had been chasing one another through her head all through this dinner, as a sort of accompaniment to their conversation. Had he found it out? she asked herself—

" The world and what it fears."

Thus she hung hesitating while Mrs. Carruthers gathered in her hands her gloves and her fan. There was a woman at the other end of the table however who would not stop talking. She was in the midst of some story and heeded not the signals of her hostess. Jane Repton wished she would go on talking for the rest of the evening, and recognised that the wish was a waste of time and grew flurried. She had to make up her mind to say something which should be true or to lie. Yet she was too staunch to betray the confidence of her friend unless the betrayal meant her friend's salvation. But just as the woman at the end of the

27

table ceased to talk an inspiration came to her. She would say nothing to Thresk, but if he had eyes to see she would place him where the view was good.

"I have this to say," she answered in a low quick voice. "Go yourself to Chitipur. You sail on Friday, I think? And to-day is Monday. You can make the journey there and back quite easily in the time."

"I can?" asked Thresk.

"Yes. Travel by the night-mail up to Ajmere to-morrow night. You will be in Chitipur on Wednesday afternoon. That gives you twenty-four hours there, and you can still catch the steamer here on Friday."

"You advise that?"

"Yes, I do," said Mrs. Repton.

Mrs. Carruthers rose from the table and Jane Repton had no further word with Thresk that night. In the drawing-room Mrs. Carruthers led him from woman to woman, allowing him ten minutes for each one.

"He might be Royalty or her pet Pekingese," cried Mrs. Repton in exasperation. For now that her blood had cooled she was not so sure that her advice had been good. The habit of respect for authority resumed its ancient place in her. She might be planting that night the seed of a very evil flower. "Respectability" had seemed to her a magnificent poem as she sat at the dinner-table. Here in the drawing-room she began to think that it was not for every-day use. She wished

28

JANE REPTON

a word now with Thresk, so that she might make light of the advice which she had given. "I had no business to interfere," she kept repeating to herself whilst she talked with her host. "People get what they want if they want it enough, but they can't control the price they have to pay. Therefore it was no business of mine to interfere."

But Thresk took his leave and gave her no chance for a private word. She drove homewards a few minutes later with her husband; and as they descended the hill to the shore of Back Bay he said:

"I had a moment's conversation with Thresk after you had left the dining-room, and what do you think?"

"Tell me!"

"He asked me for a letter of introduction to Ballantyne at Chitipur."

"But he knows Stella!" exclaimed Jane Repton.

"Does he? He didn't tell me that! He simply said that he had time to see Chitipur before he sailed and asked for a line to the Resident."

"And you promised to give him one?"

"Of course. I am to send it to the Taj Mahal hotel to-morrow morning."

Mrs. Repton was a little startled. She did not understand at all why Thresk asked for the letter and, not understanding, was the more alarmed. The request seemed to imply not merely that he had decided to make the journey but that during the hour or so

29

since they had sat at the dinner-table he had formed some definite and serious plan.

"Did you tell him anything?" she asked rather timidly.

"Not a word," replied Repton.

"Not even about—what happened in the hills at Mussoorie?"

"Of course not."

"No, of course not," Jane Repton agreed.

She leaned back against the cushions of the victoria. A clear dark sky of stars wonderfully bright stretched above her head. After the hot day a cool wind blew pleasantly on the hill, and between the trees of the gardens she could see the lights of the city and of a ship here and there in the Bay at their feet.

"But it's not very likely that Thresk will find them at Chitipur," said Repton. "They will probably be in camp."

Mrs. Repton sat forward.

"Yes, that's true. This is the time they go on their tour of inspection. He will miss them." And at once disappointment laid hold of her. Mrs. Repton was not in the mood for logic that evening. She had been afraid a moment since that the train she had laid would bring about a conflagration. Now that she knew it would not even catch fire she passed at once to a passionate regret. Thresk had inspired her with a great confidence. He was the man, she believed, for her Stella. But he was going up to Chitipur! Anything might happen! She leaned back again in the carriage and cried defiantly to the stars.

"I am glad that he's going. I am very glad." And in spite of her conscience her heart leaped joyously in her bosom.

CHAPTER V

THE QUEST

The next night Henry Thresk left Bombay and on the Wednesday afternoon he was travelling in a little white narrow-gauge train across a flat yellow desert which baked and sparkled in the sun. Here and there a patch of green and a few huts marked a railway station and at each gaily-robed natives sprung apparently from nowhere and going no-whither thronged the platform and climbed into the carriages. Thresk looked impatiently through the clouded windows, wondering what he should find in Chitipur if ever he got there. The capital of that state lies aloof from the trunk roads and is reached by a branch railway sixty miles long, which is the private possession of the Maharajah and takes four hours to traverse. For in Chitipur the ancient ways are devoutly followed. Modern ideas of speed and progress may whirl up the big central railroad from Bombay to Ajmere. But they stop at the junction. They do not travel along the Maharajah's private lines to Chitipur, where he, directly descended from an important and most authentic goddess, dispenses life and justice to his subjects without even the assistance of the Press. There is little criticism in the city and less work. A patriarchal calm sleeps in all its streets. In Chitipur it is always Sunday afternoon. Even down by the lake, where the huge white many-storeyed palace contemplates its dark-latticed windows and high balconies mirrored in still water unimaginably blue nothing which could be described as energy is visible. You may see an elephant kneeling placidly in the lake while an attendant polishes up his trunk and his forehead with a brickbat. But the elephant will be too well-mannered to trumpet his enjoyment. Or you may notice a fisherman drowsing in a boat heavy enough to cope with the surf of the Atlantic. But the fisherman will not notice you—not even though you call to him with dulcet promises of rupees. You will, if you wait long enough, see a woman coming down the steps with a pitcher balanced on her head; and indeed perhaps two women. But when your eyes have dwelt upon these wonders you will have seen what there is of movement and life about the shores of those sleeping waters.

It was in accordance with the fitness of things that the city and its lake should be three miles from the railway station and quite invisible to the traveller. The hotel however and the Residency were near to the station, and it was the Residency which had brought Thresk out of the crowds and tumult of Bombay. He put up at the hotel and enclosing Repton's introduction in a covering letter sent it by his bearer down the road. Then he waited; and no answer came.

Finally he asked if his bearer had returned. Quite half an hour he was told, and the man was sent for.

"Well? You delivered my letter?" said Thresk.

"Yes, Sahib."

"And there was no answer?"

"No. No answer, Sahib," replied the man cheerfully.

"Very well."

He waited yet another hour, and since still no acknowledgment had come he strolled along the road himself. He came to a large white house. A flagpost tapered from its roof but no flag blew out its folds. There was a garden about the house, the trim well-ordered garden of the English folk with a lawn and banks of flowers, and a gardener with a hose was busy watering it. Thresk stopped before the hedge. The windows were all shuttered, the big door closed: there was nowhere any sign of the inhabitants.

Thresk turned and walked back to the hotel. He found the bearer laying out a change of clothes for him upon his bed.

"His Excellency is away," he said.

"Yes, Sahib," replied the bearer promptly. "His Excellency gone on inspection tour."

"Then why in heaven's name didn't you tell me?" cried Thresk.

The bearer's face lost all its cheerfulness in a second and became a mask. He was a Madrassee and black as coal. To Thresk it seemed that the man had suddenly withdrawn himself altogether and left merely an image with living eyes. He shrugged his shoulders. He knew that change in his servant. It came at the first note of reproach in his voice and with such completeness that it gave him the shock of a conjurer's trick. One moment the bearer was before him, the next he had disappeared.

"What did you do with the letter?" Thresk asked and was careful that there should be no exasperation in his voice.

The bearer came to life again, his white teeth gleamed in smiles.

"I leave the letter. I give it to the gardener. All letters are sent to his Excellency."

"When?"

"Perhaps this week, perhaps next."

"I see," said Thresk. He stood for a moment or two with his eyes upon the window. Then he moved abruptly.

"We go back to Bombay to-morrow afternoon."

"The Sahib will see Chitipur to-morrow. There are beautiful palaces on the lake."

Thresk laughed, but the laugh was short and bitter.

"Oh yes, we'll do the whole thing in style to-morrow."

He had the tone of a man who has caught himself out in some childish act of folly. He seemed at once angry and ashamed.

35

None the less he was the next morning the complete tourist doing India at express speed during a cold weather. He visited the Museum, he walked through the Elephant Gate into the bazaar, he was rowed over the lake to the island palaces; he admired their marble steps and columns and floors and was confounded by their tinkling blue glass chandeliers. He did the correct thing all through that morning and early in the afternoon climbed into the little train which was to carry him back to Jarwhal Junction and the night mail to Bombay.

"You will have five hours to wait at the junction, Mr. Thresk," said the manager of the hotel, who had come to see him off. "I have put up some dinner for you and there is a dâk-bungalow where you can eat it."

"Thank you," said Thresk, and the train moved off. The sun had set before he reached the junction. When he stepped out on to the platform twilight had come— the swift twilight of the East. Before he had reached the dâk-bungalow the twilight had changed to the splendour of an Indian night. The bungalow was empty of visitors. Thresk's bearer lit a fire and prepared dinner while Thresk wandered outside the door and smoked. He looked across a plain to a long high ridge, where once a city had struggled. Its deserted towers and crumbling walls still crowned the height and made a habitation for beasts and birds. But they were quite hidden now and the sharp line of the ridge was softened. Halfway between the old city and the

36

bungalow a cluster of bright lights shone upon the plain and the red tongues of a fire flickered in the open. Thresk was in no hurry to go back to the bungalow. The first chill of the darkness had gone. The night was cool but not cold; a moon had risen, and that dusty plain had become a place of glamour. From somewhere far away came the sound of a single drum. Thresk garnered up in his thoughts the beauty of that night. It was to be his last night in India. By this time to-morrow Bombay would have sunk below the rim of the sea. He thought of it with regret. He had come up into Rajputana on a definite quest and on the advice of a woman whose judgment he was inclined to trust. And his quest had failed. He was to see for himself. He would see nothing. And still far away the beating of that drum went on—monotonous, mournful, significant—the real call of the East made audible. Thresk leaned forward on his seat, listening, treasuring the sound. He rose reluctantly when his bearer came to tell him that dinner was ready. Thresk took a look round. He pointed to the cluster of lights on the plain.

"Is that a village?" he asked.

"No, Sahib," replied the bearer. "That's his Excellency's camp."

"What!" cried Thresk, swinging round upon his heel. His bearer smiled cheerfully.

"Yes. His Excellency to whom I carried the Sahib's letter. That's his camp for to-night. The keeper of the bungalow told me so. His Excellency camped here yesterday and goes on to-morrow."

"And you never told me!" exclaimed Thresk, and he checked himself. He stood wondering what he should do, when there came suddenly out of the darkness a queer soft scuffling sound, the like of which he had never heard. He heard a heavy breathing and a bubbling noise and then into the fan of light which spread from the window of the bungalow a man in a scarlet livery rode on a camel. The camel knelt; its rider dismounted, and as he dismounted he talked to Thresk's bearer. Something passed from hand to hand and the bearer came back to Thresk with a letter in his hand.

"A chit from his Excellency."

Thresk tore open the envelope and found within it an invitation to dinner, signed "Stephen Ballantyne."

"Your letter has reached me this moment," the note ran. "It came by your train. I am glad not to have missed you altogether and I hope that you will come to-night. The camel will bring you to the camp and take you back in plenty of time for the mail."

After all then the quest had not failed. After all he was to see for himself—what a man could see within two hours, of the inner life of a married couple. Not very much certainly, but a hint perhaps, some token which would reveal to him what it was that had written so much character into Stella Ballantyne's face and driven Jane Repton into warnings and reserve.

THE QUEST

"I will go at once," said Thresk and his bearer translated the words to the camel-driver.

But even so Thresk stayed to look again at the letter. Its handwriting at the first glance, when the unexpected words were dancing before his eyes, had arrested his attention; it was so small, so delicately clear. Thresk's experience had made him quick to notice details and slow to infer from them. Yet this handwriting set him wondering. It might have been the work of some fastidious woman or of some leisured scholar; so much pride of penmanship was there. It certainly agreed with no picture of Stephen Ballantyne which his imagination had drawn.

He mounted the camel behind the driver, and for the next few minutes all his questions and perplexities vanished from his mind. He simply clung to the waist of the driver. For the camel bumped down into steep ditches and scuffled up out of them, climbed over mounds and slid down the further side of them, and all the while Thresk had the sensation of being poised uncertainly in the air as high as a church-steeple. Suddenly however the lights of the camp grew large and the camel padded silently in between the tents. It was halted some twenty yards from a great marquee. Another servant robed in white with a scarlet sash about his waist received Thresk from the camel-driver.

He spoke a few words in Hindustani, but Thresk shook his head. Then the man moved towards the marquee and Thresk followed him. He was conscious of a curious excitement, and only when he caught his breath was he aware that his heart was beating fast. As they neared the tent he heard voices within. They grew louder as he reached it—one was a man's, loud, wrathful, the other was a woman's. It was not raised but it had a ring in it of defiance. The words Thresk could not hear, but he knew the woman's voice. The servant raised the flap of the tent.

"Huzoor, the Sahib is here," he said, and at once both the voices were stilled. As Thresk stood in the doorway both the man and the woman turned. The man, with a little confusion in his manner, came quickly towards him. Over his shoulder Thresk saw Stella Ballantyne staring at him, as if he had risen from the grave. Then, as he took Ballantyne's extended hand, Stella swiftly raised her hand to her throat with a curious gesture and turned away. It seemed as if now that she was sure that Thresk stood there before her, a living presence, she had something to hide from him.

CHAPTER VI

The marquee was large and high. It had a thick lining of a dull red colour and a carpet covered the floor; cushioned basket chairs and a few small tables stood here and there; against one wall rose an open escritoire with a box of cheroots upon it; the two passages to the sleeping-tents and the kitchen were hidden by grass-screens and between them stood a great Chesterfield sofa. It was, in a word, the tent of people who were accustomed to make their home in it for weeks at a time. Even the latest books were to be seen. But it was dark.

A single lamp swinging above the round dinner-table from the cross-pole of the roof burnt in the very centre of the tent; and that was all. The corners were shadowy; the lining merely absorbed the rays and gave none back. The round pool of light which spread out beneath the lamp was behind Ballantyne when he turned to the doorway, so Thresk for a moment was only aware of him as a big heavily-built man in a smoking-jacket and a starched white shirt; and it was to that starched white shirt that he spoke,

41

making his apologies. He was glad too to delay for a second or two the moment when he must speak to Stella. In her presence this eight long years of effort and work had become a very little space.

"I had to come as I was, Captain Ballantyne," he said, "for I have only with me what I want for the night in the train."

"Of course. That's all right," Ballantyne replied with a great cordiality. He turned towards Stella. "Mr. Thresk, this is my wife."

Now she had to turn. She held out her right hand but she still covered her throat with her left. She gave no sign of recognition and she did not look at her visitor.

"How do you do, Mr. Thresk?" she said, and went on quickly, allowing him no time for a reply. "We are in camp, you see. You must just take us as we are. Stephen did not tell me till a minute ago that he expected a visitor. You have not too much time. I will see that dinner is served at once." She went quickly to one of the grass-screens and lifting it vanished from his view. It seemed to Thresk that she had just seized upon an excuse to get away. Why? he asked himself. She was nervous and distressed, and in her distress she had accepted without surprise Thresk's introduction to her as a stranger. To that relationship then he and she were bound for the rest of his stay in the Resident's camp.

IN THE TENT AT CHITIPUR

Mrs. Repton had been wrong when she had attributed Thresk's request for a formal introduction to Ballantyne to a plan already matured in his mind. He had no plan, although he formed one before that dinner was at an end. He had asked for the letter because he wished faithfully to follow her advice and see for himself. If he called upon Stella he would find her alone; the mere sending in of his name would put her on her guard; he would see nothing. She would take care of that. He had no wish to make Ballantyne's acquaintance as Mrs. Ballantyne's friend. He could claim that friendship afterwards. Now however Stella herself in her confusion had made the claim impossible. She had fled—there was no other word which could truthfully describe her swift movement to the screen.

Ballantyne however had clearly not been surprised by it.

"It was a piece of luck for me that I camped here yesterday and telegraphed for my letters," he said. "You mentioned in your note that you had only twenty-four hours to give to Chitipur, didn't you? So I was sure that you would be upon this train."

He spoke with a slow precision in a voice which he was careful—or so it struck Thresk—to keep suave and low; and as he spoke he moved towards the dinner-table and came within the round pool of light. Thresk had a clear view of him. He was a man of a gross and powerful face, with a blue heavy chin and thick eyelids over bloodshot eyes.

"Will you have a cocktail?" he asked, and he called aloud, going to the second passage from the tent: "Quai hai! Baram Singh, cocktails!"

The servant who had met Thresk at the door came in upon the instant with a couple of cocktails on a tray.

"Ah, you have them," he said. "Good!"

But he refused the glass when the tray was held out to him, refused it after a long look and with a certain violence.

"For me? Certainly not! Never in this world." He looked up at Thresk with a laugh. "Cocktails are all very well for you, Mr. Thresk, who are here during a cold weather, but we who make our homes here—we have to be careful."

"Yes, so I suppose," said Thresk. But just behind Ballantyne, on a sideboard against the wall of the tent opposite to that wall where the writing-table stood, he noticed a syphon of soda, a decanter of whisky and a long glass which was not quite empty. He looked at Ballantyne curiously and as he looked he saw him start and stare with wide-opened eyes into the dim corners of the tent. Ballantyne had forgotten Thresk's presence. He stood there, his body rigid, his mouth half-open and fear looking out from his eyes and every line in his face—stark paralysing fear. Then he saw

44

Thresk staring at him, but he was too sunk in terror to resent the stare.

"Did you hear anything?" he said in a whisper.

"No."

"I did," and he leaned his head on one side. For a moment the two men stood holding their breath; and then Thresk did hear something. It was the rustle of a dress in the corridor beyond the mat-screen.

"It's Mrs. Ballantyne," he said, and she lifted the screen and came in.

Thresk just noticed a sharp movement of revulsion in Ballantyne, but he paid no heed to him. His eyes were riveted on Stella Ballantyne. She was wearing about her throat now a turquoise necklace. It was a heavy necklace of Indian make, rather barbaric and not at all beautiful, but it had many rows of stones and it hid her throat—just as surely as her hand had hidden it when she first saw Thresk. It was to hide her throat that she had fled. He saw Ballantyne go up to his wife, he heard his voice and noticed that her face grew grave and hard.

"So you have come to your senses," he said in a low tone. Stella passed him and did not answer. It was, then, upon the question of that necklace that their voices had been raised when he reached the camp. He had heard Ballantyne's, loud and dominant, the voice of a bully. He had been ordering her to cover her throat. Stella, on the other hand, had been quiet

45

but defiant. She had refused. Now she had changed her mind.

Baram Singh brought in the soup-tureen a second afterwards and Ballantyne raised his hands in a simulation of the profoundest astonishment.

"Why, dinner's actually punctual! What a miracle! Upon my word, Stella, I shan't know what to expect next if you spoil me in this way."

"It's usually punctual, Stephen," Stella replied with a smile of anxiety and appeal.

"Is it, my dear? I hadn't noticed it. Let us sit down at once."

Upon this tone of banter the dinner began; and no doubt in another man's mouth it might have sounded good-humoured enough. There was certainly no word as yet which, it could be definitely said, was meant to wound, but underneath the raillery Thresk was conscious of a rasp, a bitterness just held in check through the presence of a stranger. Not that Thresk was spared his share of it. At the very outset he, the guest whom it was such a rare piece of good fortune for Ballantyne to meet, came in for a taste of the whip.

"So you could actually give four-and-twenty hours to Chitipur, Mr. Thresk. That was most kind and considerate of you. Chitipur is grateful. Let us drink to it! By the way what will you drink? Our cellar is rather limited in camp. There's some claret and some whisky-and-soda."

IN THE TENT AT CHITIPUR

"Whisky-and-soda for me, please," said Thresk.

"And for me too. You take claret, don't you, Stella dear?" and he lingered upon the "dear" as though he anticipated getting a great deal of amusement out of her later on. And so she understood him, for there came a look of trouble into her face and she made a little gesture of helplessness. Thresk watched and said nothing.

"The decanter's in front of you, Stella," continued Ballantyne. He turned his attention to his own tumbler, into which Baram Singh had already poured the whisky; and at once he exclaimed indignantly:

"There's much too much here for me! Good heavens, what next!" and in Hindustani he ordered Baram Singh to add to the soda-water. Then he turned again to Thresk. "But I've no doubt you exhausted Chitipur in your twenty-four hours, didn't you? Of course you are going to write a book."

"Write a book!" cried Thresk. He was surprised into a laugh. "Not I."

Ballantyne leaned forward with a most serious and puzzled face.

"You're not writing a book about India? God bless my soul! D'you hear that, Stella? He's actually twenty-four hours in Chitipur.and he's not going to write a book about it."

"Six weeks from door to door: or how I made an ass of myself in India," said Thresk. "No thank you!"

47

Ballantyne laughed, took a gulp of his whisky-and-soda and put the glass down again with a wry face.

"This is too strong for me," he said, and he rose from his chair and crossed over to the tantalus upon the sideboard. He gave a cautious look towards the table, but Thresk had bent forward towards Stella. She was saying in a low voice:

"You don't mind a little chaff, do you?" and with an appeal so wistful that it touched Thresk to the heart.

"Of course not," he answered, and he looked up towards Ballantyne. Stella noticed a change come over his face. It was not surprise so much which showed there as interest and a confirmation of some suspicion which he already had. He saw that Ballantyne was secretly pouring into his glass not soda-water at all but whisky from the tantalus. He came back with the tumbler charged to the brim and drank deeply from it with relish.

"That's better," he said, and with a grin he turned his attention to his wife, fixing her with his eyes, gloating over her like some great snake over a bird trembling on the floor of its cage. The courses followed one upon the other and while he ate he baited her for his amusement. She took refuge in silence but he forced her to talk and then shivered with ridicule everything she said. Stella was cowed by him. If she answered it was probably some small commonplace

48

which with an exaggerated politeness he would nag at her to repeat. In the end, with her cheeks on fire, she would repeat it and bend her head under the brutal sarcasm with which it was torn to rags. Once or twice Thresk was on the point of springing up in her defence, but she looked at him with so much terror in her eyes that he did not interfere. He sat and watched and meanwhile his plan began to take shape in his mind.

There came an interval of silence during which Ballantyne leaned back in his chair in a sort of stupor; and in the midst of that silence Stella suddenly exclaimed with a world of longing in her voice:

"And you'll be in England in thirteen days! To think of it!" She glanced round the tent. It seemed incredible that any one could be so fortunate.

"You go straight from Jarwhal Junction here at our tent door to Bombay. To-morrow you go on board your ship and in twelve days afterwards you'll be in England."

Thresk leaned forward across the table.

"When did you go home last?" he asked.

"I have never been home since I married."

"Never!" exclaimed Thresk.

Stella shook her head.

"Never."

She was looking down at the tablecloth while she spoke, but as she finished she raised her head.

"Yes, I have been eight years in India," she added,

49

and Thresk saw the tears suddenly glisten in her eyes. He had come up to Chitipur reproaching himself for that morning on the South Downs, a morning so distant, so aloof from all the surroundings in which he found himself that it seemed to belong to an earlier life. But his reproaches became doubly poignant now. She had been eight years in India, tied to this brute! But Stella Ballantyne mastered herself with a laugh.

"However I am not alone in that," she said lightly. "And how's London?"

It was unfortunate that just at this moment Captain Ballantyne woke up.

"Eh what!" he exclaimed in a mock surprise. "You were talking, Stella, were you? It must have been something extraordinarily interesting that you were saying. Do let me hear it."

At once Stella shrank. Her spirit was so cowed that she almost had the look of a stupid person; she became stupid in sheer terror of her husband's railleries.

"It wasn't of any importance."

"Oh, my dear," said Ballantyne with a sneer, "you do yourself an injustice," and then his voice grew harsh, his face brutal. "What was it?" he demanded.

Stella looked this way and that, like an animal in a trap. Then she caught sight of Thresk's face over against her. Her eyes appealed to him for silence; she turned quickly to her husband.

"I only said how's London?"

50

IN THE TENT AT CHITIPUR

A smile spread over Ballantyne's face.

"Now did you say that? How's London! Now why did you ask how London was? How should London be? What sort of an answer did you expect?"

"I didn't expect any answer," replied Stella. "Of course the question sounds stupid if you drag it out and worry it."

Ballantyne snorted contemptuously.

"How's London? Try again, Stella!"

Thresk had come to the limit of his patience. In spite of Stella's appeal he interrupted and interrupted sharply.

"It doesn't seem to me an unnatural question for any woman to ask who has not seen London for eight years. After all, say what you like, for women India means exile—real exile."

Ballantyne turned upon his visitor with some rejoinder on his tongue. But he thought better of it. He looked away and contented himself with a laugh.

"Yes," said Stella, "we need next-door neighbours."

The restraint which Ballantyne showed towards Thresk only served to inflame him against his wife.

"So that you may pull their gowns to pieces and unpick their characters," he said. "Never mind, Stella! The time'll come when we shall settle down to domestic bliss at Camberley on twopence-halfpenny a year. That'll be jolly, won't it? Long walks over the heather and quiet evenings—alone with me. You must look forward to that, my dear." His voice rose to a veritable menace as he sketched the future which awaited them and then sank again.

"How's London!" he growled, harping scornfully on the unfortunate phrase. Ballantyne had had luck that night. He had chanced upon two of the banalities of ordinary talk which give an easy occasion for the bully. Thresk's twenty-four hours to give to Chitipur provided the best opening. Only Thresk was a guest—not that that in Ballantyne's present mood would have mattered a great deal, but he was a guest whom Ballantyne had it in his mind to use. All the more keenly therefore he pounced upon Stella. But in pouncing he gave Thresk a glimpse into the real man that he was, a glimpse which the barrister was quick to appreciate.

"How's London? A lot of London we shall be able to afford! God! what a life there's in store for us! Breakfast, lunch and dinner, dinner, breakfast, lunch —all among the next-door neighbours." And upon that he flung himself back in his chair and reached out his arms.

"Give me Rajputana!" he cried, and even through the thickness of his utterance his sincerity rang clear as a bell. "You can stretch yourself here. The cities! Live in the cities and you can only wear yourself out hankering to do what you like. Here you can do it. Do you see that, Mr. Thresk? You can do it." And he thumped the table with his hand.

IN THE TENT AT CHITIPUR

"I like getting away into camp for two months, three months at a time—on the plain, in the jungle, alone. That's the point—alone. You've got it all then. You're a king without a Press. No one to spy on you —no one to carry tales—no next-door neighbours. How's London?" and with a sneer he turned back to his wife. "Oh, I know it doesn't suit Stella. Stella's so sociable. Stella wants parties. Stella likes frocks. Stella loves to hang herself about with beads, don't you, my darling?"

But Ballantyne had overtried her to-night. Her face suddenly flushed and with a swift and violent gesture she tore at the necklace round her throat. The clasp broke, the beads fell with a clatter upon her plate, leaving her throat bare. For a moment Ballantyne stared at her, unable to believe his eyes. So many times he had made her the butt of his savage humour and she had offered no reply. Now she actually dared him!

"Why did you do that?" he asked, pushing his face close to hers. But he could not stare her down. She looked him in the face steadily. Even her lips did not tremble.

"You told me to wear them. I wore them. You jeer at me for wearing them. I take them off."

And as she sat there with her head erect Thresk knew why he had bidden her to wear them. There were bruises upon her throat—upon each side of her throat —the sort of bruises which would be made by the grip of a man's fingers. "Good God!" he cried, and before he could speak another word Stella's moment of defiance passed. She suddenly covered her face with her hands and burst into tears.

Ballantyne pushed back his chair sulkily. Thresk sprang to his feet. But Stella held him off with a gesture of her hand.

"It's nothing," she said between her sobs. "I am foolish. These last few days have been hot, haven't they?" She smiled wanly, checking her tears. "There's no reason at all," and she got up from her chair. "I think I'll leave you for a little while. My head aches and—and—I've no doubt I have got a red nose now."

She took a step or two towards the passage into her private tent but stopped.

"I *can* leave you to get along together alone, can't I?" she said with her eyes on Thresk. "You know what women are, don't you? Stephen will tell you interesting things about Rajputana if you can get him to talk. I shall see you before you go," and she lifted the screen and went out of the room. In the darkness of the passage she stood silent for a moment to steady herself and while she stood there, in spite of her efforts, her tears burst forth again uncontrollably. She clasped her hands tightly over her mouth so that the sound of her sobbing might not reach to the table in the centre of the big marquee; and with her lips whis-

54

pering in all sincerity the vain wish that she were dead
she stumbled along the corridor.

But the sound had reached into the big marquee and
coming after the silence it wrung Thresk's heart. He
knew this of her at all events—that she did not easily
cry. Ballantyne touched him on the arm.

"You blame me for this."

"I don't know that I do," answered Thresk slowly.
He was wondering how much share in the blame he had
himself, he who had ridden with her on the Downs
eight years ago and had let her speak and had not answered. He sat in this tent to-night with shame burning at his heart. "It wasn't as if I had no confidence
in myself," he argued, unable quite to cast back to the
Thresk of those early days. "I had—heaps of it."

Ballantyne lifted himself out of his chair and lurched
over to the sideboard. Thresk, watching him, fell to
wondering why in the world Stella had married him or
he her. He knew that a blind man may see such mys-
teries on any day and that a wise one will not try to
explain them. Still he wondered. Had the man's
reputation dazzled her?—for undoubtedly he had one;
or was it that intellect which suffered an eclipse when
Ballantyne went into camp with nobody to carry tales?

He was still pondering on that problem when Ballantyne swung back to the table and set himself to
prove, drunk though he was, that his reputation was
not ill-founded.

THE WITNESS FOR THE DEFENCE

"I am afraid Stella's not very well," he said, sitting heavily down. "But she asked me to tell you things, didn't she? Well, her wishes are my law. So here goes." His manner altogether changed now that they were alone. He became confidential, intimate, friendly. He was drunk. He was a coarse heavy-featured man with bloodshot eyes; he interrupted his conversation with uneasy glances into the corners of the tent, such glances as Thresk had noticed when he was alone with him before they sat down to dinner; but he managed none the less to talk of Rajputana with a knowledge which amazed Thresk now and would have enthralled him at another time. A visitor may see the surface of Rajputana much as Thresk had done, may admire its marble palaces, its blue lakes and the great yellow stretches of its desert, but to know anything of the life underneath in that strange secret country is given to few even of those who for long years fly the British flag over the Agencies. Nevertheless Ballantyne knew— very little as he acknowledged but more than his fellows. And groping drunkenly in his mind he drew out now this queer intrigue, now that fateful piece of history, now the story of some savage punishment wreaked behind the latticed windows, and laid them one after another before Thresk's eyes—his peace-offerings. And Thresk listened. But before his eyes stood the picture of Stella Ballantyne standing alone in the dark corridor beyond the grass-screen whispering with wild lips her wish that she was dead; and in his ears was the sound of her sobbing. Here, it seemed, was another story to add to the annals of Rajputana.

Then Ballantyne tapped him on the arm.

"You're not listening," he said with a leer. "And I'm telling you good things—things that people don't know and that I wouldn't tell them—the swine. You're not listening. You're thinking I'm a brute to my wife, eh?" And Thresk was startled by the shrewdness of his host's guess.

"Well, I'll tell you the truth. I am not master of myself," Ballantyne continued. His voice sank and his eyes narrowed to two little bright slits. "I am afraid. Yes, that's the explanation. I am so afraid that when I am not alone I seek relief any way, any how. I can't help it." And even as he spoke his eyes opened wide and he sat staring intently at a dim corner of the tent, moving his head with little jerks from one side to the other that he might see the better.

"There's no one over there, eh?" he asked.

"No one."

Ballantyne nodded as he moistened his lips with the tip of his tongue.

"They make these tents too large," he said in a whisper. "One great blot of light in the middle and all around in the corners—shadows. We sit here in the blot of light—a fair mark. But what's going on in the shadows, Mr.—— What's your name? Eh? What's going on in the shadows?"

Thresk had no doubt that Ballantyne's fear was genuine. He was not putting forward merely an excuse for the scene which his guest had witnessed and might spread abroad on his return to Bombay. No, he was really terrified. He interspersed his words with sudden unexpected silences, during which he sat all ears and his face strained to listen, as though he expected to surprise some stealthy movement. But Thresk accounted for it by that decanter on the sideboard, in which the level of the whisky had been so noticeably lowered that evening. He was wrong however, for Ballantyne sprang to his feet.

"You are going away to-night. You can do me a service."

"Can I?" asked Thresk.

He understood at last why Ballantyne had been at such pains to interest and amuse him.

"Yes. And in return," cried Ballantyne, "I'll give you another glimpse into the India you don't know."

He walked up to the door of the tent and drew it aside. "Look!"

Thresk, leaning forward in his chair, looked out through the opening. He saw the moonlit plain in a soft haze, in the middle of it the green lamp of a railway signal and beyond the distant ridge, on which straggled the ruins of old Chitipur.

"Look!" cried Ballantyne. "There's tourist India all in one: a desert, a railway and a deserted city, hovels and temples, deep sacred pools and forgotten

58

palaces—the whole bag of tricks crumbling slowly to ruin through centuries on the top of a hill. That's what the good people come out for to see in the cold weather—Jarwhal Junction and old Chitipur."

He dropped the curtain contemptuously and it swung back, shutting out the desert. He took a step or two back into the tent and flung out his arms wide on each side of him.

"But bless your soul," he cried vigorously, "here's the real India."

Thresk looked about the tent and understood.

"I see," he answered—"a place very badly lit, a great blot of light in the centre and all around it dark corners and grim shadows."

Ballantyne nodded his head with a grim smile upon his lips.

"Oh, you have learnt that! Well, you shall do me a service and in return you shall look into the shadows. But we will have the table cleared first." And he called aloud for Baram Singh.

CHAPTER VII

While Baram Singh was clearing the table Ballantyne lifted the box of cheroots from the top of the bureau and held it out to Thresk.

"Will you smoke?"

Thresk, however, though he smoked had not during his stay in India acquired the taste for the cheroot; and it interested him in later times to reflect how largely he owed his entanglement in the tragic events which were to follow to that accidental distaste. For conscious of it he had brought his pipe with him, and he now fetched it out of his pocket.

"This, if I may," he said.

"Of course."

Thresk filled his pipe and lighted it, Ballantyne for his part lit a cheroot and replaced the box upon the top, close to a heavy riding-crop with a bone handle, which Thresk happened now to notice for the first time.

"Be quick!" he cried impatiently to Baram Singh, and seated himself in the swing-chair in front of the bureau, turning it so as not to have his back to Thresk

60

at the table. Baram Singh hurriedly finished his work and left the marquee by the passage leading to the kitchen. Ballantyne waited with his eyes upon that passage until the grass-mat screen had ceased to move. Then taking a bunch of keys from his pocket he stooped under the open writing-flap of the bureau and unlocked the lowest of the three drawers. From this drawer he lifted a scarlet despatch-box, and was just going to bring it to the table when Baram Singh silently appeared once more. At once Ballantyne dropped the box on the floor, covering it as well as he could with his legs.

"What the devil do you want?" he cried, speaking of course in Hindustani, and with a violence which seemed to be half made up of anger and half of fear. Baram Singh replied that he had brought an ash-tray for the Sahib, and he placed it on the round table by Thresk's side.

"Well, get out and don't come back until you are called," cried Ballantyne roughly, and in evident relief as Baram Singh once more retired he took a long draught from a fresh tumbler of whisky-and-soda which stood on the flap of the bureau beside him. He then stooped once more to lift the red despatch-box from the floor, but to Thresk's amazement in the very act of stooping he stopped. He remained with his hands open to seize the box and his body bent over his knees, quite motionless. His mouth was open, his eyes staring,

61

and upon his face such a look of sheer terror was stamped as Thresk could never find words to describe. For the first moment he imagined that the man had had a stroke. His habits, his heavy build all pointed that way. The act of stooping would quite naturally be the breaking pressure upon that overcharged brain. But before Thresk had risen to make sure Ballantyne moved an arm. He moved it upwards without changing his attitude in any other way, or even the direction of his eyes, and he groped along the flap of the bureau very cautiously and secretly and up again to the top ledge. All the while his eyes were staring intently, but with the intentness of extreme fear, not at the despatch-box but at the space of carpet—a couple of feet at the most—between the despatch-box and the tent-wall. His fingers felt along the ledge of the bureau and closed with a silent grip upon the handle of the riding-crop. Thresk jumped to the natural conclusion: a snake had crept in under the tent-wall and Ballantyne dared not move lest the snake should strike. Neither did he dare to move himself. Ballantyne was clearly within reach of its fangs. But he looked and—there was nothing. The light was not good certainly, and down by the tent-wall there close to the floor it was shadowy and dim. But Thresk's eyes were keen. The space between the despatch-box and the wall was empty. Nothing crawled there, nothing was coiled.

THE PHOTOGRAPH

Thresk looked at Ballantyne with amazement; and as he looked Ballantyne sprang from his chair with a scream of terror—the scream of a panic-stricken child. He sprang with an agility which Thresk would never have believed possible in a man of so gross a build. He leapt into the air and with his crop he struck savagely once, twice and thrice at the floor between the wall and the box. Then he turned to Thresk with every muscle working in his face.

"Did you see?" he cried. "Did you see?"

"What? There was nothing to see!"

"Nothing!" screamed Ballantyne. He picked up the box and placed it on the table, thrusting it under Thresk's hand. "Hold that! Don't let go! Stay here and don't let go," he said, and running up the tent raised his voice to a shout.

"Baram Singh!" and lifting the tent-door he called to others of his servants by name. Without waiting for them he ran out himself and in a second Thresk heard him cursing thickly and calling in panic-stricken tones just close to that point of the wall against which the bureau stood. The camp woke to clamour.

Thresk stood by the table gripping the handle of the despatch-box as he had been bidden to do. The tent-door was left open. He could see lights flashing, he heard Ballantyne shouting orders, and his voice dwindled and grew loud as he moved from spot to spot in the encampment. And in the midst of the noise the

white frightened face of Stella Ballantyne appeared at
the opening of her corridor.

"What has happened?" she asked in a whisper.
"Oh, I was afraid that you and he had quarrelled,"
and she stood with her hand pressed over her heart.

"No, no indeed," Thresk replied, and Captain Ballantyne stumbled back into the tent. His face was
livid, and yet the sweat stood upon his forehead.
Stella Ballantyne drew back, but Ballantyne saw her
as she moved and drove her to her own quarters.

"I have a private message for Mr. Thresk's ears,"
he said, and when she had gone he took out his handkerchief and wiped his forehead.

"Now you must help me," he said in a low voice.
But his voice shook and his eyes strayed again to the
ground by the wall of the tent.

"It was just there the arm came through," he said.
"Yes, just there," and he pointed a trembling finger.

"Arm?" cried Thresk. "What are you talking
about?"

Ballantyne looked away from the wall to Thresk,
his eyes incredulous.

"But you saw!" he insisted, leaning forward over
the table.

"What?"

"An arm, a hand thrust in under the tent there,
along the ground reaching out for my box."

"No. There was nothing to see."

THE PHOTOGRAPH

"A lean brown arm, I tell you, a hand thin and delicate as a woman's."

"No. You are dreaming," exclaimed Thresk; but dreaming was a euphemism for the word he meant.

"Dreaming!" repeated Ballantyne with a harsh laugh. "Good God! I wish I was. Come. Sit down here! We have not too much time." He seated himself opposite to Thresk and drew the despatch-box towards him. He had regained enough mastery over himself now to be able to speak in a level voice. No doubt too his fright had sobered him. But it had him still in its grip, for when he opened the despatch-box his hand so shook that he could hardly insert the key in the lock. It was done at last however, and feeling beneath the loose papers on the surface he drew out from the very bottom a large sealed envelope. He examined the seals to make sure they had not been tampered with. Then he tore open the envelope and took out a photograph, somewhat larger than cabinet size.

"You have heard of Bahadur Salak?" he said.

Thresk started.

"The affair at Umballa, the riots at Benares, the murder in Madras?"

"Exactly."

Ballantyne pushed the photograph into Thresk's hand.

"That's the fellow—the middle one of the group."

THE WITNESS FOR THE DEFENCE

Thresk held up the photograph to the light. It represented a group of nine Hindus seated upon chairs in a garden and arranged in a row facing the camera. Thresk looked at the central figure with a keen and professional interest. Salak was a notorious figure in the Indian politics of the day—the politics of the subterranean kind. For some years he had preached and practised sedition with so much subtlety and skill that though all men were aware that his hand worked the strings of disorder there was never any convicting evidence against him. In all the three cases which Thresk had quoted and in many others less well-known those responsible for order were sure that he had devised the crime, chosen the moment for its commission and given the order. But up till a month ago he had slipped through the meshes. A month ago, however, he had made his mistake.

"Yes. It's a clever face," said Thresk.

Ballantyne nodded his head.

"He's a Mahratta Brahmin from Poona. They are the fellows for brains, and Salak's about the cleverest of them."

Thresk looked again at the photograph.

"I see the picture was taken at Poona."

"Yes, and isn't it an extraordinary thing!" cried Ballantyne, his face flashing suddenly into interest and enjoyment. The enthusiasm of the administrator in his work got the better of his fear now, just as a

66

little earlier it had got the better of his drunkenness.
Thresk was looking now into the face of a quite different man, the man of the intimate knowledge and
the high ability for whom fine rewards were prophesied
in Bombay. "The very cleverest of them can't resist
the temptation of being photographed in group. Crime
after crime has been brought home to the Indian criminal both here and in London because they will sit in
garden-chairs and let a man take their portraits. Nothing will stop them. They won't learn. They are like
the ladies of the light opera stage. Well, let 'em go
on I say. Here's an instance."

"Is it?" asked Thresk. "Surely that photograph
was taken a long time ago."

"Nine years. But he was at the same game. You
have got the proof in your hands. There's a group of
nine men—Salak and his eight friends. Well, of his
eight friends every man jack is now doing time for
burglary, in some cases with violence—that second
ruffian, for instance, he's in for life—in some cases
without, but in each case the crime was burglary. And
why? Because Salak in the centre there set them on
to it. Because Salak nine years ago wasn't the big
swell he is now. Because Salak wanted money to
start his intrigues. That's the way he got it—bur-
glaries all round Bombay."

"I see," said Thresk. "Salak's in prison now?"

"He's in prison in Calcutta, yes. But he's awaiting
his trial. He's not convicted yet."

67

"Exactly," Thresk answered. "This photograph is a valuable thing to have just now."

Ballantyne threw up his arms in despair at the obtuseness of his companion.

"Valuable!" he cried in derision. "Valuable!" and he leaned forward on his elbows and began to talk to Thresk with an ironic gentleness as if he were a child.

"You don't quite understand me, do you? But a little effort and all will be plain."

He got no farther however upon this line of attack, for Thresk interrupted him sharply.

"Here! Say what you have got to say if you want me to help you. Oh, you needn't scowl! You are not going to bait me for your amusement. I am not your wife." And Ballantyne after a vain effort to stare Thresk down changed to a more cordial tone.

"Well, you say it's a valuable thing to have just now. I say it's an infernally dangerous thing. On the one side there's Salak the great national leader, Salak the deliverer, Salak professing from his prison in Calcutta that he has never used any but the most legitimate constitutional means to forward his propaganda. And here on the other is Salak in his garden-chair amongst the burglars. Not a good thing to possess—this photograph, Mr. Thresk. Especially because it's the only one in existence and the negative has been destroyed. So Salak's friends are naturally anxious to get it back."

"Do they know you have it?" Thresk asked.

68

THE PHOTOGRAPH

"Of course they do. You had proof that they knew five minutes ago when that brown arm wriggled in under the tent-wall."

Ballantyne's fear returned upon him as he spoke. He sat shivering; his eyes wandered furtively from corner to corner of the great tent and came always back as though drawn by a serpent to the floor by the wall of the tent. Thresk shrugged his shoulders. To dispute with Ballantyne once more upon his delusion would be the merest waste of time. He took up the photograph again.

"How do you come to possess it?" he asked. If he was to serve his host in the way he suspected he would be asked to, he must know its history.

"I was agent in a state not far from Poona before I came here."

Thresk agreed.

"I know. Bakuta."

"Oh?" said Ballantyne with a sharp look. "How did you know that?"

He was always in alarm lest somewhere in the world gossip was whispering his secret.

"A Mrs. Carruthers at Bombay."

"Did she tell you anything else?"

"Yes. She told me that you were a great man."

Ballantyne grinned suddenly.

"Isn't she a fool?" Then the grin left his face. "But how did you come to discuss me with her at all?"

That was a question which Thresk had not the slightest intention to answer. He evaded it altogether.

"Wasn't it natural since I was going to Chitipur?" he asked, and Ballantyne was appeased.

"Well, the Rajah of Bakutu had that photograph and he gave it to me when I left the State. He came down to the station to see me off. He was too near Poona to be comfortable with that in his pocket. He gave it to me on the platform in full view, the damned coward. He wanted to show that he had given it to me. He said that I should be safe with it in Chitipur."

"Chitipur's a long way from Poona," Thresk agreed.

"But don't you see, this trial that's coming along in Calcutta makes all the difference. It's known I have got it. It's not safe here now and no more am I so long as I've got it."

One question had been puzzling Thresk ever since he had seen the look of terror reappear in Ballantyne's face. It was clear that he lived in a very real fear. He believed that he was watched, and he believed that he was in danger; and very probably he actually was. There had, to be sure, been no attempt that night to rob him of it as he imagined. But none the less Salak and his friends could not like the prospect of the production of that photograph in Calcutta, and would hardly be scrupulous what means they took to prevent it. Then why had not Ballantyne destroyed it?

THE PHOTOGRAPH

Thresk asked the question and was fairly startled by the answer. For it presented to him in the most unexpected manner another and a new side of the strange and complex character of Stephen Ballantyne.

"Yes, why don't I destroy it?" Ballantyne repeated. "I ask myself that," and he took the photograph out of Thresk's hands and sat in a sort of muse, staring at it. Then he turned it over and took the edge between his forefinger and his thumb, hesitating whether he would not even at this moment tear it into strips and have done with it. But in the end he cast it upon the table as he had done many a time before and cried in a voice of violence:

"No, I can't. That's to own these fellows my masters and I won't. By God I won't! I may be every kind of brute, but I have been bred up in this service. For twenty years I have lived in it and by it. And the service is too strong for me. No, I can't destroy that photograph. There's the truth. I should hate myself to my dying day if I did."

He rose abruptly as if half ashamed of his outburst and crossing to his bureau lighted another cheroot.

"Then what do you want me to do with it?" asked Thresk.

"I want you to take it away."

Ballantyne was taking a casuistical way of satisfying his conscience, and he was aware of it. He would not destroy the portrait—no! But he wouldn't keep it

71

THE WITNESS FOR THE DEFENCE

either. "You are going straight back to England,"
he said. "Take it with you. When you get home you
can hand it to one of the big-wigs at the India Office,
and he'll put it in a pigeon-hole, and some day an old
charwoman cleaning the office will find it, and she'll
take it home to her grandchildren to play with and one
of them'll drop it on the fire, and there'll be an end of
it."

"Yes," replied Thresk slowly. "But if I do that, it
won't be useful at Calcutta, will it?"

"Oh," said Ballantyne with a sneer. "You've got
a conscience too, eh? Well, I'll tell you. I don't
think that photograph will be needed at Calcutta."

"Are you sure of that?"

"Yes. Salak's friends don't know it, but I do."

Thresk sat still in doubt. Was Ballantyne speaking
the truth or did he speak in fear? He was still standing by the bureau looking down upon Thresk and behind him, so that Thresk had not the expression of his
face to help him to decide. But he did not turn in his
chair to look. For as he sat there it dawned upon him
that the photograph was the very thing which he himself needed. The scheme which had been growing in
his mind all through this evening, which had begun to
grow from the very moment when he had entered the
tent, was now complete in every detail except one. He
wanted an excuse, a good excuse which should explain
why he missed his boat, and here it was on the table

72

in front of him. Almost he had refused it! Now it seemed to him a Godsend.

"I'll take it," he cried, and Baram Singh silently appeared at the outer doorway of the tent.

"Huzoor," he said. "Railgharri hai."

Ballantyne turned to Thresk.

"Your train is signalled," and as Thresk started up he reassured him. "There's no hurry. I have sent word that it is not to start without you." And while Baram Singh still stood waiting for orders in the doorway of the tent Ballantyne walked round the table, took up the portrait very deliberately and handed it to Thresk.

"Thank you," he said. "Button it in your coat pocket."

He waited while Thresk obeyed.

"Thus," said Thresk with a laugh, "did the Rajah of Bakutu," and Ballantyne replied with a grin.

"Thank you for mentioning that name." He turned to Baram Singh. "The camel, quick!"

Baram Singh went out to the enclosure within the little village of tents and Thresk asked curiously:

"Do you distrust him?"

Ballantyne looked steadily at his visitor and said:

"I don't answer such questions. But I'll tell you something. If that man were dying he would ask for leave. And if he would ask for leave because he would not die with my scarlet livery on his back. Are you answered?"

"Yes," said Thresk.

"Very well." And with a brisk change of tone Ballantyne added: "I'll see that your camel is ready." He called aloud to his wife: "Stella! Stella! Mr. Thresk is going," and he went out through the doorway into the moonlight.

CHAPTER VIII

Thresk, alone in the tent, looked impatiently towards the grass-screen. He wanted half-a-dozen words with Stella alone. Here was the opportunity, the unhoped-for opportunity, and it was slipping away. Through the open doorway of the tent he saw Ballantyne standing by a big fire and men moving quickly in obedience to his voice. Then he heard the rustle of a dress in the corridor, and she was in the room. He moved quickly towards her, but she held up her hand and stopped him.

"Oh, why did you come?" she said, and the pallor of her face reproached him no less than the regret in her voice.

"I heard of you in Bombay," he replied. "I am glad that I did come."

"And I am sorry."

"Why?"

She looked about the tent as though he might find his answer there. Thresk did not move. He stood near to her, watching her face intently with his jaw rather set.

75

"Oh, I didn't say that to wound you," said Stella, and she sat down on one of the cushioned basket-chairs. "You mustn't think I wasn't glad to see you. I was —at the first moment I was very glad;" and she saw his face lighten as she spoke. "I couldn't help it. All the years rolled away. I remembered the Sussex Downs and—and—days when we rode there high up above the weald. Do you remember?"

"Yes."

"How long was that ago?"

"Eight years."

Stella laughed wistfully.

"To me it seems a century." She was silent for a moment, and though he spoke to her urgently she did not answer. She was carried back to the high broad hills of grass with the curious clumps of big beech-trees upon their crests.

"Do you remember Halnaker Gallop?" she asked with a laugh. "We found it when the chains weren't up and had the whole two miles free. Was there ever such grass?"

She was looking straight at the bureau, but she was seeing that green lane of shaven turf in the haze of an August morning. She saw it rise and dip in the open between long brown grass. There was a tree on the left-hand side just where the ride dipped for the first time. Then it ran straight to the big beech-trees and passed between them, a wide glade of sunlight, and curved out at the upper end by the road and dipped down again to the two lodges.

"And the ridge at the back of Charlton forest, all the weald to Leith Hill in view?" She rose suddenly from her chair. "Oh, I am sorry that you came."

"And I am glad," repeated Thresk.

The stubbornness with which he repeated his words arrested her. She looked at him—was it with distrust, he asked himself? He could not be sure. But certainly there was a little hard note in her voice which had not been there before, when in her turn she asked:

"Why?"

"Because I shouldn't have known," he said in a quick whisper. "I should have gone back. I should have left you here. I shouldn't have known."

Stella recoiled.

"There is nothing to know," she said sharply, and Thresk pointed at her throat.

"Nothing?"

Stella Ballantyne raised her hand to cover the blue marks.

"I—I fell and hurt myself," she stammered.

"It was he—Ballantyne."

"No," she cried and she drew herself erect. But Thresk would not accept the denial.

"He ill-treats you," he insisted. "He drinks and ill-treats you."

Stella shook her head.

"You asked questions in Bombay where we are known. You were not told that," she said confidently. There was only one person in Bombay who knew the truth and Jane Repton, she was very sure, would never have betrayed her.

"That's true," Thresk conceded. "But why? Because it's only here in camp that he lets himself go. He told us as much to-night. You were here at the table. You heard. He let his secret slip: no one to carry tales, no one to spy. In the towns he sets a guard upon himself. Yes, but he looks forward to the months of camp when there are no next-door neighbours."

"No, that's not true," she protested and cast about for explanations. "He—he has had a long day and to-night he was tired—and when you are tired—— Oh, as a rule he's different." And to her relief she heard Ballantyne's voice outside the tent.

"Thresk! Thresk!"

She came forward and held out her hand.

"There! Your camel's ready," she said. "You must go! Goodbye," and as he took it the old friendliness transfigured her face. "You are a great man now. I read of you. You always meant to be, didn't you? Hard work?"

"Very," said Thresk. "Four o'clock in the morning till midnight;" and she suddenly caught him by the arm.

"But it's worth it." She let him go and clasped her hands together. "Oh, you have got everything!" she cried in envy.

"No," he answered. But she would not listen.

"Everything you asked for," she said and she added hurriedly, "Do you still collect miniatures? No time for that now I suppose." Once more Ballantyne's voice called to them from the camp-fire.

"You must go."

Thresk looked through the opening of the tent. Ballantyne had turned and was coming back towards them.

"I'll write to you from Bombay," he said, and utter disbelief showed in her face and sounded in her laugh.

"That letter will never reach me," she said lightly, and she went up to the door of the tent. Thresk had a moment whilst her back was turned and he used it. He took his pipe out of his pocket and placed it silently and quickly on the table. He wanted a word with her when Ballantyne was out of the way and she was not upon her guard to fence him off. The pipe might be his friend and give it him. He went up to Stella at the tent-door and Ballantyne, who was half-way between the camp-fire and the tent, stopped when he caught sight of him.

"That's right," he said. "You ought to be going;" and he turned again towards the camel. Thus for another moment they were alone together, but it was Stella who seized it.

79

"There go!" she said. "You must go," and in the same breath she added:

"Married yet?"

"No," answered Thresk.

"Still too busy getting on?"

"That's not the reason"—and he lowered his voice to a whisper—"Stella."

Again she laughed in frank and utter disbelief.

"Nor is Stella. That's mere politeness and good manners. We must show the dear creatures the great part they play in our lives." And upon that all her fortitude suddenly deserted her. She had played her part so far, she could play it no longer. An extraordinary change came over her face. The smiles, the laughter slipped from it like a loosened mask. Thresk saw such an agony of weariness and hopeless longing in her eyes as he had never seen even with his experience in the Courts of Law. She drew back into the shadow of the tent.

"In thirteen days you'll be steaming up the Channel," she whispered, and with a sob she covered her face with her hands. Thresk saw the tears trickle between her fingers.

Ballantyne at the fire was looking back towards the tent. Thresk hurried out to him. The camel was crouching close to the fire saddled and ready.

"You have time," said Ballantyne. "The train's not in yet," and Thresk walked to the side of the camel, where a couple of steps had been placed for him to mount. He had a foot on the step when he suddenly clapped his hand to his pocket.

"I've left my pipe," he cried, "and I've a night's journey in front of me. I won't be a second."

He ran back with all his speed to the tent. The hangings at the door were closed. He tore them aside and rushed in.

"Stella!" he said in a whisper, and then he stopped in amazement. He had left her on the very extremity of distress. He found her, though to be sure the stains of her tears were still visible upon her face, busy with one of the evening preparations natural in a camp-life —quietly, energetically busy. She looked up once when he raised the hanging over the door, but she dropped her eyes the next instant to her work.

She was standing by the table with a small rook-rifle in her hands. The breech was open. She looked down the barrel, holding up the weapon so that the light might shine into the breech.

"Yes?" she said, and with so much indifference that she did not lift her eyes from her work. "I thought you had gone."

"I left my pipe behind me," said Thresk.

"There it is, on the table."

"Thank you."

He put it in his pocket. Of the two he was disconcerted and at a loss, she was entirely at her ease.

81

"You are looking at my little rifle," she said.

"No! Stella! I have only a moment——" But Stella went on as though he had not spoken.

"I am seeing that it is clean and ready for to-morrow," and Ballantyne's voice was heard speaking with some urgency close to the tent.

"Have you found it?" he called and he pushed his way in. "The train's coming into the station now. It has a ten minutes' wait, but it will take you all that time and more and I don't want to keep it longer than can be helped." He noticed Stella's occupation. "You are looking at Stella's pop-gun," he said contemptuously. "My wife's pretty smart with it. She allows no back-talk from the rabbits, I can tell you. Come along."

"Yes," said Stella, "it's time. Once more, goodbye, Mr. Thresk;" and there was a little note of emphasis in her voice. Thresk turned with a sudden abruptness.

"Goodbye," he said, and he went up with Ballantyne to the door. But he was to hear her voice again that night, though it was not to him she spoke, for as they were passing out into the open she said to her husband:

"I suppose you are going to the station with Mr. Thresk?"

"No," he replied. "I am just going to see him start from the camp."

It struck Thresk that a shadow of disappointment

passed across Stella's face, but at that distance and in the dim light he was not sure. The curtain closed behind them and hid her from his sight.

Thresk climbed up on to the camel behind the driver, whilst a servant held the beast's head.

"Sit firm," said Ballantyne, "or you'll be pitched off as he gets up."

The camel rose, unfolding himself in sections, while Thresk was shot forwards and backwards like a child upon a rocking-horse.

"There, you are all right now," cried Ballantyne. "Hold on and good-night."

"Good-night," said Thresk.

The camel moved out of the glare of the fire into the haze of the moonlight. The noise of the camp dropped away behind him. He heard only the soft padding of the camel's feet.

CHAPTER IX

The Reptons lived upon the Khamballa Hill and the bow-window of their drawing-room looked down upon the Arabian Sea and southwards along the coast towards Malabar Point. In this embrasure Mrs. Repton sat through a morning, denying herself to her friends. A book lay open on her lap but her eyes were upon the sea. A few minutes after the clock upon her mantelpiece had struck twelve she saw that for which she watched: the bowsprit and the black bows of a big ship pushing out from under the hill and the water boiling under its stem. The whole ship came into view with its awnings and its saffron funnels and headed to the north-west for Aden.

Jane Repton rose up from her chair and watched it go. In the sunlight its black hull was so sharply outlined on the sea, its lines and spars were so trim that it looked a miniature ship which she could reach out her hand and snatch. But her eyes grew dim as she watched, so that it became shapeless and blurred, and long before the liner was out of sight it was quite lost to her.

84

AN EPISODE IN BALLANTYNE'S LIFE

"I am foolish," she said as she turned away, and she bit her handkerchief hard. This was midday of the Friday and ever since that dinner-party at the Carruthers' on the Monday night she had been alternating between wild hopes and arguments of prudence. But until this moment of disappointment she had not realised how completely the hopes had gained the upper hand with her and how extravagantly she had built upon Thresk's urgent questioning of her at the dinner-table.

"Very likely he never found the Ballantynes at all," she argued. But he might have sent her word. All that morning she had been expecting a telephone message or a telegram or a note scribbled on board the steamer and sent up the Khamballa Hill by a messenger. But not a token had come from him and now of the boat which was carrying him to England there was nothing left but the stain of its smoke upon the sky.

Mrs. Repton put her handkerchief in her pocket and was going about the business of her house when the butler opened the door.

"I am not in——" Mrs. Repton began and cut short the sentence with a cry of welcome and surprise, for close upon the heels of the servant Thresk was standing.

"You!" she cried. "Oh!"

She felt her legs weakening under her and she sat down abruptly on a chair.

"Thank Heaven it was there," she said. "I should have sat on the floor if it hadn't been." She dismissed the butler and held out her hand to Thresk. "Oh, my friend," she said, "there's your steamer on its way to Aden."

Her voice rang with enthusiasm and admiration. Thresk only nodded his head gloomily.

"I have missed it," he replied. "It's very unfortunate. I have clients waiting for me in London."

"You missed it on purpose," she declared and Thresk's face relaxed into a smile. He turned away from the window to her. He seemed suddenly to wear the look of a boy.

"I have the best of excuses," he replied, "the perfect excuse." But even he could not foresee how completely that excuse was to serve him.

"Sit down," said Jane Repton, "and tell me. You went to Chitipur, I know. From your presence here I know too that you found—them—there."

"No," said Thresk, "I didn't." He sat down and looked straight into Jane Repton's eyes. "I had a stroke of luck. I found them—in camp."

Jane Repton understood all that the last two words implied.

"I should have wished that," she answered, "if I had dared to think it possible. You talked with Stella?"

"Hardly a word alone. But I saw."

86

AN EPISODE IN BALLANTYNE'S LIFE

"What did you see?"

"I am here to tell you." And he told her the story of his night at the camp so far as it concerned Stella Ballantyne, and indeed not quite all of that. For instance he omitted altogether to relate how he had left his pipe behind in the tent and had returned for it. That seemed to him unimportant. Nor did he tell her of his conversation with Ballantyne about the photograph. "He was in a panic. He had delusions," he said and left the matter there. Thresk had the lawyer's mind or rather the mind of a lawyer in big practice. He had the instinct for the essential fact and the knowledge that it was most lucid when presented in a naked simplicity. He was at pains to set before Jane Repton what he had seen of the life which Stella lived with Stephen Ballantyne and nothing else.

"Now," he said when he had finished, "you sent me to Chitipur. I must know why."

And when she hesitated he overbore her.

"You can be guilty of no disloyalty to your friend," he insisted, "by being frank with me. After all I have given guarantees. I went to Chitipur upon your word. I have missed my boat. You bade me go to Chitipur. That told me too little or too much. I say too little. I have got to know all now." And he rose up and stood before her. "What do you know about Stephen Ballantyne?"

"I'll tell you," said Jane Repton. She looked at the

87

clock. "You had better stay and lunch with us if you will. We shall be alone. I'll tell you afterwards. Meanwhile——" and in her turn she stood up. The sense of responsibility was heavy upon her.

She had sent this man upon his errand of knowledge. He had done, in consequence of it, a stronger, a wilder thing than she had thought, than she had hoped for. She had a panicky feeling that she had set great forces at work.

"Meanwhile——" asked Thresk; and she drew a breath of relief. The steadiness of his eyes and voice comforted her. His quiet insistence gave her courage. None of her troubles and doubts had any place apparently in his mind. A nervous horse in the hands of a real horseman—thus she thought of herself in Thresk's presence.

"Meanwhile I'll give you one reason why I wanted you to go. My husband's time in India is up. We are leaving for England altogether in a month's time. We shall not come back at all. And when we have gone Stella will be left without one intimate friend in the whole country."

"Yes," said Thresk. "That wouldn't do, would it?" and they went in to their luncheon.

All through that meal, before the servants, they talked what is written in the newspapers. And of the two she who had fears and hesitations was still the most impatient to get it done. She had her curiosity and

88

it was beginning to consume her. What had Thresk known of Stella and she of him before she had come out to India and become Stella Ballantyne? Had they been in love? If not why had Thresk gone to Chitipur? Why had he missed his boat and left all his clients over there in England in the lurch? If so, why hadn't they married—the idiots? Oh, how she wanted to know all the answers to all these questions! And what he proposed to do now! And she would know nothing unless she was frank herself. She had read his ultimatum in his face.

"We'll have coffee in my sitting-room. You can smoke there," she said and led the way to it. "A cheroot?"

Thresk smiled with amusement. But the amusement annoyed her for she did not understand it.

"I have got a Havana cigar here," he said. "May I?"

"Of course."

He lit it and listened. But it was not long before it went out and he did not stir to light it again. The incident of which Mrs. Repton had been the witness, and which she related now, invested Ballantyne with horror. Thresk had left the camp at Chitipur with an angry contempt for him. The contempt passed out of his feelings altogether as he sat in Mrs. Repton's drawing-room.

"I am not telling you what Stella has confided to

me," said Mrs. Repton. "Stella's loyal even when there's no cause for loyalty; and if loyalty didn't keep her mouth closed, self-respect would. I tell you what I saw. We were at Agra at the time. My husband was Collector there. There was a Durbar held there and the Rajah of Chitipur came to it with his elephants and his soldiers, and naturally Captain Ballantyne and his wife came too. They stayed with us. You are to understand that I knew nothing—absolutely nothing—up to that time. I hadn't a suspicion—until the afternoon of the finals in the Polo Tournament. Stella and I went together alone and we came home about six. Stella went upstairs and I—I walked into the library."

She had found Ballantyne sitting in a high arm-chair, his eyes glittering under his black thick eyebrows and his face livid. He looked at her as she entered, but he neither moved nor spoke, and she thought that he was ill. But the decanter of whisky stood empty on a little table at his side and she noticed it.

"We have some people coming to dinner to-night, Captain Ballantyne," she said. "We shall dine at eight, so there's an hour and a half still."

She went over to a book-case and took out a book. When she turned back into the room a change had taken place in her visitor. Life had flickered into his face. His eyes were wary and cunning.

"And why do you tell me that?" he asked in a voice which was thick and formidable. She had a notion

90

that he did not know who she was and then suddenly she became afraid. She had discovered a secret—his secret. For once in the towns he had let himself go. She had a hope now that he could not move and that he knew it; he sat as still as his arm-chair.

"I had forgotten to tell you," she replied. "I thought you might like to know beforehand."

"Why should I like to know beforehand?"

She had his secret, he plied her with questions to know if she had it. She must hide her knowledge. Every instinct warned her to hide it.

"The people who are coming are strangers to India," she said, "but I have told them of you and they will come expectant."

"You are very kind."

She had spoken lightly and with a laugh. Ballantyne replied without irony or amusement and with his eyes fixed upon her face. Mrs. Repton could not account for the panic which seized hold upon her. She had dined in Captain Ballantyne's company before often enough; he had now been for three days in her house; she had recognised his ability and had neither particularly liked nor disliked him. Her main impression had been that he was not good enough for Stella, and it was an impression purely feminine and instinctive. Now suddenly he had imposed himself upon her as a creature dangerous, beastlike. She wanted to get out of the room but she dared not, for she was sure

91

that her careful steps would, despite herself, change into a run. She sat down, meaning to read for a few moments, compose herself and then go. But no sooner had she taken her seat than her terror increased tenfold, for Ballantyne rose swiftly from his chair and walking in a circle round the room with an extraordinarily light and noiseless step disappeared behind her. Then he sat down. Mrs. Repton heard the slight grating of the legs of a chair upon the floor. It was a chair at a writing-table close by the window and exactly at her back. He could see every movement which she made, and she could see nothing, not so much as the tip of one of his fingers. And of his fingers she was now afraid. He was watching her from his point of vantage; she seemed to feel his eyes burning upon the nape of her neck. And he said nothing; and he did not stir.

It was broad daylight, she assured herself. She had but to cross the room to the bell beside the fireplace. Nay, she had only to scream—and she was very near to screaming—to bring the servants to her rescue. But she dared not do it. Before she was half-way to the bell, before the cry was out of her mouth she would feel his fingers close about her throat.

Mrs. Repton had begun to tell her story with reluctance, dreading lest Thresk should attribute it to a woman's nerves and laugh. But he did not. He listened gravely, seriously; and, as she continued, that

92

nightmare of an evening so lived again in her recollections that she could not but make it vivid in her words.

"I had more than a mere sense of danger," she said. "I felt besides a sort of hideous discomfort, almost physical discomfort, which made me believe that there was something evil in that room beyond the power of language to describe."

She felt her self-control leaving her. If she stayed she must betray her alarm. Even now she had swallowed again and again, and she wondered that he had not detected the working of her throat. She summoned what was left of her courage and tossing her book aside rose slowly and deliberately.

"I think I shall copy Stella's example and lie down for an hour," she said without turning her head towards Ballantyne, and even while she spoke she knew that she had made a mistake in mentioning Stella. He would follow her to discover whether she went to Stella's room and told what she had seen to her. But he did not move. She reached the door, turned the handle, went out and closed the door behind her.

For a moment then her strength failed her; she leaned against the wall by the side of the door, her heart racing. But the fear that he would follow urged her on. She crossed the hall and stopped deliberately before a cabinet of china at the foot of the stairs, which stood against the wall in which the library door was placed. While she stood there she saw the door open very slowly and Ballantyne's livid face appear at the opening. She turned towards the stairs and mounted them without looking back. Halfway up a turn hid the hall from her, and the moment after she had passed the turn she heard him crossing the hall after her, again with a lightness of step which seemed to be uncanny and inhuman in so heavy and gross a creature.

"I was appalled," she said to Thresk frankly. "He had the step of an animal. I felt that some great baboon was tracking me stealthily."

Mrs. Repton came to Stella Ballantyne's door and was careful not to stop. She reached her own room, and once in shot the bolt; and in a moment or two she heard him breathing just outside the panels.

"And to think that Stella is alone with him in the jungle months at a time!" she cried, actually wringing her hands. "That thought was in my mind all the time—a horror of a thought. Oh, I could understand now the loss of her spirits, her colour, her youth."

Pictures of lonely camps and empty rest-houses, far removed from any habitation in the silence of Indian nights, rose before her eyes. She imagined Stella propped up on her elbow in bed, wide-eyed with terror, listening and listening to the light footsteps of the drunken brute beyond the partition-wall, shivering when they approached, dropping back with the dew of her sweat upon her forehead when they retired; and these pictures she translated in words for Thresk in her house on the Khamballa Hill.

Thresk was moved and showed that he was moved. He rose and walked to the window, turning his back to her.

"Why did she marry him?" he exclaimed. "She was poor, but she had a little money. Why did she marry him?" and he turned back to Mrs. Repton for an answer.

She gave him one quick look and said:

"That is one of the things she has never told me and I didn't meet her until after she had married him."

"And why doesn't she leave him?"

Mrs. Repton held up her hands.

"Oh, the easy questions, Mr. Thresk! How many women endure the thing that is because it is? Even to leave your husband you want a trifle of spirit. And what if your spirit's broken? What if you are cowed? What if you live in terror day and night?"

"Yes. I am a fool," said Thresk, and he sat down again. "There are two more questions I want to ask. Did you ever talk to Stella"—the Christian name slipped naturally from him and only Jane Repton of the two remarked that he had used it—"of that incident in the library at Agra?"

"Yes."

"And did she in consequence of what you told her give you any account of her life with her husband?"

Mrs. Repton hesitated not because she was any longer in doubt as to whether she would speak the whole truth or not—she had committed herself already too far—but because the form of the question nettled her. It was a little too forensic for her taste. She was anxious to know the man; she could dispense with the barrister altogether.

"Yes, she did," she replied, "and don't cross-examine me, please."

"I beg your pardon," said Thresk with a laugh which made him human on the instant.

"Well, it's true," said Jane Repton in a rush. "She told me the truth—what you know and more. He stripped when he was drunk, stripped to the skin. Think of it! Stella told me that and broke down. Oh, if you had seen her! For Stella to give way— that alone must alarm her friends. Oh, but the look of her! She sat by my side on the sofa, wringing her hands, with the tears pouring down her face . . ." Thresk rose quickly from his chair.

"Thank you," he said, cutting her short. He wanted to hear no more. He held out his hand to her with a certain abruptness.

Mrs. Repton rose too.

"What are you going to do?" she asked breathlessly. "I must know I have a right to, I think. I have told you so much. I was in great doubt whether I should tell you anything. But——" Her voice broke and she ended her plea lamely enough: "I am very fond of Stella."

"I know that," said Thresk, and his voice was grateful and his face most friendly.

"Well, what are you going to do?"

"I am going to write to her to ask her to join me in Bombay," he replied.

CHAPTER X

A long silence followed upon his words. Jane Repton turned to the mantelshelf and moved an ornament here and another one there. She had contemplated this very consequence of Thresk's journey to Chitipur. She had actually worked for it herself. She was frank enough to acknowledge that. None the less his announcement, quietly as he had made it, was a shock to her. She did not, however, go back upon her work; and when she spoke it was rather to make sure that he was not going to act upon an unconsidered impulse.

"It will damage your career," she said. "Of course you have thought of that."

"It will alter it," he answered, "if she comes to me. I shall go out of Parliament, of course."

"And your practice?"

"That will suffer too for a while no doubt. But even if I lost it altogether I should not be a poor man."

"You have saved money?"

"No. There has not been much time for that, but for a good many years now I have collected silver and miniatures. I know something about them and the collection is of value."

"I see."

98

Mrs. Repton looked at him now. Oh, yes, he had thought his proposal out during the night journey to Bombay—not a doubt of it.

"Stella, too, will suffer," she said.

"Worse than she does now?" asked Thresk.

"No. But her position will be difficult for awhile at least," and she came towards Thresk and pleaded.

"You will be thoughtful of her, for her? Oh, if you should play her false—how I should hate you!" and her eyes flashed fire at him.

"I don't think that you need fear that."

But he was too calm for her, too quiet. She was in the mood to want heroics. She clamoured for protestations as a drug for her uneasy mind. And Thresk stood before her without one. She searched his face with doubtful eyes. Oh, there seemed to her no tenderness in it.

"She will need—love," said Mrs. Repton. "There—that's the word. Can you give it her?"

"If she comes to me—yes. I have wanted her for eight years," and then suddenly she got, not heroics, but a glimpse of a real passion. A spasm of pain convulsed his face. He sat down and beat with his fist upon the table. "It was horrible to me to ride away from that camp and leave her there—miles away from any friend. I would have torn her from him by force if there had been a single hope that way. But his levies would have barred the road. No, this was the

99

only chance: to come away to Bombay, to write to her that the first day, the first night she is able to slip out and travel here she will find me waiting."

Mrs. Repton was satisfied. But while he had been speaking a new fear had entered into her.

"There's something I should have thought of," she exclaimed.

"Yes?"

"Captain Ballantyne is not generous. He is just the sort of man not to divorce his wife."

Thresk raised his head. Clearly that possibility had no more occurred to him than it had to Jane Repton. He thought it over now.

"Just the sort of man," he agreed. "But we must take that risk—if she comes."

"The letter's not yet written," Mrs. Repton suggested.

"But it will be," he replied, and then he stood and confronted her. "Do you wish me not to write it?"

She avoided his eyes, she looked upon the floor, she began more than one sentence of evasion; but in the end she took both his hands in hers and said stoutly:

"No, I don't! Write! Write!"

"Thank you!"

He went to the door, and when he had reached it she called to him in a low voice.

"Mr. Thresk, what did you mean when you repeated and repeated if she comes?"

100

NEWS FROM CHITIPUR

Thresk came slowly back into the room.

"I meant that eight years ago I gave her a very good reason why she should put no faith in me."

He told her that quite frankly and simply, but he told her no more than that, and she let him go. He went back to the great hotel on the Apollo Bund and sent off a number of cablegrams to London saying that he had missed his steamer and that the work waiting for him must go to other hands. The letter to Stella Ballantyne he kept to the last. It could not reach her immediately in any case since she was in camp. For all he knew it might be weeks before she read it; and he had need to go warily in the writing of it. Certain words she had used to him were an encouragement; but there were others which made him doubt whether she would have any faith in him. Every now and then there had been a savour of bitterness. Once she had been shamed because of him, on Bignor Hill where Stane Street runs to Chichester, and a second time in front of him in the tent at Chitipur. No, it was not an easy letter which he had to write, and he took the night and the greater part of the next day to decide upon its wording. It could not in any case go until the night-mail. He had finished it and directed it by six o'clock in the evening and he went down with the letter in his hand into the big lounge to post it in the box there. But it never was posted.

Close to the foot of the staircase stood a tape ma-

chine, and as Thresk descended he heard the clicking
of the instrument and saw the usual small group of
visitors about it. They were mostly Americans, and
they were reading out to one another the latest prices
of the stock-markets. Some of the chatter reached to
Thresk's inattentive ears, and when he was only two
steps from the floor one carelessly-spoken phrase in-
terjected between the values of two securities brought
him to a stop. The speaker was a young man with a
squarish face and thick hair parted accurately in the
middle. He was dressed in a thin grey suit and he
was passing the tape between his fingers as it ran out.
The picture of him was impressed during that instant
upon Thresk's mind, so that he could never afterwards
forget it.

"Copper's up one point," he was saying, "that's
fine. Who's Captain Ballantyne, I wonder? United
Steel has dropped seven-eighths. Well, that doesn't
affect me," and so he ran on.

Thresk heard no more of what he said. He stood
wondering what news could have come up on the tape
of Captain Ballantyne who was out in camp in the
state of Chitipur, or if there was another Captain
Ballantyne. He joined the little group in front of the
machine, and picking up the ribbon from the floor
ran his eyes backwards along it until he came to
"United Steel." The sentence in front of that ran as
follows:

NEWS FROM CHITIPUR

"Captain Ballantyne was found dead early yesterday morning outside his tent close to Jarwhal Junction."

Thresk read the sentence twice and then walked away. The news might be false, of course, but if it were true here was a revolution in his life. There was no need for this letter which he held in his hand. The way was smoothed out for Stella, for him. Not for a moment could he pretend to do anything but welcome the news, to wish with all his heart that it was true. And it seemed probable news. There was the matter of that photograph. Thresk had carried it out to the Governor's house on Malabar Point on the very morning of his arrival in Bombay. He had driven on to Mrs. Repton's house after he had left it there. But he had taken it away from Chitipur at too late a day to save Ballantyne. Ballantyne had, after all, had good cause to be afraid while he possessed it, and the news had not yet got to Salak's friends that it had left his possession. Thus he made out the history of Captain Ballantyne's death.

The tape machine, however, might have ticked out a mere rumour with no truth in it at all. He went to the office and obtained a copy of *The Advocate of India*, —the evening newspaper of the city. He looked at the stop-press telegrams. There was no mention of Ballantyne's death. Nor on glancing down the columns could he find in any paragraph a statement that any mishap had befallen him. But on the other hand he read that he himself, Henry Thresk, having brought his case to a successful conclusion, had left India yesterday by the mail-steamer *Madras*, bound for Marseilles. He threw down the paper and went to the telephone-box. If the news were true the one person likely to know of it was Mrs. Repton. Thresk rang up the house on the Khamballa Hill and asked to speak to her. An answer was returned to him at once that Mrs. Repton had given orders that she was not to be disturbed. Thresk however insisted:

"Will you please give my name to her—Henry Thresk," and he waited with his ear to the receiver for a century. At last a voice spoke to him, but it was again the voice of the servant.

"The Memsahib very sorry, sir, but cannot speak to any one just now;" and he heard the jar of the instrument as the receiver at the other end was sharply hung up and the connection broken.

Thresk came out from the telephone-box with a face puzzled and very grave. Mrs. Repton refused to speak to him!

It was a fact, an inexplicable fact, and it alarmed him. It was impossible to believe that mere reflection during the last twenty-four hours had brought about so complete a revolution in her feelings. He to whom she had passionately cried "Write! Write!" only yesterday could hardly be barred out from mere

104

speech with her to-day for any fault of his. He had done nothing, had seen no one. Thresk was certain now that the news upon the tape was true. But it could not be all the truth. There was something behind it—something rather grim and terrible.

Thresk walked to the door of the hotel and called up a motor-car. "Tell him to drive to the Khamballa Hill," he said to the porter. "I'll let him know when to stop."

The porter translated the order and Thresk stopped him at Mrs. Repton's door.

"The Memsahib does not receive any one to-day," said the butler.

"I know," replied Thresk. He scribbled on a card and sent it in. There was a long delay. Thresk stood in the hall looking out through the open door. Night had come. There were lights upon the roadway, lights a long way below at the water's edge on Breach Candy, and there was a light twinkling far out on the Arabian Sea. But in the house behind him all was dark. He had come to an abode of desolation and mourning; and his heart sank and he was attacked with forebodings. At last in the passage behind him there was a shuffling of feet and a gleam of white. The Memsahib would receive him.

Thresk was shown into the drawing-room. That room too was unlit. But the blinds had not been lowered and light from a street lamp outside turned the

105

darkness into twilight. No one came forward to greet him, but the room was not empty. He saw Repton and his wife huddled close together on a sofa in a recess by the fireplace.

"I thought that I had better come up from Bombay," said Thresk, as he stood in the middle of the room. No answer was returned to him for a few moments, and then it was Repton himself who spoke.

"Yes, yes," he said, and he got up from the sofa. "I think we had better have some light," he added in a strange indifferent voice. He turned the light on in the central chandelier, leaving the corners of the room in shadow, like—the parallel forced its way into Thresk's mind—like the tent in Chitipur. Then very methodically he pulled down the blinds. He did not look at Thresk and Jane Repton on the couch never stirred. Thresk's forebodings became a dreadful certainty. Some evil thing had happened. He might have been in a house of death. He knew that he was not wanted there, that husband and wife wished to be alone and silently resented his presence. But he could not go without more knowledge than he had.

"A message came up on the tape half an hour ago," he said in a low voice. "It reported that Ballantyne was dead."

"Yes," replied Repton. He was leaning forward over a table and looking up to the chandelier as if he fancied that its light burnt more dimly than was usual.

106

"That's true," and he spoke in the same strange mechanical voice he had used before.

"That he was found dead outside his tent," Thresk added.

"It's quite true," Repton agreed. "We are very sorry."

"Sorry!"

The exclamation burst from Thresk's lips.

"Yes."

Repton moved away from the chandelier. He had not looked at Thresk once since he had entered the room; nor did he look towards his wife. His face was very pale and he was busy now setting a chair in place, moving a photograph, doing any one of the little unnecessary things people restlessly do when there is an importunate visitor in the room who will not go.

"You see, there's terribly bad news," he added.

"What news?"

"He was shot, you know. That wasn't in the telegram on the tape, of course. Yes, he was shot—on the same night you dined there—after you had gone."

"Shot!"

Thresk's voice dropped to a whisper.

"Yes," and the dull quiet voice went on, speaking apparently of some trivial affair in which none of them could have any interest. "He was shot by a bullet from a little rook-rifle which belonged to Stella, and which she was in the habit of using."

Thresk's heart stood still. A picture flashed before his eyes. He saw the inside of that dimly lit tent with its red lining and Stella standing by the table. He could hear her voice: "This is my little rook-rifle. I was seeing that it was clean for to-morrow." She had spoken so carelessly, so indifferently that it wasn't conceivable that what was in all their minds could be true. Yet she had spoken, after all, no more indifferently than Repton was speaking now; and he was in a great stress of grief. Then Thresk's mind leaped to the weak point in all this chain of presumption.

"But Ballantyne was found *outside* the tent," he cried with a little note of triumph. But it had no echo in Repton's reply.

"I know. That makes everything so much worse."

"What do you mean?"

"Ballantyne was found in the morning outside the tent stone-cold. But no one had heard the shot, and there were sentries on the edge of the encampment. He had been dragged outside after he was dead or when he was dying."

A low cry broke from Thresk. The weak point became of a sudden the most deadly, the most terrible element in the whole case. He could hear the prosecuting counsel making play with it. He stood for a moment lost in horror. Repton had no further word to say to him. Mrs. Repton had never once spoken. They wanted him away, out of the room, out of the house. Some insight let him into the meaning of her silence. In the presence of this tragedy remorse had gripped her. She was looking upon herself as one who had plotted harm for Stella. She would never forgive Thresk for his share in the plot.

Thresk went out of the room without a word more to either Repton or his wife. Whatever he did now he must do by himself. He would not be admitted into that house again. He closed the door of the room behind him, and hardly had he closed it when he heard the snap of a switch and the line of light under the door vanished. Once more there was darkness in the drawing-room. Repton no doubt had returned to his wife's side and they were huddled again side by side on the sofa. Thresk walked down the hill with a horrible feeling of isolation and loneliness. But he shook it off as he neared the lights of Bombay.

CHAPTER XI

Thresk reached his hotel with some words ringing in his head which Jane Repton had spoken to him at Mrs. Carruthers' dinner-party:

"You can get any single thing in life you want if you want it enough, but you cannot control the price you will have to pay for it. That you will only learn afterwards and gradually."

He had got what he had wanted—the career of distinction, and he wondered whether he was to begin now to learn its price.

He mounted to his sitting-room on the second floor, avoiding the lounge and the lift and using a small side staircase instead of the great central one. He had passed no one on the way. In his room he looked upon the mantelshelf and on the table. No visitor had called on him that day; no letter awaited him. For the first time since he had landed in India a day had passed without some resident leaving on him a card or a note of invitation. The newspapers gave him the reason. He was supposed to have left on the *Madras* for England. To make sure he rang for his waiter; no message of any kind had come.

"Shall I ask at the office?" the waiter asked.

110

"By no means," answered Thresk, and he added: "I will have dinner served up here to-night."

There was just a possibility, he thought, that he might after all escape this particular payment. He took from his pocket his unposted letter to Stella Ballantyne. There was no longer any use for it and even its existence was now dangerous to Stella. For let it be discovered, however she might plead that she knew nothing of its contents, a motive for the death of Ballantyne might be inferred from it. It would be a false motive, but just the sort of motive which the man in the street would immediately accept. Thresk burnt the letter carefully in a plate and pounded up each black flake of paper until nothing was left but ashes. Then for the moment his work was done. He had only to wait and he did not wait long. On the very next morning his newspaper informed him that Inspector Coulson of the Bombay Police had left for Chitipur.

The Inspector was a young man devoted to his work, but he travelled now upon a duty which he would gladly have handed to any other of his colleagues. He had met Stella Ballantyne in Bombay upon one of her rare visits to Jane Repton. He had sat at the same dinner-table with her, and he did not find it pleasant to reflect on the tragic destiny which she must now fulfil. For the facts were fatal.

At daybreak on the morning of the Friday a sentry on the outer edge of the camp at Jarwhal Junction had

111

noticed something black lying upon the ground in the open just outside the door of the Agent's big marquee. He ran across the ground and discovered Captain Ballantyne sprawling, face downwards, in the smoking-suit which he had worn at dinner the night before. The sentry shook him gently by the shoulder, but the limpness of the body frightened him. Then he noticed that there was blood upon the ground, and calling loudly for help he ran to the guard-room tent. He returned with others of the native levies and they lifted Ballantyne up. He was dead and the body was cold. The levies carried him into the tent and opened his shirt. He had been shot through the heart. They then roused Mrs. Ballantyne's ayah and bade her wake her mistress. The ayah went into Mrs. Ballantyne's room and found her mistress sound asleep. She waked her up and told her what had happened. Stella Ballantyne said not a word. She got out of bed, and flinging on some clothes went into the outer tent, where the servants were standing about the body. Stella Ballantyne went quite close to it and looked down upon the dead man's face for a long time. She was pale, but there was no shrinking in her attitude—no apprehension in her eyes.

"He has been killed," she said at length; "telegrams must be sent at once: to Ajmere for a doctor, to Bombay, and to His Highness the Maharajah."

Baram Singh salaamed.

"It is as your Excellency wills," he said.

"I will write them," said Stella quietly. And she sat down at her own writing-table there and then.

The doctor from Ajmere arrived during the day, made an examination and telegraphed a report to the Chief Commissioner at Ajmere. That report contained the three significant points which Repton had enumerated to Thresk, but with some still more significant details. The bullet which pierced Captain Ballantyne's heart had been fired from Mrs. Ballantyne's small rook-rifle, and the exploded cartridge was still in the breech. The rifle was standing up against Mrs. Ballantyne's writing-table in a corner of the tent, when the doctor from Ajmere discovered it. In the second place, although Ballantyne was found in the open, there was a patch of blood upon the carpet within the tent and a trail of blood from that spot to the door. There could be no doubt that Ballantyne was killed inside. There was the third point to establish that theory. Neither the sentry on guard nor any one of the servants sleeping in the adjacent tents had heard the crack of the rifle. It would not be loud in any case, but if the weapon had been fired in the open it would have been sufficiently sharp and clear to attract the attention of the men on guard. The heavy double lining of the tent however was thick enough so to muffle and deaden the sound that it would pass unnoticed.

113

The report was considered at Ajmere and forwarded. It now brought Inspector Coluson of the Police up the railway from Bombay. He found Mrs. Ballantyne waiting for him at the Residency of Chitipur.

"I must tell you who I am," he said awkwardly.

"There is no need to," she answered, "I know."

He then cautioned her in the usual way, and producing his pocket-book asked her whether she wished to throw any light upon her husband's death.

"No," she said. "I have nothing to say. I was asleep and in bed when my ayah came into my room with the news of his death."

"Yes," said the Inspector uncomfortably. That detail, next to the dragging of the body out of the tent, seemed to him the grimmest part of the whole tragedy.

He shut up his book.

"I am afraid it is all very unsatisfactory," he said. "I think we must go back to Bombay."

"It is as your Excellency wills," said Stella in Hindustani, and the Inspector was startled by the bad taste of the joke. He had not the knowledge of her life with Ballantyne, which alone would have given him the key to understand her. But he was not a fool, and a second glance at her showed to him that she was not speaking in joke at all. He had an impression that she was so tired that she did not at the moment care what happened to her at all. The fatigue would wear off, no doubt, when she realised that she

114

must fight for her life, but now she stood in front of him indifferent and docile—much as one of the native levies was wont to stand before her husband. The words which the levies used and the language in which they spoke them rose naturally to her lips, as the only words and language suitable to the occasion.

"You see, Mrs. Ballantyne," he said gently, "there is no reason to suspect a single one of your servants or of your escort."

"And there is reason to suspect me," she added, looking at him quietly and steadily.

The Inspector for his part looked away. He was a young man—no more than a year or two older than Stella Ballantyne herself. They both came from the same kind of stock. Her people and his people might have been friends in some pleasant country village in one of the English counties. She was pretty, too, disconcertingly pretty, in spite of the dark circles under her eyes and the pallor of her face. There was a delicacy in her looks and in her dress which appealed to him for tenderness. The appeal was all the stronger because it was only in that way and unconsciously that she appealed. In her voice, in her bearing, in her eyes there was no request, no prayer.

"I have been to the Palace," he said, "I have had an audience with the Maharajah."

"Of course," she answered. "I shall put no difficulties in your way."

THE WITNESS FOR THE DEFENCE

He was standing in her own drawing-room, noticing with what skill comfort had been combined with daintiness, and how she had followed the usual instinct of her kind in trying to create here in this room a piece of England. Through the window he looked out upon a lawn which was being watered by a garden-sprinkler, and where a gardener was at work attending to a bed of bright flowers. There, too, she had been making the usual pathetic attempt to convert a half-acre of this country of yellow desert into a green garden of England. Coulson had not a shadow of doubt in his mind Stella Ballantyne would exchange this room with its restful colours and its outlook on a green lawn for—at the best—many years of solitary imprisonment in Poona Gaol. He shut up his book with a snap.

"Will you be ready to go in an hour?" he asked roughly.

"Yes," said she.

"If I leave you unwatched during that hour you will promise to me that you *will* be ready to go in an hour?"

Stella Ballantyne nodded her head.

"I shall not kill myself now," she said, and he looked at her quickly, but she did not trouble to explain her words. She merely added: "I may take some clothes, I suppose?"

"Whatever you need," said the Inspector. And he took her down to Bombay.

She was formally charged next morning before the

stipendiary for the murder of her husband and remanded for a week.

She was remanded at eleven o'clock in the morning,
and five minutes later the news was ticked off on the
tape at the Taj Mahal Hotel. Within another five
minutes the news was brought upstairs to Thresk.
He had been fortunate. He was in a huge hotel,
where people flit through its rooms for a day and are
gone the next, and no one is concerned with the doings
of his neighbour, a place of arrival and departure like
the platform of a great railway station. There was no
place in all Bombay where Thresk could so easily pass
unnoticed. And he had passed unnoticed. A single
inquiry at the office, it is true, would have revealed his
presence, but no one had inquired, since by this time
he should be nearing Aden. He had kept to his rooms
during the day and had only taken the air after it was
dark. This was in the early stages of wireless teleg-
raphy, and the *Madras* had no installation. It might
be that inquiries would be made for him at Aden. He
could only wait with Jane Repton's words ringing in
his ears: "You cannot control the price you will have
to pay."

Stella Ballantyne was brought up again in a week's
time and the case then proceeded from day to day.
The character of Ballantyne was revealed, his brutali-
ties, his cunning. Detail by detail he was built up
into a gross sinister figure secret and violent which

117

lived again in that crowded court and turned the eyes of the spectators with a shiver of discomfort upon the young and quiet woman in the dock. And in that character the prosecution found the motive of the crime. Sympathy at times ran high for Stella Ballantyne, but there were always the two grim details to keep it in check: she had been found asleep by her ayah, quietly restfully asleep within a few hours of Ballantyne's death; and she had, according to the theory of the Crown, found in some violence of passion the strength to drag the dying man from the tent and to leave him to gasp out his life under the stars.

Thresk watched the case from his rooms at the Taj Mahal Hotel. Every fact which was calculated to arouse sympathy for her was also helping to condemn her. No one doubted that she had shot Stephen Ballantyne. He deserved shooting—very well. But that did not give her the right to be his executioner. What was her defence to be? A sudden intolerable provocation? How would that square with the dragging of his body across the carpet to the door? There was the fatal insuperable act.

Thresk read again and again the reports of the proceedings for a hint as to the line of the defence. He got it the day when Repton appeared in the witness-box on a subpœna from the Crown to bear testimony to the violence of Stephen Ballantyne. He had seen

Stella with her wrist bruised so that in public she could not remove her gloves.

"What kind of bruises?" asked the counsel.

"Such bruises as might be made by some one twisting her arms," he answered, and then Mr. Travers, a young barrister who was enjoying his first leap into the public eye, rose to cross-examine.

Thresk read through that cross-examination and rose to his feet. "You cannot control the price you will have to pay," he said to himself. That day, when Mrs. Ballantyne's solicitor returned to his office after the rising of the Court, he found Thresk waiting for him.

"I wish to give evidence for Mrs. Ballantyne," said Thresk—"evidence which will acquit her."

He spoke with so much certainty that the solicitor was fairly startled.

"And with evidence so positive in your possession it is only this afternoon that you come here with it! Why?"

Thresk was prepared for the question.

"I have a great deal of work waiting for me in London," he returned. "I hoped that it might not be necessary for me to appear at all. Now I see that it is."

The solicitor looked straight at Thresk.

"I knew from Mrs. Repton that you dined with the Ballantynes that night, but she was sure that you knew nothing of the affair. You had left the tent before it happened."

"That is true," answered Thresk.

"Yet you have evidence which will acquit Mrs. Ballantyne?"

"I think so."

"How is it, then," the lawyer asked, "that we have heard nothing of this evidence at all from Mrs. Ballantyne herself?"

"Because she knows nothing of it," replied Thresk.

The lawyer pointed to a chair. The two men sat down together in the office and it was long before they parted.

Within an hour of Thresk's return from the solicitor's office an Inspector of Police waited on him at his hotel and was instantly shown up.

"We did not know until to-day," he said, "that you were still in Bombay, Mr. Thresk. We believed you to be on the *Madras*, which reached Marseilles early this morning."

"I missed it," replied Thresk. "Had you wanted me you could have inquired at Port Said five days ago."

"Five days ago we had no information."

The native servants of Ballantyne had from the first shrouded themselves in ignorance. They would answer what questions were put to them; they would not go one inch beyond. The crime was an affair of the Sahibs and the less they had to do with it the better, until at all events they were sure which way the wind was setting from Government House. Of their own initiative they knew nothing. It was thus only by the discovery of Thresk's letter to Captain Ballantyne, which was found crumpled up in a waste-paper basket, that his presence that night in the tent was suspected.

"It is strange," the Inspector grumbled, "that you did not come to us of your own accord when you had missed your boat and tell us what you knew."

"I don't think it is strange at all," answered Thresk, "for I am a witness for the defence. I shall give my evidence when the case for the defence opens."

The Inspector was disconcerted and went away. Thresk's policy had so far succeeded. But he had taken a great risk and now that it was past he realised with an intense relief how serious the risk had been. If the Inspector had called upon him before he had made known his presence to Mrs. Ballantyne's solicitor and offered his evidence, his position would have been difficult. He would have had to discover some other good reason why he had lain quietly at his hotel during these last days. But fortune had favoured him. He had to thank, above all, the secrecy of the native servants.

CHAPTER XII

Thresk's fears were justified. Sympathy for Stella Ballantyne had already begun to wane. The fact that Ballantyne had been found outside the door of the tent was already assuming a sinister importance. Mrs. Ballantyne's counsel slid discreetly over that awkward incident. Very fortunately, as it was now to prove, he did not cross-examine the doctor from Ajmere at all. But there are always the few who oppóse the general opinion—the men and women who are in the minority because it is the minority; those whom the hysterical glorification made of Stella Ballantyne had offended; the austere, the pedantic, the just, the jealous, all were quick to seize upon this disconcerting fact: Stella Ballantyne had dragged her dying husband from the tent. It was either sheer callousness or blind fury—you might take your choice. In either case it dulled the glow of martyrdom which for a week or two had been so radiant upon Stella Ballantyne's forehead; and the few who argued thus attracted adherents daily. And with the sympathy for Stella Ballantyne interest in the case began to wane too.

The magisterial inquiry threatened to become tedious.

122

THRESK GIVES EVIDENCE

The pictures of the witnesses and the principals occupied less and less space in the newspapers. In another week the case would be coldly left with a shrug of the shoulders to the Law Courts. But unexpectedly curiosity was stirred again, for the day after Thresk had called upon the lawyer, when the case for the Crown was at an end, Mrs. Ballantyne's counsel, Mr. Travers, asked permission to recall Baram Singh. Permission was granted, and Baram Singh once more took his place in the witness-box.

Mr. Travers leant against the desk behind him and put his questions with the most significant slowness.

"I wish to ask you, Baram Singh," he said, "about the dinner-table on the Thursday night. You laid it?"

"Yes," replied Baram Singh.

"For how many?"

"For three."

There was a movement through the whole court.

"Yes," said Mr. Travers, "Captain Ballantyne had a visitor that night."

Baram Singh agreed.

"Look round the court and tell the magistrate if you can see here the man who dined with Captain Ballantyne and his wife that night."

For a moment the court was filled with the noise of murmuring. The usher cried "Silence!" and the murmuring ceased. A hush of expectation filled that crowded room as Baram Singh's eyes travelled slowly

123

round the walls. He dropped them to the well of the court, and even his unexpressive face flashed with a look of recognition.

"There," he cried, "there!" and he pointed to a man who was sitting just underneath the counsel's bench.

Mr. Travers leant forward and in a quiet but particularly clear voice said:

"Will you kindly stand up, Mr. Thresk?"

Thresk stood up. To many of those present—the idlers, the people of fashion, the seekers after a thrill of excitement who fill the public galleries and law-courts —his long conduct of the great Carruthers trial had made him a familiar figure. To the others his name, at all events, was known, and as he stood up on the floor of the court a swift and regular movement like a ripple of water passed through the throng. They leant forward to get a clearer view of him and for a moment there was a hiss of excited whispering.

"That is the man who dined with Captain and Mrs. Ballantyne on the night when Captain Ballantyne was killed?" said Mr. Travers.

"Yes," replied Baram Singh.

No one understood what was coming. People began to ask themselves whether Thresk was concerned in the murder. Word had been published that he had already left for England. How was it he was here now? Mr. Travers, for his part, was enjoying to the full the suspense which his question had aroused. Not by any intonation did he allow a hint to escape him whether he looked upon Thresk as an enemy or friend.

"You may sit down, sir, now," he said, and Thresk resumed his seat.

"Will you tell us what you know of Mr. Thresk's visit to the Captain?" Travers resumed, and Baram Singh told how a camel had been sent to the dâk-house by the station of Jarwhal Junction.

"Yes," said Mr. Travers, "and he dined in the tent. How long did he stay?"

"He left the camp at eleven o'clock on the camel to catch the night train to Bombay. The Captain-sahib saw him off from the edge of the camp."

"Ah," said Mr. Travers, "Captain Ballantyne saw him off?"

"Yes—from the edge of the camp."

"And then went back to the tent?"

"Yes."

"Now I want to take you to another point. You waited at dinner?"

"Yes."

"And towards the close of dinner Mrs. Ballantyne left the room?"

"Yes."

"She did not come back again?"

"No."

"No. The two men were then left alone?"

125

"Yes."

"After dinner was the table cleared?"

"Yes," said Baram Singh, "the Captain-sahib called to me to clear the table quickly."

"Yes," said Travers. "Now, will you tell me what the Captain-sahib was doing while you were clearing the table?"

Baram Singh reflected.

"First of all the Captain-sahib offered a box of cheroots to his visitor, and his visitor refused and took a pipe from his pocket. The Captain-sahib then lit a cheroot for himself and replaced the box on the top of the bureau."

"And after that?" asked Travers.

"After that," said Baram Singh, "he stooped down, unlocked the bottom drawer of his bureau and then turned sharply to me and told me to hurry and get out."

"And that order you obeyed?"

"Yes."

"Now, Baram Singh, did you enter the room again?"

Baram Singh explained that after he had gone out with the table-cloth he returned in a few moments with an ash-tray, which he placed beside the visitor-sahib.

"Yes," said Travers. "Had Captain Ballantyne altered his position?"

Baram Singh then related that Captain Ballantyne

was still sitting in his chair by the bureau, but that the drawer of the bureau was now open, and that on the ground close to Captain Ballantyne's feet there was a red despatch-box.

"The Captain-sahib," he continued, "turned to me with great anger, and drove me again out of the room."

"Thank you," said Mr. Travers, and he sat down.

The prosecuting counsel rose at once.

"Now, Baram Singh," he said with severity, "why did you not mention when you were first put in the witness-box that this gentleman was present in the camp that night?"

"I was not asked."

"No, that is quite true," he continued, "you were not asked specifically, but you were asked to tell all that you knew."

"I did not interfere," replied Baram Singh. "I answered what questions were asked. Besides, when the sahib left the camp the Captain-sahib was alive."

At this moment Mr. Travers leaned across to the prosecuting counsel and said: "It will all be made clear when Mr. Thresk goes into the box."

And once more, as Mr. Travers spoke these words, a rustle of expectancy ran round the court.

Travers opened the case for the defence on the following morning. He had been originally instructed, he declared, to reserve the defence for the actual trial

127

before the jury, but upon his own urgent advice that plan was not to be followed. The case which he had to put before the stipendiary must so infallibly prove that Mrs. Ballantyne was free from all complicity in this crime that he felt he would not be doing his duty to her unless he made it public at the first opportunity. That unhappy lady had already, as every one who had paid even the most careless attention to the facts that had been presented by the prosecution must know, suffered so much distress and sorrow in the course of her married life that he felt it would not be fair to add to it the strain and suspense which even the most innocent must suffer when sent for trial upon such a serious charge. He at once proposed to call Mr. Thresk, and Thresk rose and went into the witness-box.

Thresk told the story of that dinner-party word for word as it had occurred, laying some emphasis on the terror which from time to time had taken possession of Stephen Ballantyne, down to the moment when Baram Singh had brought the ash-tray and left the two men together, Thresk sitting by the table in the middle of the room and Ballantyne at his bureau with the despatch-box on the floor at his feet.

"Then I noticed an extraordinary look of fear disfigure his face," he continued, "and following the direction of his eyes I saw a lean brown arm with a thin hand as delicate as a woman's wriggle forward

128

from beneath the wall of the tent towards the despatch-box."

"You saw that quite clearly?" asked Mr. Travers.

"The tent was not very brightly lit," Thresk explained. "At the first glance I saw something moving. I was inclined to believe it a snake and to account in that way for Captain Ballantyne's fear and the sudden rigidity of his attitude. But I looked again and I was then quite sure that it was an arm and hand."

The evidence roused those present to such a tension of excitement and to so loud a burst of murmuring that it was quite a minute before order was restored and Thresk took up his tale again. He described Ballantyne's search for the thief.

"And what were you doing," Mr. Travers asked, "whilst the search was being made?"

"I stood by the table holding the despatch-box firmly in my hands as Ballantyne had urgently asked me to do."

"Quite so," said Mr. Travers; and the attention of the court was now directed to that despatch-box and the portrait of Bahadur Salak which it contained. The history of the photograph, its importance at this moment when Salak's trial impended, and Ballantyne's conviction of the extreme danger which its possessor ran—a conviction established by the bold attempt to steal it made under their very eyes—was laid before the stipendiary. He sent the case to trial as he was bound to do, but the verdict in most people's eyes was a foregone conclusion. Thresk had supplied a story which accounted for the crime, and cross-examination could not shake him. It was easy to believe that at the very moment when Thresk was saying goodbye to Captain Ballantyne by the fire on the edge of the camp the thief slipped into the marquee, and when discovered by Ballantyne either on his return or later shot him with Mrs. Ballantyne's rifle. It was clear that no conviction could be obtained while this story held the field and in due course Mrs. Ballantyne was acquitted. Of Thresk's return to the tent just before leaving the camp nothing was said. Thresk himself did not mention it and the counsel for the Crown had no hint which could help him to elicit it.

Thus the case ended. The popular heroine of a criminal trial loses, as all observers will have noticed, her crown of romance the moment she is set free; and that good fortune awaited Stella Ballantyne. Thresk called the next day upon Jane Repton and was coldly told that Stella had already gone from Bombay. He betook himself to her solicitor, who was cordial but uncommunicative. The Reptons, it appeared, were responsible to him for the conduct of the case. He had not any knowledge of Stella Ballantyne's destination, and he pointed to a stack of telegrams and letters as confirmation of his words.

THRESK GIVES EVIDENCE

"They will all go up to Khamballa Hill," he said. "I have no other address."

The next day, however, a little note of gratitude came to Thresk through the post. It was unsigned and without any address. But it was in Stella Ballantyne's handwriting and the post-mark was Kurrachee. That she did not wish to see him he could quite understand; Kurrachee was a port from which ships sailed to many destinations; he could hardly set out in a blind search for her across the world. So here, it seemed, was that chapter closed. He took the next steamer westwards from Bombay, landed at Brindisi and went back to his work in the Law Courts and in Parliament.

CHAPTER XIII

But though she disappeared Stella Ballantyne was not in flight from men and women. She avoided them because they did not for the moment count in her thoughts, except as possible hindrances. She was not so much running away as running to the place of her desires. She yielded to an impulse with which they had nothing whatever to do, an impulse so overmastering that even to the Reptons her precipitancy wore a look of ingratitude. She drove home with Jane Repton as soon as she was released, to the house on Khamballa Hill, and while she was still in the carriage she said:

"I must go away to-morrow morning."

She was sitting forward with a tense and eager look upon her face and her hands clenched tightly in her lap.

"There is no need for that. Make your home with us, Stella, for a little while and hold your head high."

Jane Repton had talked over this proposal with her husband. Both of them recognised that the acceptance of it would entail on them some little sacrifice. Prejudice would be difficult. But they had thrust these

considerations aside in the loyalty of their friendship
and Jane Repton was a little hurt that Stella waved
away their invitation without ceremony.

"I can't. I can't," she said irritably. "Don't try
to stop me."

Her nerves were quite on edge and she spoke with
a greater violence than she knew. Jane Repton tried
to persuade her.

"Wouldn't it be wiser for you to face things here,
even though it means some effort and pain?"

"I don't know," answered Stella, still in the quick
peremptory tone of one who will not be argued with.
"I don't care either. I have nothing to do with wis-
dom just now. I don't want people at all. I want—
oh, how I want——" She stopped and then she
added vaguely: "Something else," and her voice trailed
away into silence. She sat without a word, all tingling
impatience, during the rest of that drive and continued
so to sit after the carriage had stopped. When Jane
Repton descended, and she woke up with a start and
looked at the house, it was as though she brought her
eyes down from heaven to earth. Once within the
house she went straight up to Repton. He had left
his wife behind with Stella at the Law Courts and had
come home in advance of them. He had not spoken
a word to Stella that day, and he had not the time now,
for she began immediately in an eager voice and a look
of fever in her eyes:

133

"You won't try to stop me, will you? I must go away to-morrow."

Repton used more tact now than his wife had done. He took the troubled and excited woman's hand and answered her very gently:

"Of course, Stella. You shall go when you like."

"Oh, thank you," she cried, and was freed to remember the debt which she owed to these good friends of hers. "You must think me a brute, Jane! I haven't said a word to you about all your kindness. But—oh, you'll think me ridiculous, when you know"—and she began to laugh and to sob in one breath. Stella Ballantyne had remained so sunk in apathy through all that long trial that her friends were relieved at her outburst of tears. Jane Repton led her upstairs and put her to bed just as if she had been a child.

"There! You can get up for dinner if you like, Stella, or stay where you are. And if you'll tell us what you want to do we'll make the arrangements for you and not ask you a question."

Jane Repton kissed her and left her alone; and it was while Stella was sleeping upstairs that Henry Thresk called at the house and was told that there was no news for him.

"No doubt she will write to you, Mr. Thresk, if she wishes you to know what she is doing. But I should not count upon it if I were you," said Jane Repton, in a sweet voice and with eyes like pebbles. "She did not

134

mention you, I am sorry to say, when the trial was over."

She could not forgive him because of her own share in what she now called his "treachery" towards Stella. She had no more of the logician in her composition than Thresk had of the hero. He had committed under a great stress of emotion and sympathy what the whole experience and method of his life told him was one of the worst of crimes. And now that its object was achieved, and Stella Ballantyne free, he was in the mood to see only the harm which he had done to the majesty of the law; he was uneasy; he was not troubled by the thought that discovery would absolutely ruin him. That indeed did not enter into his thoughts. But he could not but make a picture of himself in the robe of a King's Counsel, claiming sternly the anger of the Law against some other man who should have done just what he had done, no more and no less. And so when Mrs. Repton's door was finally closed upon him, and no message was given to him from the woman he had saved, he was at once human and unheroic enough to visit a little of his resentment upon her. He had not spoken to her at all since the night at Chitipur; he had no knowledge of the stupor and the prostration into which, after her years of misery, she had fallen; he had no insight into the one compelling passion which now had her, body and soul, in its grip. He turned away from the door and went back to the Taj Mahal. A

135

steamer would be starting for Port Said in two days and by that steamer he would travel. That Stella was in the house on the Khamballa Hill he did not doubt, but since she had no word or thought to spare for him he could not but turn his back and go.

Stella herself got up to dinner, and after it was over she told her friends of the longing which filled her soul.

"All through the trial," she said shyly, with the shrinking of those who reveal a very secret fancy and are afraid that it will be ridiculed, "in the heat of the court, in the close captivity of my cell, I was conscious of just one real unconquerable passion—to feel the wind blowing against my face upon the Sussex Downs. Can you understand that? Just to see the broad green hills with the white chalk hollows in their sides and the forests marching down to the valleys like the Roman soldiers from Chichester—oh! I was mad for the look and the smell and the sounds of them! It was all that I thought about. I used to close my eyes in the dock and I was away in a second riding through Charlton Forest or over Farm Hill, or looking down to Slindon from Gumber Corner, and over its woods to the sea. And now that I am free"—she clasped her hands and her face grew radiant—"oh, I don't want to see people." She reached out a hand to each of her friends. "I don't call *you* people, you know. But even you— you'll understand and forgive and not be hurt—I don't want to see for a little while."

136

The beaten look of her took the sting of ingratitude out of her words. She stood between them, her delicate face worn thin, her eyes unnaturally big; she had the strange transparent beauty of people who have been lying for months in a mortal sickness. Jane Repton's eyes filled with tears and her hand sought for her handkerchief.

"Let's see what can be done," said Repton. "There's a mail-steamer of course, but you won't want to travel by that."

"No."

Repton worked out the sailings from Bombay and the other ports on the western coast of India while Stella leaned over his shoulder.

"Look!" he said. "This is the best way. There's a steamer going to Kurrachee to-morrow, and when you reach Kurrachee you'll just have time to catch a German Lloyd boat which calls at Southampton. You won't be home in thirteen days to be sure, but on the other hand you won't be pestered by curious people."

"Yes, yes," cried Stella eagerly. "I can go to-morrow."

"Very well."

Repton looked at the clock. It was still no more than half-past ten. He saw with what a fever of impatience Stella was consumed.

"I believe I could lay my hand on the local manager of the line to-night and fix your journey up for you."

"You could?" cried Stella. He might have been offering her a crown, so brightly her thanks shone in her eyes.

"I think so."

He got up from the table and stood looking at her, and then away from her with his lips pursed in doubt.

"Yes?" said she.

"I was thinking. Will you travel under another name? I don't suggest it really, only it might save you —annoyance."

Repton's hesitation was misplaced, for Stella Ballantyne's pride was quite beaten to the ground.

"Yes," she said at once. "I should wish to do that"; and both he and his wife understood from that ready answer more completely than they ever had before how near Stella had come to the big blank wall at the end of life. For seven years she had held her head high, never so much as whispering a reproach against her husband, keeping with a perpetual guard the secret of her misery. Pride had been her mainspring; now even that was broken. Repton went out of the house and returned at midnight.

"It's all settled," he said. "You will have a cabin on deck in both steamers. I gave your name in confidence to the manager here and he will take care that everything possible is done for you. There will be very few passengers on the German boat. The season is too early for either the tourists or the people on leave."

138

LITTLE BEEDING AGAIN

Thus Stella Ballantyne crept away from Bombay and in five weeks' time she landed at Southampton. There she resumed her name. She travelled into Sussex and stayed for a few nights at the inn whither Henry Thresk had come years before on his momentous holiday. She had a little money—the trifling income which her parents had left to her upon their death—and she began to look about for a house. By a piece of good fortune she discovered that the cottage in which she had lived at Little Beeding would be empty in a few months. She took it and before the summer was out she was once more established there. It was on an afternoon of August when Stella made her home in it again. She passed along the yellow lane driven deep between high banks of earth where the roots of great elm-trees cropped out. Every step was familiar to her. The lane with many twists under overarching branches ran down a steep hill and came out into the open by the big house with its pillared portico and its light grey stone and its wonderful garden of lawn and flowers and cedars. A tiny church with a narrow grave-yard and strange carefully-trimmed square bushes of yew stood next to the house, and beyond the church the lane dipped to the river and the cottage.

Stella went from room to room. She had furnished the cottage simply and daintily; the walls were bright, her servant-girl had gathered flowers and set them about. Outside the window the sunlight shone on a green garden. She was alone. It was the home-coming she had wished for.

For three or four months she was left alone; and then one afternoon as she came into the cottage after a walk she found a little white card upon the table. It bore the name of Mr. Hazlewood.

CHAPTER XIV

In the quiet country town obvious changes had taken place during the eight years of Stella's absence. They were not changes of importance, however, and one sentence can symbolize them all—there was now tarmac upon its roads. But in the cluster of houses a mile away at the end of the deep lane the case was different. Mr. Harold Hazlewood had come to Little Beeding. He now lived in the big house to which the village owed its name and indeed its existence. He lived—and spread consternation amongst the gentry for miles round.

"Lord, how I wish poor Arthur hadn't died!" old John Chubble used to cry. He had hunted the West Sussex hounds for thirty years and the very name of Little Beeding turned his red face purple. "There was a man. But this fellow! And to think he's got that beautiful house! Do you know there's hardly a pheasant on the place. And I've hashed them down out of the sky in the old days there by the dozen. Well, he's got a son in the Coldstream, Dick Hazlewood, who's not so bad. But Harold! Oh, pass me the port!"

Harold indeed had inherited Little Beeding by an accident during the first summer after Stella had gone

141

out to India. Arthur Hazlewood, the owner and Harold's nephew, had been lost with his yacht in a gale of wind off the coast of Portugal. Arthur was a bachelor and thus Harold Hazlewood came quite unexpectedly into the position of a country squire when he was already well on in middle age. He was a widower and a man of a noticeable aspect. At the first glance you knew that he was not as other men; at the second you suspected that he took a pride in his dissimilarity. He was long, rather shambling in his gait, with a mild blue eye and fair thin hair now growing grey. But length was the chief impression left by his physical appearance. His legs, his arms, his face, even his hair, unless his son in the Coldstream happened to be at home at the time, were long.

"Is your father mad?" Mr. Chubble once asked of Dick Hazlewood. The two men had met in the broad street of Great Beeding at midday, and the elder one, bubbling with indignation, had planted himself in front of Dick.

"Mad?" Dick repeated reflectively. "No, I shouldn't go as far as that. Oh no! What has he done now?"

"He has paid out of his own pocket the fines of all the people in Great Beeding who have just been convicted for not having their babies vaccinated."

Dick Hazlewood stared in surprise at his companion's indignant face.

142

"But of course he'd do that, Mr. Chubble," he answered cheerfully. "He's anti-everything—everything, I mean, which experience has established or prudence could suggest."

"In addition he wants to sell the navy for old iron and abolish the army."

"Yes," said Dick, nodding his head amicably. "He's like that. He thinks that without an army and a navy we should be less aggressive. I can't deny it."

"I should think not indeed," cried Mr. Chubble. "Are you walking home?"

"Yes."

"Let us walk together." Mr. Chubble took Dick Hazlewood by the arm and as they went filled the lane with his plaints.

"I should think you can't deny it. Why, he has actually written a pamphlet to enforce his views upon the subject."

"You should bless your stars, Mr. Chubble, that there is only one. He suffers from pamphlets. He writes 'em and prints 'em and every member of Parliament gets one of 'em for nothing. Pamphlets do for him what the gout does for other old gentlemen—they carry off from his system a great number of disquieting ailments. He's at prison reform now," said Dick with a smile of thorough enjoyment. "Have you heard him on it?"

"No, and I don't want to," Mr. Chubble exploded.

He struck viciously at an overhanging bough, as though it was the head of Harold Hazlewood, and went on with the catalogue of crimes. "He made a speech last week in the town-hall," and he jerked his thumb backwards towards the town they had left. "Intolerable I call it. He actually denounced his own countrymen as a race of oppressors."

"He would," answered Dick calmly. "What did I say to you a minute ago? He's advanced, you know."

"Advanced!" sneered Mr. Chubble, and then Dick Hazlewood stopped and contemplated his companion with a thoughtful eye.

"I really don't think you understand my father, Mr. Chubble," said Dick with a gentle remonstrance in his voice which Mr. Chubble was at a loss whether to take seriously or no.

"Can you give me the key to him?" he cried.

"I can."

"Then out with it, my lad."

Mr. Chubble disposed himself to listen but with so bristling an expression that it was clear no explanation could satisfy him. Dick, however, took no heed of that. He spoke slowly as one lecturing to an obtuse class of scholars.

"My father was born predestined to believe that all the people whom he knows are invariably wrong, and all the people he doesn't know are invariably right.

144

And when I feel inclined to deplore his abuse of his own country I console myself with the reflection that he would be the staunchest friend of England that England ever had—if only he had been born in Germany."

Mr. Chubble grunted and turned the speech suspiciously over in his mind. Was Dick poking fun at him or at his father?

"That's bookish," he said.

"I am afraid it is," Dick Hazlewood agreed humbly. "The fact is I am now an Instructor at the Staff College and much is expected of me."

They had reached the gate of Little Beeding House. It was summer time. A yellow drive of gravel ran straight between long broad flower-beds to the door.

"Won't you come in and see my father?" Dick asked innocently. "He's at home."

"No, my lad, no." Mr. Chubble hastened to add: "I haven't the time. But I am very glad to have met *you*. You are here for long?"

"No. Only just for luncheon," said Dick, and he walked along the drive into the house. He was met in the hall by Hubbard the butler, an old colourless man of genteel movements which seemed slow and were astonishingly quick. He spoke in gentle purring tones and was the very butler for Mr. Harold Hazlewood.

"Your father has been asking for you, sir," said

145

Hubbard. "He seems a little anxious. He is in the big room."

"Very well," said Dick, and he crossed the hall and the drawing-room, wondering what new plan for the regeneration of the world was being hatched in his father's sedulous brains. He had received a telegram at Camberley the day before urgently calling upon him to arrive at Little Beeding in time for luncheon. He went into the library as it was called, but in reality it was the room used by everybody except upon ceremonial occasions. It was a big room; half of it held a billiard table, the other half had writing-tables, lounges, comfortable chairs and a table for bridge. The carpet was laid over a parquet floor so that young people, when they stayed there, rolled it up and danced. There were windows upon two sides of the room. Here a row of them looked down the slope of the lawn to the cedar-trees and the river, the other, a great bay which opened to the ground, gave a view of a corner of the high churchyard wall and of a meadow and a thatched cottage beyond. In this bay Mr. Hazlewood was standing when Dick entered the room.

"I got your telegram, father, and here I am."

Mr. Hazlewood turned back from the window with a smile upon his face.

"It is good of you, Richard. I wanted you to-day."

A very genuine affection existed between these two, dissimilar as they were in physique and mind. Dick

THE HAZLEWOODS

Hazlewood was at this time thirty-four years old, an officer of hard work and distinction, one of the younger men to whom the generals look to provide the brains in the next great war. He had the religion of his type. To keep physically fit for the hardest campaigning and mentally fit for the highest problems of modern strategy and to boast about neither the one qualification nor the other—these were the articles of his creed. In appearance he was a little younger than his years, lithe, long in the leg, with a thin brown face and grey eyes which twinkled with humour. Harold Hazlewood was intensely proud of him, though he professed to detest his profession. And no doubt he found at times that the mere healthful, well-groomed look of his son was irritatingly conventional. What was quite wholesome could never be quite right in the older man's philosophy. To Dick, on the other hand, his father was an intense enjoyment. Here was a lovable innocent with the most delightful illusion that he understood the world. Dick would draw out his father by the hour, but, as he put it, he wouldn't let the old boy down. He stopped his chaff before it could begin to hurt.

"Well, I am here," he said. "What scrape have you got into now?"

"I am in no scrape, Richard. I don't get into scrapes," replied his father. He shifted from one foot to the other uneasily. "I was wondering, Richard— you have been away all this last year, haven't you?—

147

I was wondering whether you could give me any of your summer."

Dick looked at his father. What in the world was the old boy up to now? he asked himself.

"Of course I can. I shall get my leave in a day or two. I thought of playing some polo here and there. There are a few matches arranged. Then no doubt ——" He broke off. "But look here, sir! You didn't send me an urgent telegram merely to ask me that."

"No, Richard, no." Everybody else called his son Dick, but Harold Hazlewood never. He was Richard. From Richard you might expect much, the awakening of a higher nature, a devotion to the regeneration of the world, humanitarianism, even the cult of all the "antis." From Dick you could expect nothing but health and cleanliness and robustious conventionality. Therefore Richard Captain Hazlewood of the Coldstream and the Staff Corps remained. "No, there was something else."

Mr. Hazlewood took his son by the arm and led him into the bay window. He pointed across the field to the thatched cottage.

"You know who lives there?"

"No."

"Mrs. Ballantyne."

Dick put his head on one side and whistled softly.

He knew the general tenor of that *cause célèbre*. Mr. Hazlewood raised remonstrating hands.

148

THE HAZLEWOODS

"There! You are like the rest, Richard. You take the worst view. Here is a good woman maligned and slandered. There is nothing against her. She was acquitted in open trial by a jury of responsible citizens under a judge of the Highest Court in India. Yet she is left alone—like a leper. She is the victim of gossip and *such* gossip. Richard," said the old man solemnly, "for uncharitableness, ill-nature and stupid malice the gossip of a Sussex village leaves the most deplorable efforts of Voltaire and Swift entirely behind."

"Father, you *are* going it," said Dick with a chuckle. "Do you mean to give me a step-mother?"

"I do not, Richard. Such a monstrous idea never entered my thoughts. But, my boy, I have called upon her."

"Oh, you have!"

"Yes. I have seen her too. I left a card. She left one upon me. I called again. I was fortunate."

"She was in?"

"She gave me tea, Richard."

Richard cocked his head on one side.

"What's she like, father? Topping?"

"Richard, she gave me tea," said the old man, dwelling insistently upon his repetition.

"So you said, sir, and it was most kind of her to be sure. But that fact won't help me to form even the vaguest picture of her looks."

"But it will, Richard," Mr. Hazlewood protested

with a nervousness which set Dick wondering again. "She gave me tea. Therefore, don't you see, I must return the hospitality, which I do with the utmost eagerness. Richard, I look to you to help me. We must champion that slandered lady. You will see her for yourself. She is coming here to luncheon."

The truth was out at last. Yet Dick was aware that he might very easily have guessed it. This was just the quixotic line his father could have been foreseen to take.

"Well, we must just keep our eyes open and see that she doesn't slip anything into the decanters while our heads are turned," said Dick with a chuckle. Old Mr. Hazlewood laid a hand upon his son's shoulder.

"That's the sort of thing they say. Only you don't mean it, Richard, and they do," he remarked with a mild and reproachful shake of the head. "Ah, some day, my boy, your better nature will awaken."

Dick expressed no anxiety for the quick advent of that day.

"How many are there of us to be at luncheon?" asked Dick.

"Only the two of us."

"I see. We are to keep the danger in the family. Very wise, sir, upon my word."

"Richard, you pervert my meaning," said Mr. Hazlewood. "The neighbourhood has not been kind to Mrs. Ballantyne. She has been made to suffer. The Vicar's wife, for instance—a most uncharitable person. And my sister, your Aunt Margaret, too, in Great Beeding —she is what you would call——"

"Hot stuff," murmured Dick.

"Quite so," replied Mr. Hazlewood, and he turned to his son with a look of keen interest upon his face. "I am not familiar with the phrase, Richard, but not for the first time I notice that the crude and inelegant vulgarisms in which you abound and which you no doubt pick up in the barrack squares compress a great deal of forcible meaning into very few words."

"That is indeed true, sir," replied Dick with an admirable gravity, "and if I might be allowed to suggest it, a pamphlet upon that interesting subject would be less dangerous work than coquetting with the latest edition of the Marquise de Brinvilliers."

The word pamphlet was a bugle-call to Mr. Hazlewood.

"Ah! Speaking of pamphlets, my boy," he began, and walked over to a desk which was littered with papers.

"We have not the time, sir," Dick interrupted from the bay of the window. A woman had come out from the cottage. She unlatched a little gate in her garden which opened on to the meadow. She crossed it. Yet another gate gave her entrance to the garden of Little Beeding. In a moment Hubbard announced:

"Mrs. Ballantyne"; and Stella came into the room

and stood near to the door with a certain constraint in her attitude and a timid watchfulness in her big eyes. She had the look of a deer. It seemed to Dick that at one abrupt movement she would turn and run.

Mr. Hazlewood pressed forward to greet her and she smiled with a warmth of gratitude. Dick, watching her from the bay window, was surprised by the delicacy of her face, by a look of fragility. She was dressed very simply in a coat and short skirt of white, her shoes and her gloves were of white suède, her hat was small.

"And this is my son Richard," said Mr. Hazlewood; and Dick came forward out of the bay. Stella Ballantyne bowed to him but said no word. She was taking no risks even at the hands of the son of her friend. If advances of friendliness were to be made they must be made by him, not her. There was just one awkward moment of hesitation. Then Dick Hazlewood held out his hand.

"I am very glad to meet you, Mrs. Ballantyne," he said cordially, and he saw the blood rush into her face and the fear die out in her eyes.

The neighbourhood, to quote Mr. Hazlewood, had not been kind to Stella Ballantyne. She had stood in the dock and the fact tarnished her. Moreover here and there letters had come from India. The verdict was inevitable, but—but—there was a doubt about its justice. The full penalty—no. No one desired or would have thought it right, but something betwixt and between in the proper spirit of British compromise would not have been amiss. Thus gossip ran. Moreover Stella Ballantyne was too good-looking, and she wore her neat and simple clothes too well. To some of the women it was an added offence when they considered what she might be wearing if only the verdict had been different. Thus for a year Stella had been left to her own company except for a couple of visits which the Reptons had paid to her. At the first she had welcomed the silence, the peace of her loneliness. It was a balm to her. She recovered like a flower in the night. But she was young—she was twenty-eight this year—and as her limbs ceased to be things of lead and became once more aglow with life there came to her a need of companionship. She tried to tramp the need away on the turf of her well-loved downs, but she failed. A friend to share with her the joy of these summer days! Her blood clamoured for one. But she was an outcast. Friends did not come her way. Therefore she had gratefully received old Mr. Hazlewood in her house, and had accepted, though with some fear, his proposal that she should lunch at the big house and make the acquaintance of his son.

She was nervous at the beginning of that meal, but both father and son were at the pains to put her at her ease; and soon she was talking naturally, with a colour in her cheeks, and now and then a note of laughter in her voice. Dick worked for the recurrence of that laughter. He liked the clear sound of it and the melting of all her face into sweetness and tender humour which came with it. And for another thing he had a thought, and a true one, that it was very long since she had known the pleasure of good laughter.

They took their coffee out on the lawn under the shade of a huge cedar-tree. The river ran at their feet and a Canadian canoe and a rowing-boat were tethered close by in a little dock. The house, a place of grey stone with grey weathered and lichen-coloured slates, raised its great oblong chimneys into a pellucid air. The sunlight flashed upon its rows of tall windows— they were all flat to the house, except the one great bay on the ground floor in the library—and birds called from all the trees. The time slipped away. Dick Hazlewood found himself talking of his work, a practice into which he seldom fell, and was surprised that she could talk of it with him. He realised with a start how it was that she knew. But she talked naturally and openly, as though he must know her history. Once even some jargon of the Staff College slipped from her. "You were doing let us pretend at Box Hill last week, weren't you?" she said, and when he started at the phrase she imagined that he started at the extent of her information. "It was in the papers," she said. "I read every word of them," and then for a second her face clouded, and she added: "I have time, you see."

She looked at her watch and sprang to her feet.

"I must go," she said. "I didn't know it was so late. I have enjoyed myself very much." She did not hesitate now to offer her hand. "Goodbye."

Dick Hazlewood went with her as far as the gate and came back to his father.

"You were asking me," he said carelessly, "if I could give you some part of the summer. I don't see why I shouldn't come here in a day or two. The polo matches aren't so important."

The old man's eyes brightened.

"I shall be delighted, Richard, if you will." He looked at his son with something really ecstatic in his expression. At last then his better nature was awakening. "I really believe——" he exclaimed and Dick cut him short.

"Yes, it may be that, sir. On the other hand it may not. What is quite clear is that I must catch my train. So if I might order the car?"

"Of course, of course."

He came out with his son into the porch of the house.

"We have done a fine thing to-day, Richard," he said with enthusiasm and a nod towards the cottage beyond the meadow.

"We have indeed, sir," returned Dick cheerily. "Did you ever see such a pair of ankles?"

"She lost the tragic look this afternoon, Richard. We must be her champions."

"We will put in the summer that way, father," said

Dick, and waving his hand was driven off to the station.

Mr. Hazlewood walked back to the library. But "walked" is a poor word. He seemed to float on air. A great opportunity had come to him. He had enlisted the services of his son. He saw Dick and himself as Toreadors waving red flags in the face of a bull labelled Conventionality. He went back to the pamphlet on which he was engaged with renewed ardour and laboured diligently far into the night.

CHAPTER XV

"I was in Great Beeding this morning," said Dick, as he sat at luncheon with his father, "and the blinds were up in Aunt Margaret's house."

"They have returned from their holiday then," his father observed with a tremor in his voice. He looked afraid. Then he looked annoyed.

"Pettifer will break down if he doesn't take care," he exclaimed petulantly. "No man with any sense would work as hard as he does. He ought to have taken two months this year at the least."

"We should still have to meet Aunt Margaret at the end of them," said Dick calmly. He had no belief in Mr. Hazlewood's distress at the overwork of Pettifer.

A month had passed since the inauguration of the great Crusade, and though talk was rife everywhere and indignation in many places loud, a certain amount of success had been won. But all this while Mrs. Pettifer had been away. Now she had returned. Mr. Hazlewood stood in some awe of his sister. She was not ill-natured, but she knew her mind and expressed it forcibly and without delay. She was of a practical limited nature; she saw very clearly what she saw, but

157

she walked in blinkers, and had neither comprehension of nor sympathy with those of a wider vision. She was at this time a woman of forty, comfortable to look upon and the wife of Mr. Robert Pettifer, the head of the well-known firm of solicitors, Pettifer, Gryll and Musgrave. Mrs. Pettifer had very little patience to spare for the idiosyncrasies of her brother, though she owed him a good deal more than patience. For at the time, some twenty years before, when she had married Robert Pettifer, then merely a junior partner of the firm, Harold Hazlewood had alone stood by her. To the rest of the family she was throwing herself away; to her brother Harold she was doing a fine thing, not because it was a fine thing but because it was an exceptional thing. Robert Pettifer however had prospered, and though he had reached an age when he might have claimed his leisure the nine o'clock train still took him daily to London.

"Aunt Margaret isn't after all so violent," said Dick, for whom she kept a very soft place in her heart. But Harold shook his head.

"Your aunt, Richard, has all the primæval ferocity of the average woman." And then the fires of the enthusiast were set alight in his blue eyes. "I'll tell you what I'll do: I'll send her my new pamphlet, Richard. It may have a humanising influence upon her. I have some advance copies. I'll send her one this afternoon."

Dick's eyes twinkled.

158

"I should if I were you, though to be sure, sir, we have tried that plan before without any prodigious effect."

"True, Richard, true, but I have never before risen to such heights as these." Mr. Hazlewood threw down his napkin and paced the room. "Richard, I am not inclined to boast. I am a humble man."

"It is only humility, sir, which achieves great work," said Dick, as he went contentedly on with his luncheon.

"But the very title of this pamphlet seems to me calculated to interest the careless and attract the thoughtful. It is called *The Prison Walls must Cast no Shadow.*"

With an arm outstretched he seemed to deliver the words of the title one by one from the palm of his hand. Then he stood smiling, confident, awaiting applause. Dick's face, which had shown the highest expectancy, slowly fell in a profound disappointment. He laid down his knife and fork.

"Oh, come, father. All walls cast shadows. It entirely depends upon the altitude of the sun."

Mr. Hazlewood returned to his seat and spoke gently.

"The phrase, my boy, is a metaphor. I develop in this pamphlet my belief that a convict, once he has expiated his offence, should upon his release be restored to the precise position in society which he held before with all its privileges unimpaired."

Dick chuckled in the most unregenerate delight.

159

"You are going it, father," he said, and disappointment came to Mr. Hazlewood.

"Richard," he remonstrated mildly, "I hoped that I should have had your approval. It seemed to me that a change was taking place in you, that the player of polo, the wild hunter of an inoffensive little white ball, was developing into the humanitarian."

"Well, sir," rejoined Dick, "I won't deny that of late I have been beginning to think that there is a good deal in your theories. But you mustn't try me too high at the beginning, you know. I am only in my novitiate. However, please send it to Aunt Margaret, and—oh, how I would like to hear her remarks upon it!"

An idea occurred to Mr. Hazlewood.

"Richard, why shouldn't you take it over yourself this afternoon?"

Dick shook his head.

"Impossible, father, I have something to do." He looked out of the window down to the river running dark in the shade of trees. "But I'll go to-morrow morning," he added.

And the next morning he walked over early to Great Beeding. His aunt would have received the pamphlet by the first post and he wished to seize the first fine careless rapture of her comments. But he found her in a mood of distress rather than of wordy impatience.

The Pettifers lived in a big house of the Georgian period at the bottom of an irregular square in the middle of the little town. Mrs. Pettifer was sitting in a room facing the garden at the back with the pamphlet on a little table beside her. She sprang up as Dick was shown into the room, and before he could utter a word of greeting she cried:

"Dick, you are the one person I wanted to see."

"Oh?"

"Yes. Sit down."

Dick obeyed.

"Dick, I believe you are the only person in the world who has any control over your father."

"Yes. Even in my pinafores I learnt the great lesson that to control one's parents is the first duty of the modern child."

"Don't be silly," his aunt rejoined sharply. Then she looked him over. "Yes, you must have some control over him, for he lets you remain in the army, though an army is one of his abominations."

"Theoretically it's a great grief to him," replied Dick. "But you see I have done fairly well, so actually he's ready to burst with pride. Every sentimental philosopher sooner or later breaks his head against his own theories."

Mrs. Pettifer nodded her head in commendation.

"That's an improvement on your last remark, Dick. It's true. And your father's going to break his head very badly unless you stop him."

"How?"

161

"Mrs. Ballantyne."

All the flippancy died out of Dick Hazlewood's face. He became at once grave, wary.

"I have been hearing about him," continued Mrs. Pettifer. "He has made friends with her—a woman who has stood in the dock on a capital charge."

"And has been acquitted," Dick Hazlewood added quietly and Mrs. Pettifer blazed up.

"She wouldn't have been acquitted if I had been on the jury. A parcel of silly men who are taken in by a pretty face!" she cried, and Dick broke in:

"Aunt Margaret, I am sorry to interrupt you. But I want you to understand that I am with my father heart and soul in this."

He spoke very slowly and deliberately and Mrs. Pettifer was utterly dismayed.

"You!" she cried. She grew pale, and alarm so changed her face it was as if a tragic mask had been slipped over it. "Oh, Dick, not you!"

"Yes, I. I think it is cruelly hard," he continued with his eyes relentlessly fixed upon Mrs. Pettifer's face, "that a woman like Mrs. Ballantyne, who has endured all the horrors of a trial, the publicity, the suspense, the dread risk that justice might miscarry, should have afterwards to suffer the treatment of a leper."

There was for the moment no room for any anger now in Mrs. Pettifer's thoughts. Consternation possessed her. She weighed every quiet firm word that fell from Dick, she appreciated the feeling which gave them wings, she searched his face, his eyes. Dick had none of his father's flightiness. He was level-headed, shrewd and with the conventions of his times and his profession. If Dick spoke like this, with so much certitude and so much sympathy, why then—— She shrank from the conclusion with a sinking heart. She became very quiet.

"Oh, she shouldn't have come to Little Beeding," she said in a low voice, staring now upon the ground. It was to herself she spoke, but Dick answered her, and his voice rose to a challenge.

"Why shouldn't she? Here she was born, here she was known. What else should she do but come back to Little Beeding and hold her head high? I respect her pride for doing it."

Here were reasons no doubt why Stella should come back; but they did not include the reason why she had. Dick Hazlewood was well aware of it. He had learnt it only the afternoon before when he was with her on the river. But he thought it a reason too delicate, of too fine a gossamer to be offered to the prosaic mind of his Aunt Margaret. With what ridicule and disbelief she would rend it into tatters! Reasons so exquisite were not for her. She could never understand them.

Mrs. Pettifer abandoned her remonstrances and was

163

for dropping the subject altogether. But Dick was obstinate.

"You don't know Mrs. Ballantyne, Aunt Margaret. You are unjust to her because you don't know her. I want you to," he said boldly.

"What!" cried Mrs. Pettifer. "You actually—— Oh!" Indignation robbed her of words. She gasped.

"Yes, I do," continued Dick calmly. "I want you to come one night and dine at Little Beeding. We'll persuade Mrs. Ballantyne to come too."

It was a bold move, and even in his eyes it had its risks for Stella. To bring Mrs. Pettifer and her together was, so it seemed to him, to mix earth with delicate flame. But he had great faith in Stella Ballantyne. Let them but meet and the earth might melt— who could tell? At the worst his aunt would bristle, and there were his father and himself to see that the bristles did not prick.

"Yes, come and dine."

Mrs. Pettifer had got over her amazement at her nephew's audacity. Curiosity had taken its place— curiosity and fear. She must see this woman for herself.

"Yes," she answered after a pause. "I will come. I'll bring Robert too."

"Good. We'll fix up a date and write to you. Goodbye."

Dick went back to Little Beeding and asked for his father. The old gentleman added to his other foibles

164

that of a collector. It was the only taste he had which was really productive, for he owned a collection of miniatures, gathered together throughout his life, which would have realised a fortune if it had been sold at Christie's. He kept it arranged in cabinets in the library and Dick found him bending over one of the drawers and rearranging his treasures.

"I have seen Aunt Margaret," he said. "She will meet Stella here at dinner."

"That will be splendid," cried the old man with enthusiasm.

"Perhaps," replied his son; and the next morning the Pettifers received their invitation.

Mrs. Pettifer accepted it at once. She had not been idle since Dick had left her. Before he had come she had merely looked upon the crusade as one of Harold Hazlewood's stupendous follies. But after he had gone she was genuinely horrified. She saw Dick speaking with the set dogged look and the hard eyes which once or twice she had seen before. He had always got his way, she remembered, on those occasions. She drove round to her friends and made inquiries. At each house her terrors were confirmed. It was Dick now who led the crusade. He had given up his polo, he was spending all his leave at Little Beeding and most of it with Stella Ballantyne. He lent her a horse and rode with her in the morning, he rowed her on the river in the afternoon. He bullied his friends to call on her. He brandished his friendship with her like a flag. Love me, love my Stella was his new motto. Mrs. Pettifer drove home with every fear exaggerated. Dick's career would be ruined altogether—even if nothing worse were to happen. To any view that Stella Ballantyne might hold she hardly gave a thought. She was sure of what it would be. Stella Ballantyne would jump at her nephew. He had good looks, social position, money and a high reputation. It was the last quality which would give him a unique value in Stella Ballantyne's eyes. He was not one of the chinless who haunt the stage doors; nor again one of that more subtly decadent class which seeks to attract sensation by linking itself to notoriety. No. From Stella's point of view Dick Hazlewood must be the ideal husband.

Mrs. Pettifer waited for her husband's return that evening with unusual impatience, but she was wise enough to hold her tongue until dinner was over and he with a cigar between his lips and a glass of old brandy on the table-cloth in front of him, disposed to amiability and concession.

Then, however, she related her troubles.

"You see it must be stopped, Robert."

Robert Pettifer was a lean wiry man of fifty-five whose brown dried face seemed by a sort of climatic change to have taken on the colour of the binding of his law-books. He, too, was a little troubled by the story, but he was of a fair and cautious mind.

"Stopped?" he said. "How? We can't arrest Mrs. Ballantyne again."

"No," replied Mrs. Pettifer. "Robert, you must do something."

Robert Pettifer jumped in his chair.

"I, Margaret! Lord love you, no! I decline to mix myself up in the matter at all. Dick's a grown man and Mrs. Ballantyne has been acquitted."

Margaret Pettifer knew her husband.

"Is that your last word?" she asked ruefully.

"Absolutely."

"It isn't mine, Robert."

Robert Pettifer chuckled and laid a hand upon his wife's.

"I know that, Margaret."

"We are going to dine next Friday night at Little Beeding to meet Stella Ballantyne."

Mr. Pettifer was startled but he held his tongue.

"The invitation came this morning after you had left for London," she added.

"And you accepted it at once?"

"Yes."

Pettifer was certain that she had before she opened her mouth to answer him.

"I shall dine at Little Beeding on Friday," he said, "because Harold always gives me an admirable glass of vintage port"; and with that he dismissed the subject. Mrs. Pettifer was content to let it smoulder in his mind. She was not quite sure that he was as disturbed as she wished him to be, but that he was proud of Dick she knew, and if by any chance uneasiness grew strong in him, why, sooner or later he would let fall some little sentence; and that little sentence would probably be useful.

CHAPTER XVI

The dinner-party at Little Beeding was a small affair. There were but ten altogether who sat down at Mr. Hazlewood's dinner-table and with the exception of the Pettifers all, owing to Dick Hazlewood's insistence, were declared partisans of Stella Ballantyne. None the less Stella came to it with hesitation. It was the first time that she had dined abroad since she had left India, now the best part of eighteen months ago, and she went forth to it as to an ordeal. For though friends of hers would be present to enhearten her she was to meet the Pettifers. The redoubtable Aunt Margaret had spoilt her sleep for a week. It was for the Pettifers she dressed, careful to choose neither white nor black, lest they should find something symbolic in the colour of her gown and make of it an offence. She put on a frock of pale blue satin trimmed with some white lace which had belonged to her mother, and she wore not so much as a thin gold chain about her neck. But she did not need jewels that night. The months of quiet had restored her to her beauty, the excitement of this evening had given life and colour to her face, the queer little droop at the corners of her lips which had betrayed so much misery and bitterness of spirit had

169

vanished altogether. Yet when she was quite dressed and her mirror bade her take courage she sat down and wrote a note of apology pleading a sudden indisposition. But she did not send it. Even in the writing her cowardice came home to her and she tore it up before she had signed her name. The wheels of the cab which was to take her to the big house rattled down the lane under her windows, and slipping her cloak over her shoulders she ran downstairs.

The party began with a little constraint. Mr. Hazlewood received his guests in his drawing-room and it had the chill and the ceremony of a room which is seldom used. But the constraint wore off at the table. Most of those present were striving to set Stella Ballantyne at her ease, and she was at a comfortable distance from Mrs. Pettifer, with Mr. Hazlewood at her side. She was conscious that she was kept under observation and from time to time the knowledge made her uncomfortable.

"I am being watched," she said to her host.

"You mustn't mind," replied Mr. Hazlewood, and the smile came back to her lips as she glanced round the table.

"Oh, I don't, I don't," she said in a low voice, "for I have friends here."

"And friends who will not fail you, Stella," said the old man. "To-night begins the great change. You'll see."

CONSEQUENCES

Robert Pettifer puzzled her indeed more than his wife. She was plain to read. She was frigidly polite, her enemy. Once or twice, however, Stella turned her head to find Robert Pettifer's eyes resting upon her with a quiet scrutiny which betrayed nothing of his thoughts. As a matter of fact he liked her manner. She was neither defiant nor servile, neither loud nor over-silent. She had been through fire; that was evident. But it was evident only because of a queer haunting look which came and went in her dark eyes. The fire had not withered her. Indeed Pettifer was surprised. He had not formulated his expectations at all, but he had not expected what he saw. The clear eyes and the fresh delicate colour, her firm white shoulders and her depth of bosom, forced him to think of her as wholesome. He began to turn over in his mind his recollections of her case, recollections which he had been studious not to revive.

Halfway through the dinner Stella lost her uneasiness. The lights, the ripple of talk, the company of men and women, the bright dresses had their effect on her. It was as though after a deep plunge into dark waters she had come to the surface and flung out her arms to the sun. She ceased to notice the scrutiny of the Pettifers. She looked across the table to Dick and their eyes met; and such a look of tenderness transfigured her face as made Mrs. Pettifer turn pale.

"That woman's in love," she said to herself and

171

she was horrified. It wasn't Dick's social position then or the shelter of his character that Stella Ballantyne coveted. She was in love. Mrs. Pettifer was honest enough to acknowledge it. But she knew now that the danger which she had feared was infinitely less than the danger which actually was.

"I must have it out with Harold to-night," she said, and later on, when the men came from the dining-room, she looked out for her husband. But at first she did not see him. She was in the drawing-room and the wide double doors which led to the big library stood open. It was through those doors that the men had come. Some of the party were gathered there. She could hear the click of the billiard balls and the voices of women mingling with those of the men. She went through the doors and saw her husband standing by Harold Hazlewood's desk, and engrossed apparently in some little paper-covered book which he held in his hand. She crossed to him at once.

"Robert," she said, "don't be in a hurry to go to-night. I must have a word with Harold."

"All right," said Pettifer, but he said it in so absent a voice that his wife doubted whether he had understood her words. She was about to repeat them when Harold Hazlewood himself approached.

"You are looking at my new pamphlet, Pettifer, *The Prison Walls must Cast no Shadow*. I am hoping that it will have a great influence."

172

"No," replied Pettifer. "I wasn't. I was looking at this," and he held up the little book.

"Oh, that?" said Hazlewood, turning away with disappointment.

"Yes, that," said Pettifer with a strange and thoughtful look at his brother-in-law. "And I am not sure," he added slowly, "that in a short time you will not find it the more important publication of the two."

He laid the book down and in his turn he moved away towards the billiard-table. Margaret Pettifer remained. She had been struck by the curious deliberate words her husband had used. Was this the hint for which she was looking out? She took up the little book. It was a copy of *Notes and Queries*. She opened it.

It was a small periodical magazine made up of printed questions which contributors sent in search of information and answers to those questions from the pens of other contributors. Mrs. Pettifer glanced through the leaves, hoping to light upon the page which her husband had been studying. But he had closed the book when he laid it down and she found nothing to justify his remark. Yet he had not spoken without intention. Of that she was convinced, and her conviction was strengthened the next moment, for as she turned again towards the drawing-room Robert Pettifer looked once sharply towards her and as sharply away. Mrs.

173

Pettifer understood that glance. He was wondering whether she had noticed what in that magazine had interested him. But she did not pursue him with questions. She merely made up her mind to examine the copy of *Notes and Queries* at a time when she could bring more leisure to the task.

She waited impatiently for the party to break up but eleven o'clock had struck before any one proposed to go. Then all took their leave at once. Robert Pettifer and his wife went out into the hall with the rest, lest others seeing them remain should stay behind too; and whilst they stood a little apart from the general bustle of departure Margaret Pettifer saw Stella Ballantyne come lightly down the stairs, and a savage fury suddenly whirled in her head and turned her dizzy. She thought of all the trouble and harm this young woman was bringing into their ordered family and she would not have it that she was innocent. She saw Stella with her cloak open upon her shoulders radiant and glistening and slender against the dark panels of the staircase, youth in her face, enjoyment sparkling in her eyes, and her fingers itched to strip her of her bright frock, her gloves, her slim satin slippers, the delicate white lace which nestled against her bosom. She clothed her in the heavy shapeless garments, the coarse shoes and stockings of the convict; she saw her working desperately against time upon an ignoble task with black and

broken finger-nails.   If longing could have worked the
miracle, thus at this hour would Stella Ballantyne
have sat and worked, all the colour of her faded to a
hideous drab, all the grace of her withered.   Mrs.
Pettifer turned away with so abrupt a movement
and so disordered a face that Robert asked her if she
was ill.

"No, it's nothing," she said and against her will
her eyes were drawn back to the staircase.   But Stella
Ballantyne had disappeared and Margaret Pettifer
drew her breath in relief.   She felt that there had
been danger in her moment of passion, danger and
shame; and already enough of those two evils waited
about them.

Stella, meanwhile, with a glance towards Dick
Hazlewood, had slipped back into the big room.
Then she waited for a moment until the door opened
and Dick came in.

"I had not said good-night to you," she exclaimed,
coming towards him and giving him her hands, "and I
wanted to say it to you here, when we were alone.
For I must thank you for to-night, you and your
father.   Oh, I have no words."

The tears were very near to her eyes and they were
audible in her low voice.   Dick Hazlewood was quick
to answer her.

"Good!   For there's need of none.   Will you ride
to-morrow?"

Stella took her hands from his and moved across the room towards the great bay window with its glass doors.

"I should love to," she said.

"Eight. Is that too early after to-night?"

"No, that's the good time," she returned with a smile. "We have the day at its best and the world to ourselves."

"I'll bring the same horse round. He knows you now, doesn't he?"

"Thank you," said Stella. She unlatched the glass door and opened it. "You'll lock it after me, won't you?"

"No," said Dick. "I'll see you to your door."

But Stella refused his company. She stood in the doorway.

"There's no need! See what a night it is!" and the beauty of it crept into her soul and stilled her voice. The moon rode in a blue sky, a disc of glowing white, the great cedar-trees flung their shadows wide over the bright lawns and not a branch stirred.

"Listen," said Stella in a whisper and the river rippling against its banks with now a deep sob and now a fairy's laugh sang to them in notes most musical and clear. That liquid melody and the flutter of a bird's wings in the bough of a tree were the only sounds. They stood side by side, she looking out over the garden to the dim and pearly hills, he gazing at her

176

uplifted face and the pure column of her throat. They stood in a most dangerous silence. The air came cool and fresh to their nostrils. Stella drew it in with a smile.

"Good-night!" She laid her hand for a second on his arm. "Don't come with me!"

"Why not?"

And the answer came in a clear whisper:

"I am afraid."

Stella seemed to feel the man at her side suddenly grow very still. "It's only a step," she went on quickly and she passed out of the window on to the pathway. Dick Hazlewood followed but she turned to him and raised her hand.

"Don't," she pleaded; the voice was troubled but her eyes were steady. "If you come with me I shall tell you."

"What?" he interrupted, and the quickness of the interruption broke the spell which the night had laid upon her.

"I shall tell you again how much I thank you," she said lightly. "I shall cross the meadow by the garden gate. That brings me to my door."

She gathered her skirt in her hand and crossed the pathway to the edge of the grass.

"You can't do that," exclaimed Dick and he was at her side. He stooped and felt the turf. "Even the lawn's drenched. Crossing the meadow you'll be

177

ankle-deep in dew. You must promise never to go home across the meadow when you dine with us."

He spoke, chiding her as if she had been a mutinous child, and with so much anxiety that she laughed.

"You see, you have become rather precious to me," he added.

Though the month was July she that night was all April, half tears, half laughter. The smile passed from her lips and she raised her hands to her face with the swiftness of one who has been struck.

"What's the matter?" he asked, and she drew her hand away.

"Don't you understand?" she asked, and answered the question herself. "No, why should you?" She turned to him suddenly, her bosom heaving, her hands clenched. "Do you know what place I fill .here, in my own county? Years ago, when I was a child, there was supposed to be a pig-faced woman in Great Beeding. She lived in a small yellow cottage in the Square. It was pointed out to strangers as one of the sights of the town. Sometimes they were shown her shadow after dusk between the lamp and the blind. Sometimes you might have even caught a glimpse of her slinking late at night along the dark alleys. Well, the pig-faced woman has gone and I have taken her place."

"No," cried Dick. "That's not true."

"It is," she answered passionately. "I am the

curiosity. I am the freak. The townspeople take a pride in me, yes, just the same pride they took in her, and I find that pride more difficult to bear than all the aversion of the Pettifers. I too slink out early in the morning or late after night has fallen. And you"
—the passion of bitterness died out of her voice, her hands opened and hung at her sides, a smile of tenderness shone on her face—"you come with me. You ride with me early. With you I learn to take no heed. You welcome me to your house. You speak to me as you spoke just now." Her voice broke and a cry of gladness escaped from her which went to Dick Hazlewood's heart. "Oh, you shall see me to my door. I'll not cross the meadow. I'll go round by the road." She stopped and drew a breath.

"I'll tell you something."

"What?"

"It's rather good to be looked after. I know. It has never happened to me before. Yes, it's very good," and she drew out the words with a low laugh of happiness.

"Stella!" he said, and at the mention of her name she caught her hands up to her heart. "Oh, thank you!"

The hall-door was closed and all but one car had driven away when they turned the corner of the house and came out in the broad drive. They walked in the moonlight with a perfume of flowers in the air and the big yellow cups of the evening primroses gleaming on either side. They walked slowly. Stella knew that she should quicken her feet but she could not bring herself to do more than know it. She sought to take into her heart every tiniest detail of that walk so that in memory she might, years after, walk it again and so never be quite alone. They passed out through the great iron gates and turned into the lane. Here great elms overhung and now they walked in darkness, and now again were bathed in light. A twig snapped beneath her foot; even so small a thing she would remember.

"We must hurry," she said.

"We are doing all that we can," replied Dick. "It's a long way—this walk."

"You feel it so?" said Stella, tempting him—oh, unwisely! But the spell of the hour and the place was upon her.

"Yes," he answered her. "It's a long way in a man's life," and he drew close to her side.

"No!" she cried with a sudden violence. But she was awake too late. "No, Dick, no," she repeated, but his arms were about her.

"Stella, I want you. Oh, life's dull for a man without a woman; I can tell you," he exclaimed passionately.

"There are others—plenty," she said, and tried to thrust him away.

"Not for me," he rejoined, and he would not let her

go. Her struggles ceased, she buried her face in his coat, her hands caught his shoulders, she stood trembling and shivering against him.

"Stella," he whispered. "Stella!"

He raised her face and bent to it. Then he straightened himself.

"Not here!" he said.

They were standing in the darkness of a tree. He put his arms about her waist and lifted her into an open space where the moonlight shone bright and clear and there were no shadows.

"Here," he said, and he kissed her on the lips. She thrust her head back, her face uplifted to the skies, her eyes closed.

"Oh, Dick," she murmured, "I meant that this should never be. Even now—you shall forget it."

"No—I couldn't."

"So one says. But—oh, it would be your ruin."

She started away from him.

"Listen!"

"Yes," he answered.

She stood confronting him desperately a yard or so away, her bosom heaving, her face wet with her tears. Dick Hazlewood did not stir. Stella's lips moved as though she were speaking but no words were audible, and it seemed that her strength left her. She came suddenly forward, groping with her hands like a blind person.

181

"Oh, my dear," she said as he caught them. They went on again together. She spoke of his father, of the talk of the countryside. But he had an argument for each of hers.

"Be brave for just a little, Stella. Once we are married there will be no trouble," and with his arms about her she was eager to believe.

Stella Ballantyne sat late that night in the arm-chair in her bedroom, her eyes fixed upon the empty grate, in a turmoil of emotion. She grew cold and shivered. A loud noise of birds suddenly burst through the open window. She went to it. The morning had come. She looked across the meadow to the silent house of Little Beeding in the grey broadening light. All the blinds were down. Were they all asleep or did one watch like her? She came back to the fireplace. In the grate some torn fragments of a letter caught her eyes. She stooped and picked them up. They were fragments of the letter of regret which she had written earlier that evening.

"I should have sent it," she whispered. "I should not have gone. I should have sent the letter."

But the regret was vain. She had gone. Her maid found her in the morning lying upon her bed in a deep sleep and still wearing the dress in which she had gone out.

182

CHAPTER XVII

When Dick and Stella walked along the drive to the lane Harold Hazlewood, who was radiant at the success of his dinner-party, turned to Robert Pettifer in the hall.

"Have a whisky-and-soda, Robert, before you go," he said. He led the way back into the library. Behind him walked the Pettifers, Robert ill-at-ease and wishing himself a hundred miles away, Margaret Pettifer boiling for battle. Hazlewood himself dropped into an arm-chair.

"I am very glad that you came to-night, Margaret," he said boldly. "You have seen for yourself."

"Yes, I have," she replied. "Harold, there have been moments this evening when I could have screamed."

Robert Pettifer hurriedly turned towards the table in the far corner of the room where the tray with the decanters and the syphons had been placed.

"Margaret, I pass my life in a scream at the injustice of the world," said Harold Hazlewood, and Robert Pettifer chuckled as he cut off the end of a cigar. "It is strange that an act of reparation should move you in the same way."

183

THE WITNESS FOR THE DEFENCE

"Reparation!" cried Margaret Pettifer indignantly. Then she noticed that the window was open. She looked around the room. She drew up a chair in front of her brother.

"Harold, if you have no consideration for us, none for your own position, none for the neighbourhood, if you will at all costs force this woman upon us, don't you think that you might still spare a thought for your son?"

Robert Pettifer had kept his eyes open that evening as well as his wife. He took a step down into the room. He was anxious to take no part in the dispute; he desired to be just; he was favourably inclined towards Stella Ballantyne; looking at her he had been even a little moved. But Dick was the first consideration. He had no children of his own, he cared for Dick as he would have cared for his son, and when he went up each morning by the train to his office in London there lay at the back of his mind the thought that one day the fortune he was amassing would add a splendour to Dick's career. Harold Hazlewood alone of the three seemed to have his eyes sealed.

"Why, what on earth do you mean, Margaret?"

Margaret Pettifer sat down in her chair.

"Where was Dick yesterday afternoon?"

"Margaret, I don't know."

"I do. I saw him. He was with Stella Ballantyne on the river—in the dusk—in a Canadian canoe." She

184

uttered each fresh detail in a more indignant tone, as though it aggravated the crime. Yet even so she had not done. There was, it seemed, a culminating offence. "She was wearing a white lace frock with a big hat."

"Well," said Mr. Hazlewood mildly, "I don't think I have anything against big hats."

"She was trailing her hand in the water—that he might notice its slenderness of course. Outrageous I call it!"

Mr. Hazlewood nodded his head at his indignant sister.

"I know that frame of mind very well, Margaret," he remarked. "She cannot do right. If she had been wearing a small hat she would have been Frenchified."

But Mrs. Pettifer was not in a mood for argument.

"Can't you see what it all means?" she cried in exasperation.

"I can. I do," Mr. Hazlewood retorted and he smiled proudly upon his sister. "The boy's better nature is awakening."

Margaret Pettifer lifted up her hands.

"The boy!" she exclaimed. "He's thirty-four if he's a day."

She leaned forward in her chair and pointing up to the bay asked: "Why is that window open, Harold?"

Harold Hazlewood showed his first sign of discomfort. He shifted in his chair.

"It's a hot night, Margaret."

"That is not the reason," Mrs. Pettifer retorted implacably. "Where is Dick?"

"I expect that he is seeing Mrs. Ballantyne home."

"Exactly," said Mrs. Pettifer with a world of significance in her voice. Mr. Hazlewood sat up and looked at his sister.

"Margaret, you want to make me uncomfortable," he exclaimed pettishly. "But you shan't. No, my dear, you shan't." He let himself sink back again and joining the tips of his fingers contemplated the ceiling. But Margaret was in the mind to try. She shot out her words at him like so many explosive bullets.

"Being friends is one thing, Harold. Marrying is another."

"Very true, Margaret, very true."

"They are in love with one another."

"Rubbish, Margaret, rubbish."

"I watched them at the dinner-table and afterwards. They are man and woman, Harold. That's what you don't understand. They are not illustrations of your theories. Ask Robert."

"No," exclaimed Robert Pettifer. He hurriedly lit a cigar. "Any inference I should make must be purely hypothetical."

"Yes, we'll ask Robert. Come, Pettifer!" cried Mr. Hazlewood. "Let us have your opinion."

Robert Pettifer came reluctantly down from his corner.

TROUBLE FOR MR. HAZLEWOOD

"Well, if you insist, I think they were very friendly."

"Ah!" cried Hazlewood in triumph. "Being friends is one thing, Margaret. Marrying is another."

Mrs. Pettifer shook her head over her brother with a most aggravating pity.

"Dick said a shrewd thing the other day to me, Harold."

Mr. Hazlewood looked doubtfully at his sister.

"I am sure of it," he answered, but he was careful not to ask for any repetition of the shrewd remark. Margaret, however, was not in the mind to let him off.

"He said that sentimental philosophers sooner or later break their heads against their own theories. Mark those words, Harold! I hope they won't come true of you. I hope so very much indeed."

But it was abundantly clear that she had not a shadow of doubt that they would come true. Mr. Hazlewood was stung by the slighting phrase.

"I am not a sentimental philosopher," he said hotly. "Sentiment I altogether abhor. I hold strong views, I admit."

"You do indeed," his sister interrupted with an ironical laugh. "Oh, I have read your pamphlet, Harold. The prison walls must cast no shadow and convicts, once they are released, have as much right to sit down at our dinner-tables as they had before. Well, you carry your principles into practice, that I will say. We had an illustration to-night."

"You are unjust, Margaret," and Mr. Hazlewood rose from his chair with some dignity. "You speak of Mrs. Ballantyne, not for the first time, as if she had been tried and condemned. In fact she was tried and acquitted," and in his turn he appealed to Pettifer.

"Ask Robert!" he said.

But Pettifer was slow to answer, and when he did it was without assurance.

"Ye-es," he replied with something of a drawl. "Undoubtedly Mrs. Ballantyne was tried and acquitted"; and he left the impression on the two who heard him that with acquittal quite the last word had not been said. Mrs. Pettifer looked at him eagerly. She drew clear at once of the dispute. She left the questions now to Harold Hazlewood, and Pettifer had spoken with so much hesitation that Harold Hazlewood could not but ask them.

"You are making reservations, Robert?"

Pettifer shrugged his shoulders.

"I think we have a right to know them," Hazlewood insisted. "You are a solicitor with a great business and consequently a wide experience."

"Not of criminal cases, Hazlewood. I bring no more authority to judge them than any other man."

"Still you have formed an opinion. Please let me have it," and Mr. Hazlewood sat down again and crossed his knees. But a little impatience was now audible in his voice.

TROUBLE FOR MR. HAZLEWOOD

"An opinion is too strong a word," replied Pettifer guardedly. "The trial took place nearly eighteen months ago. I read the accounts of it certainly day by day as I travelled in the train to London. But they were summaries."

"Full summaries, Robert," said Hazlewood.

"No doubt. The trial made a great deal of noise in the world. But they were not full enough for me. Even if my memory of those newspaper reports were clear I should still hesitate to sit in judgment. But my memory isn't clear. Let us see what I do remember."

Pettifer took a chair and sat for a few moments with his forehead wrinkled in a frown. Was he really trying to remember? His wife asked herself that question as she watched him. Or had he something to tell them which he meant to let fall in his own cautiously careless way? Mrs. Pettifer listened alertly.

"The—well—let us call it the catastrophe—took place in a tent in some state of Rajputana."

"Yes," said Mr. Hazlewood.

"It took place at night. Mrs. Ballantyne was asleep in her bed. The man Ballantyne was found outside the tent in the doorway."

"Yes."

Pettifer paused. "So many law cases have engaged my attention since," he said in apology for his hesitation. He seemed quite at a loss. Then he went on:

189

"Wait a moment! A man had been dining with them at night—oh yes, I begin to remember."

Harold Hazlewood made a tiny movement and would have spoken, but Margaret held out a hand towards him swiftly.

"Yes, a man called Thresk," said Pettifer, and again he was silent.

"Well," asked Hazlewood.

"Well—that's all I remember," replied Pettifer briskly. He rose and put his chair back. "Except——" he added slowly.

"Yes?"

"Except that there was left upon my mind when the verdict was published a vague feeling of doubt."

"There!" cried Mrs. Pettifer triumphantly. "You hear him, Harold."

But Hazelwood paid no attention to her. He was gazing at his brother-in-law with a good deal of uneasiness.

"Why?" he asked. "Why were you in doubt, Robert?"

But Pettifer had said all that he had any mind to say.

"Oh, I can't remember why," he exclaimed. "I am very likely quite wrong. Come, Margaret, it's time that we were getting home."

He crossed over to Hazlewood and held out his hand. Hazlewood, however, did not rise.

"I don't think that's quite fair of you, Robert," he said. "You don't disturb my confidence, of course— I have gone into the case thoroughly—but I think you ought to give me a chance of satisfying you that your doubts have no justification."

"No really," exclaimed Pettifer. "I absolutely re- fuse to mix myself up in the affair at all." A step sounded upon the gravel path outside the window. Pettifer raised a warning finger. "It's midnight, Mar- garet," he said. "We must go"; and as he spoke Dick Hazlewood walked in through the open window.

He smiled at the group of his relations with a grim amusement. They certainly wore a guilty look. He was surprised to remark some embarrassment even upon his father's face.

"You will see your aunt off, Richard," said Mr. Hazlewood.

"Of course."

The Pettifers and Dick went out into the hall, leav- ing the old man in his chair, a little absent, perhaps a little troubled.

"Aunt Margaret, you have been upsetting my father," said Dick.

"Nonsense, Dick," she replied, and her face flushed. She stepped into the carriage quickly to avoid questions, and as she stepped in Dick noticed that she was carry- ing a little paper-covered book. Pettifer followed. "Good-night, Dick," he said, and he shook hands with his nephew very warmly. In spite of his cordiality, however, Dick's face grew hard as he watched the carriage drive away. Stella was right. The Pettifers were the enemy. Well, he had always known there would be a fight, and now the sooner it came the better. He went back to the library and as he opened the door he heard his father's voice. The old man was sitting sunk in his chair and repeating to himself:

"I won't believe it. I won't believe it."

He stopped at once when Dick came in. Dick looked at him with concern.

"You are tired, father," he said.

"Yes, I think I am a little. I'll go to bed."

Hazlewood watched Dick walk over to the corner table where the candles stood beside the tray, and his face cleared. For the first time in his life the tidy well-groomed conventional look of his son was a real pleasure to him. Richard was of those to whom the good-will of the world meant much. He would never throw it lightly away. Hazlewood got up and took one of the candles from his son. He patted him on the shoulder. He became quite at ease as he looked into his face.

"Good-night, my boy," he said.

"Good-night, sir," replied Dick cheerfully. "There's nothing like acting up to one's theories, is there?"

"Nothing," said the old man heartily. "Look at my life!"

"Yes," replied Dick. "And now look at mine. I am going to marry Stella Ballantyne."

For a moment Mr. Hazlewood stood perfectly still. Then he murmured lamely:

"Oh, are you? Are you, Richard?" and he shuffled quickly out of the room.

CHAPTER XVIII

As Dick was getting out of bed at half-past seven a troubled little note was brought to him written hurriedly and almost incoherent.

"Dick, I can't ride with you this morning. I am too tired . . . and I don't think we should meet again. You must forget last night. I shall be very proud always to remember it, but I won't ruin you, Dick. You mustn't think I shall suffer so very much . . . " Dick read it all through with a smile of tenderness upon his face. He wrote a line in reply. "I will come and see you at eleven, Stella. Meanwhile sleep, my dear," and sent it across to the cottage. Then he rolled back into bed again and took his own advice. It was late when he came down into the dining-room and he took his breakfast alone.

"Where's my father?" he asked of Hubbard the butler.

"Mr. Hazlewood breakfasted half an hour ago, sir. He's at work now."

"Capital," said Dick. "Give me some sausages. Hubbard, what would you say if I told you that I was going to be married?"

194

MR. HAZLEWOOD SEEKS ADVICE

Hubbard placed a plate in front of him.

"I should keep my head, sir," he answered in his gentle voice. "Will you take tea?"

"Thank you."

Dick looked out of the window. It was a morning of clear skies and sunlight, a very proper morning for this the first of all the remarkable days which one after the other were going especially to belong to him. He was of the gods now. The world was his property, or rather he held it in trust for Stella. It was behaving well; Dick Hazlewood was contented. He ate a large breakfast and strolling into the library lit his pipe. There was his father bending over his papers at his writing-table before the window, busy as a bee no doubt at some new enthusiasm which was destined to infuriate his neighbours. Let him go on! Dick smiled benignly at the old man's back. Then he frowned. It was curious that his father had not wished him a good-morning, curious and unusual.

"I hope, sir, that you slept well," he said.

"I did not, Richard," and still the back was turned to him. "I lay awake considering with some care what you told me last night about—about Stella Ballantyne."

Of late she had been simply Stella to Harold Hazlewood. The addition of Ballantyne was significant. It replaced friendliness with formality.

"Yes, we agreed to champion her cause, didn't

195

we?" said Dick cheerily. "You took one good step forward last night, I took another."

"You took a long stride, Richard, and I think you might have consulted me first."

Dick walked over to the table at which his father sat.

"Do you know, that's just what Stella said," he remarked, and he seemed to find the suggestion rather unintelligible. Mr. Hazlewood snatched at any support which was offered to him.

"Ah!" he exclaimed, and for the first time that morning he looked his son in the face. "There now, Richard, you see!"

"Yes," Richard returned imperturbably. "But I was able to remove all her fears. I was able to tell her that you would welcome our marriage with all your heart, for you would look upon it as a triumph for your principles and a sure sign that my better nature was at last thoroughly awake."

Dick walked away from the table. The old man's face lengthened. If he was a philosopher at all, he was a philosopher in a piteous position, for he was having his theories tested upon himself, he was to be the experiment by which they should be proved or disproved.

"No doubt," he said in a lamentable voice. "Quite so, Richard. Yes," and he caught at vague hopes of delay. "There's no hurry of course. For one thing

196

I don't want to lose you. . . . And then you have your career to think of, haven't you?" Mr. Hazlewood found himself here upon ground more solid and leaned his weight on it. "Yes, there's your career."

Dick returned to his father, amazement upon his face. He spoke as one who cannot believe the evidence of his ears.

"But it's in the army, father! Do you realise what you are saying? You want me to think of my career in the British Army?"

Consistency however had no charms for Mr. Hazlewood at this moment.

"Exactly," he cried. "We don't want to prejudice that—do we? No, no, Richard! Oh, I hear the finest things about you. And they push the young men along nowadays. You don't have to wait for grey hairs before you're made a General, Richard, so we must keep an eye on our prospects, eh? And for that reason it would be advisable perhaps"—and the old man's eyes fell from Dick's face to his papers— "yes, it would certainly be advisable to let your engagement remain for a while just a private matter between the three of us."

He took up his pen as though the matter was decided and discussion at an end. But Dick did not move from his side. He was the stronger of the two and in a little while the old man's eyes wandered up to his face again. There was a look there which Mar-

197

garet Pettifer had seen a week ago. Dick spoke and
the voice he used was strange and formidable to his
father.

"There must be no secrecy, father. I remember
what you said: for uncharitable slander an English
village is impossible to beat. Our secret would be
known within a week and by attempting to keep it we
invite suspicion. Nothing could be more damaging
to Stella than secrecy. Consequently nothing could
be more damaging to me. I don't deny that things
are going to be a little difficult. But of this I am sure"
—and his voice, though it still was quiet, rang deep
with confidence—"our one chance is to hold our heads
high. No secrecy, father! My hope is to make a life
which has been very troubled know some comfort and
a little happiness."

Mr. Hazlewood had no more to say. He must renounce his gods or hold his tongue. And renounce
his gods—no, that he could not do. He heard in
imagination the whole neighbourhood laughing—he
saw it a sea of laughter overwhelming him. He
shivered as he thought of it. He, Harold Hazlewood,
the man emancipated from the fictions of society, caught
like a silly struggling fish in the net of his own theories!
No, that must never be. He flung himself at his work.
He was revising the catalogue of his miniatures and
in a minute he began to fumble and search about his
over-loaded desk.

MR. HAZLEWOOD SEEKS ADVICE

"Everybody is trying to thwart me this morning," he cried angrily.

"What's the matter, father?" asked Dick, laying down the *Times*. "Can I help?"

"I wrote a question to *Notes and Queries* about the Marie Antoinette miniature which I bought at Lord Mirliton's sale and there was an answer in the last number, a very complete answer. But I can't find it. I can't find it anywhere"; and he tossed his papers about as though he were punishing them.

Dick helped in the search, but beyond a stray copy or two of *The Prison Walls must Cast no Shadow*, there was no publication to be found at all.

"Wait a bit, father," said Dick suddenly. "What is *Notes and Queries* like? The only notes and queries I read are contained in a pink paper. They are very amusing but they do not deal with miniatures."

Mr. Hazlewood described the appearance of the little magazine.

"Well, that's very extraordinary," said Dick, "for Aunt Margaret took it away last night."

Mr. Hazlewood looked at his son in blank astonishment.

"Are you sure, Richard?"

"I saw it in her hand as she stepped into her carriage."

Mr. Hazlewood banged his fist upon the table.

"It's extremely annoying of Margaret," he exclaimed. "She takes no interest in such matters. She is not, if I may use the word, a virtuoso. She did it solely to annoy me."

"Well, I wonder," said Dick. He looked at his watch. It was eleven o'clock. He went out into the hall, picked up a straw hat and walked across the meadow to the thatched cottage on the river-bank. But while he went he was still wondering why in the world Margaret had taken away that harmless little magazine from his father's writing-table. "Pettifer's at the bottom of it," he concluded. "There's a foxy fellow for you. I'll keep my eye on Uncle Robert." He was near to the cottage. Only a rail separated its garden from the meadow. Beyond the garden a window stood open and within the room he saw the flutter of a lilac dress.

From the window of the library Mr. Hazlewood watched his son open the garden gate. Then he un-locked a drawer of his writing-table and took out a large sealed envelope. He broke the seal and drew from the envelope a sheaf of press cuttings. They were the verbatim reports of Stella Ballantyne's trial, which had been printed day by day in the *Times of India*. He had sent for them months ago when he had blithely taken upon himself the defence of Stella Ballantyne. He had read them with a growing ardour. So harshly had she lived; so shadowless was her innocence. He turned to them now in a different

200

spirit. Pettifer had been left by 'the English summaries of the trial with a vague feeling of doubt. Mr.
Hazlewood respected Robert Pettifer. The lawyer
was cautious, deliberate, unemotional—qualities with
which Hazlewood had instinctively little sympathy.
But on the other hand he was not bound hand and
foot in prejudice. He could be liberal in his judg-
ments. He had a mind clear enough to divide what
reason had to say and the presumptions of convention.
Suppose that Pettifer was after all right! The old
man's heart sank within him. Then indeed this
marriage must be prevented—and the truth must be
made known—yes, widely known. He himself had
been deceived—like many another man before him.
It was not ridiculous to have been deceived. He remained at all events consistent to his principles.
There was his pamphlet to be sure, *The Prison Walls
must Cast no Shadow:* that gave him an uncomfortable twinge. But he reassured himself.

"There I argue that, once the offence has been expiated, all the privileges should be restored. But if
Pettifer is right there has been no expiation."

That saving clause let him out. He did not thus
phrase the position even to himself. He clothed it in
other and high-sounding words. It was after all a sort
of convention to accept acquittal as the proof of innocence. But at the back of his mind from first to last
there was an immense fear of the figure which he him-

self would cut if he refused his consent to the marriage on any ground except that of Stella Ballantyne's guilt. For Stella herself, the woman, he had no kindness to spare that morning. Yesterday he had overflowed with it. For yesterday she had been one more proof to the world how high he soared above it.

"Since Pettifer's in doubt," he said to himself, "there must be some flaw in this trial which I overlooked in the heat of my sympathy"; and to discover that flaw he read again every printed detail of it from the morning when Stella first appeared before the stipendiary magistrate to that other morning a month later when the verdict was given. And he found no flaw. Stella's acquittal was inevitable on the evidence. There was much to show what provocation she had suffered, but there was no proof that she had yielded to it. On the contrary she had endured so long, the presumption must be that she would go on enduring to the end. And there was other evidence—positive evidence given by Thresk which could not be gainsaid.

Mr. Hazlewood replaced his cuttings in the drawer; and he was utterly discontented. He had hoped for another result. There was only one point which puzzled him and that had nothing really to do with the trial, but it puzzled him so much that it slipped out at luncheon.

"Richard," he said, "I cannot understand why the name of Thresk is so familiar to me."

MR. HAZLEWOOD SEEKS ADVICE

Dick glanced quickly at his father.

"You have been reading over again the accounts of the trial."

Mr. Hazlewood looked confused.

"And a very natural proceeding, Richard," he declared. "But while reading over the trial I found the name Thresk familiar to me in another connection, but I cannot remember what the connection is."

Dick could not help him, nor was he at that time concerned by the failure of his father's memory. He was engaged in realising that here was another enemy for Stella. Knowing his father, he was not greatly surprised, but he thought it prudent to attack without delay.

"Stella will be coming over to tea this afternoon," he said.

"Will she, Richard?" the father replied, twisting uncomfortably in his chair. "Very well—of course."

"Hubbard knows of my engagement, by the way," Dick continued implacably.

"Hubbard! God bless my soul!" cried the old man. "It'll be all over the village already."

"I shouldn't wonder," replied Dick cheerfully. "I told him before I saw you this morning, whilst I was having breakfast."

Mr. Hazlewood remained silent for a while. Then he burst out petulantly:

"Richard, there's something I must speak to you

seriously about: the lateness of your hours in the morning. I have noticed it with great regret. It is not considerate to the servants and it cannot be healthy for you. Such indolence too must be enervating to your mind."

Dick forbore to remind his father that he was usually out of the house before seven.

"Father," he said, at once a very model of humility, "I will endeavour to reform."

Mr. Hazlewood concealed his embarrassment at teatime under a show of over-work. He had a great deal to do—just a moment for a cup of tea—no more. There was to be a meeting of the County Council the next morning when a most important question of small holdings was to come up for discussion. Mr. Hazlewood held the strongest views. He was engaged in shaping them in the smallest possible number of words. To be brief, to be vivid—there was the whole art of public speaking. Mr. Hazlewood chattered feverishly for five minutes; he had come in chattering, he went out chattering.

"That's all right, Stella, you see," said Dick cheerfully when they were left alone. Stella nodded her head. Mr. Hazlewood had not said one word in recognition of her engagement but she had made her little fight that morning. She had yielded and she could not renew it. She had spent three miserable hours framing reasonable arguments why last night should be forgotten. But the sight of her lover coming across the meadow had set her heart so leaping that she could only stammer out a few tags and phrases.

"Oh, I wish you hadn't come!" she had repeated and repeated and all the while her blood was leaping in her body for joy that he had. She had promised in the end to stand firm, to stand by his side and brave— what, after all, but the clamour of a week? So he put it and so she was eager to believe.

Mr. Hazelwood, busy though he made himself out to be, found time that evening to drive in his motor-car into Great Beeding, and when the London train pulled up at the station he was on the platform. He looked anxiously at the passengers who descended until he saw Robert Pettifer. He went up to him at once.

"What in the world are you doing here?" asked the lawyer.

"I came on purpose to catch you, Robert. I want to speak to you in private. My car is here. If you will get into it with me we can drive slowly towards your house."

Pettifer's face changed, but he could not refuse. Hazlewood was agitated and nervous; of his ordinary complacency there was no longer a trace. Pettifer got into the car and as it moved away from the station he asked:

"Now what's the matter?"

"I have been thinking over what you said last night, Robert. You had a vague feeling of doubt. Well, I have the verbatim reports of the trial in Bombay here in this envelope and I want you to read them carefully through and give me your opinion." He held out the envelope as he spoke, but Pettifer thrust his hands into his pockets.

"I won't touch it," he declared. "I refuse to mix myself up in the affair at all. I said more than I meant to last night."

"But you did say it, Robert."

"Then I withdraw it now."

"But you can't, Robert. You must go further. Something has happened to-day, something very serious."

"Oh?" said Pettifer.

"Yes," replied Mr. Hazlewood. "Margaret really has more insight than I credited her with. They propose to get married."

Pettifer sat upright in the car.

"You mean Dick and Stella Ballantyne?"

"Yes."

And for a little while there was silence in the car. Then Mr. Hazlewood continued to bleat.

"I never suspected anything of the kind. It places me, Robert, in a very difficult position."

"I can quite see that," answered Pettifer with a grim smile. "It's really the only consoling element in the whole business. You can't refuse your consent without looking a fool and you can't give it while you are in any doubt as to Mrs. Ballantyne's innocence."

Mr. Hazlewood was not, however, quite prepared to accept that definition of his position.

"You don't exhaust the possibilities, Robert," he said. "I can quite well refuse my consent and publicly refuse it if there are reasonable grounds for believing that there was in that trial a grave miscarriage of justice."

Mr. Pettifer looked sharply at his companion. The voice no less than the words fixed his attention. This was not the Mr. Hazlewood of yesterday. The champion had dwindled into a figure of meanness. Harold Hazlewood would be glad to discover those reasonable grounds; and he would be very much obliged if Robert Pettifer would take upon himself the responsibility of discovering them.

"Yes, I see," said Pettifer slowly. He was half inclined to leave Harold Hazlewood to find his way out of his trouble by himself. It was all his making after all. But other and wider considerations began to press upon Pettifer. He forced himself to omit altogether the subject of Hazlewood's vanities and entanglements.

"Very well. Give the cuttings to me! I will read them through and I will let you know my opinion. Their intention to marry may alter everything—my point of view as much as yours."

THE WITNESS FOR THE DEFENCE

Mr. Pettifer took the envelope in his hand and got out of the car as soon as Hazlewood had stopped it.

"You have raised no objections to the engagement?" he asked.

"A word to Richard this morning. Of not much effect I am afraid."

Mr. Pettifer nodded.

"Right. I should say nothing to anybody. You can't take a decided line against it at present and to snarl would be the worst policy imaginable. To-day's Thursday. We'll meet on Saturday. Good-night," and Robert Pettifer walked away to his own house.

He walked slowly, wondering at the eternal mystery by which this particular man and that individual woman select each other out of the throng. He owed the greater part of his fortune to the mystery like many another lawyer. But to-night he would willingly have yielded a good portion of it up if that process of selection could be ordered in a more reasonable way. Love? The attraction of Sex? Yes, no doubt. But why these two specimens of Sex? Why Dick and Stella Ballantyne?

When he reached his house his wife hurried forward to meet him. Already she had the news. There was an excitement in her face not to be misunderstood. The futile time-honoured phrase of triumph so ready on the lips of those who have prophesied evil was trembling upon hers.

MR. HAZLEWOOD SEEKS ADVICE

"Don't say it, Margaret," said Pettifer very seriously. "We have come to a pass where light words will lead us astray. Hazlewood has been with me. I have the reports of the trial here."

Margaret Pettifer put a check upon her tongue and they dined together almost in complete silence. Pettifer was methodically getting his own point of view quite clearly established in his mind, so that whatever he did or advised he might be certain not to swerve from it afterwards. He weighed his inclinations and his hopes, and when the servants had left the dining-room and he had lit his cigar he put his case before his wife.

"Listen, Margaret! You know your brother. He is always in extremes. He swings from one to the other. He is terrified now lest this marriage should take place."

"No wonder," interposed Mrs. Pettifer.

Pettifer made no comment upon the remark.

"Therefore," he continued, "he is anxious that I should discover in these reports some solid reason for believing that the verdict which acquitted Stella Ballantyne was a grave miscarriage of justice. For any such reason must have weight."

"Of course," said Mrs. Pettifer.

"And will justify him—this is his chief consideration—in withholding publicly his consent."

"I see."

THE WITNESS FOR THE DEFENCE

Only a week ago Dick himself had observed that sentimental philosophers had a knack of breaking their heads against their own theories. The words had been justified sooner than she had expected. Mrs. Pettifer was not surprised at Harold Hazlewood's swift change any more than her husband had been. Harold, to her thinking, was a sentimentalist and sentimentality was like a fir-tree—a thing of no deep roots and easily torn up.

"But I do not take that view, Margaret," continued her husband, and she looked at him with consternation. Was he now to turn champion, he who only yesterday had doubted? "And I want you to consider whether you can agree with me. There is to begin with the woman herself, Stella Ballantyne. I saw her for the first time yesterday, and to be quite honest I liked her, Margaret. Yes. It seemed to me that there was nothing whatever of the adventuress about her. And I was impressed—I will go further, I was moved—dry-as-dust old lawyer as I am, by something—— How shall I express it without being ridiculous?" He paused and searched in his vocabulary and gave up the search. "No, the epithet which occurred to me yesterday at the dinner-table and immediately, still seems to me the only true one—I was moved by something in this woman of tragic experiences which was strangely virginal."

One quick movement was made by Margaret Pettifer. The truth of her husband's description was a revelation, so exact it was. Therein lay Stella Ballantyne's charm, and her power to create champions and friends. Her history was known to you, the miseries of her marriage, the suspicion of crime. You expected a woman of adventures and lo! there stood before you one with "something virginal" in her appearance and her manner, which made its soft and irresistible appeal.

"I recognise that feeling of mine," Pettifer resumed, "and I try to put it aside. And putting it aside I ask myself and you, Margaret, this: Here's a woman who has been through a pretty bad time, who has been unhappy, who has stood in the dock, who has been acquitted. Is it quite fair that when at last she has floated into a haven of peace two private people like Hazlewood and myself should take it upon ourselves to review the verdict and perhaps reverse it?"

"But there's Dick, Robert," cried Mrs. Pettifer. "There's Dick. Surely he's our first thought."

"Yes, there's Dick," Mr. Pettifer repeated. "And Dick's my second point. You are all worrying about Dick from the social point of view—the external point of view. Well, we have got to take that into our consideration. But we are bound to look at him, the man, as well. Don't forget that, Margaret! Well, I find the two points of view identical. But our neighbours won't. Will you?"

211

Mrs. Pettifer was baffled.

"I don't understand," she said.

"I'll explain. From the social standpoint what's really important as regards Dick? That he should go out to dinner? No. That he should have children? Yes!"

And here Mrs. Pettifer interposed again.

"But they must be the right children," she exclaimed. "Better that he should have none than that he should have children——"

"With an hereditary taint," Pettifer agreed. "Admitted, Margaret. If we come to the conclusion that Stella Ballantyne did what she was accused of doing we, in spite of all the verdicts in the world, are bound to resist this marriage. I grant it. Because of that conviction I dismiss the plea that we are unfair to the woman in reviewing the trial. There are wider, greater considerations."

These were the first words of comfort which Mrs. Pettifer had heard since her husband began to expound. She received them with enthusiasm.

"I am so glad to hear that."

"Yes, Margaret," Pettifer retorted drily. "But please ask yourself this question: (it is where, to my thinking, the social and the personal elements join) if this marriage is broken off, is Dick likely to marry at all?"

"Why not?" asked Margaret.

MR. HAZLEWOOD SEEKS ADVICE

"He is thirty-four. He has had, no doubt, many opportunities of marriage. He must have had. He is good-looking, well off and a good fellow. This is the first time he has wanted to marry. If he is disappointed here will he try again?"

Mrs. Pettifer laughed, moved by the remarkable depreciation of her own sex which women of her type so often have. It was for man to throw the handkerchief. Not a doubt but there would be a rush to pick it up!

"Widowers who have been devoted to their wives marry again," she argued.

"A point for me, Margaret!" returned Pettifer. "Widowers—yes. They miss so much—the habit of a house with a woman its mistress, the companionship, the order, oh, a thousand small but important things. But a man who has remained a bachelor until he's thirty-four—that's a different case. If he sets his heart at that age, seriously, for the first time on a woman and does not get her, that's the kind of man who, my experience suggests to me—I put it plainly, Margaret—will take one or more mistresses to himself but no wife."

Mrs. Pettifer deferred to the worldly knowledge of her husband but she clung to her one clear argument.

"Nothing could be worse," she said frankly, "than that he should marry a guilty woman."

"Granted, Margaret," replied Mr. Pettifer imper-

213

turbably. "Only suppose that she's not guilty. There are you and I, rich people, and no one to leave our money to—no one to carry on your name—no one we care a rap about to benefit by my work and your brother's fortune—no one of the family to hand over Little Beeding to."

Both of them were silent after he had spoken. He had touched upon their one great sorrow. Margaret herself had her roots deep in the soil of Little Beeding. It was hateful to her that the treasured house should ever pass to strangers, as it would do if this the last branch of the family failed.

"But Stella Ballantyne was married for seven years," she said at last, "and there were no children."

"No, that's true," replied Pettifer. "But it does not follow that with a second marriage there will be none. It's a chance, I know, but——" and he got up from his chair. "I do honestly believe that it's the only chance you and I will have, Margaret, of dying with the knowledge that our lives have not been altogether vain. We've lighted our little torch. Yes, and it burns merrily enough, but what's the use unless at the appointed mile-stone there's another of us to take it and carry it on?"

He stood looking down at his wife with a wistful and serious look upon his face.

"Dick's past the age of calf-love. We can't expect him to tumble from one passion to another; and he's not easily moved. Therefore I hope very sincerely that these reports which I am now going to read will enable me to go boldly to Harold Hazlewood and say: 'Stella Ballantyne is as guiltless of this crime as you or I.' "

Mr. Pettifer took up the big envelope which he had placed on the table beside him and carried it away to his study.

CHAPTER XIX

On the Saturday morning Mr. Hazlewood drove over early to Great Beeding. His impatience had so grown during the last few days that his very sleep was broken at night and in the daytime he could not keep still. The news of Dick's engagement to Stella Ballantyne was now known throughout the countryside and the blame for it was laid upon Harold Hazlewood's shoulders. For blame was the general note, blame and chagrin. A few bold and kindly spirits went at once to see Stella; a good many more seriously and at great length debated over their tea-tables whether they should call after the marriage. But on the whole the verdict was an indignant No. Disgrace was being brought upon the neighbourhood. Little Beeding would be impossible. Dick Hazlewood only laughed at the constraint of his acquaintances, and when three of them crossed the road hurriedly in Great Beeding to avoid Stella and himself he said good-humouredly:

"They are like an ill-trained company of bad soldiers. Let one of them break from the ranks and they'll all stream away so as not to be left behind. You'll see, Stella. One of them will come and the

216

rest will tumble over one another to get into your drawing-room."

How much he believed of what he said Stella did not inquire. She had a gift of silence. She just walked a little nearer to him and smiled, lest any should think she had noticed the slight. The one man, in a word, who showed signs of wear and tear was Mr. Hazlewood himself. So keen was his distress that he had no fear of his sister's sarcasms.

"I—think of it!" he exclaimed in a piteous bewilderment, "actually I have become sensitive to public opinion," and Mrs. Pettifer forbore from the comments which she very much longed to make. She was in the study when Harold Hazlewood was shown in, and Pettifer had bidden her to stay.

"Margaret knows that I have been reading these reports," he said. "Sit down, Hazlewood, and I'll tell you what I think."

Mr. Hazlewood took a seat facing the garden with its old red brick wall, on which a purple clematis was growing.

"You have formed an opinion then, Robert?"

"One."

"What is it?" he asked eagerly.

Robert Pettifer clapped the palm of his hand down upon the cuttings from the newspapers which lay before him on his desk.

"This—no other verdict could possibly have been

217

given by the jury. On the evidence produced at the trial in Bombay Mrs. Ballantyne was properly and inevitably acquitted."

"Robert!" exclaimed his wife. She too had been hoping for the contrary opinion. As for Hazlewood himself the sunlight seemed to die off that garden. He drew his hand across his forehead. He half rose to go when again Robert Pettifer spoke.

"And yet," he said slowly, "I am not satisfied."

Harold Hazlewood sat down again. Mrs. Pettifer drew a breath of relief.

"The chief witness for the defence, the witness whose evidence made the acquittal certain, was a man I know —a barrister called Thresk."

"Yes," interrupted Hazlewood. "I have been puzzled about that man ever since you mentioned him before. His name I am somehow familiar with."

"I'll explain that to you in a minute," said Pettifer, and his wife leaned forward suddenly in her chair. She did not interrupt but she sat with a look of keen expectancy upon her face. She did not know whither Pettifer was leading them but she was now sure that it was to some carefully pondered goal.

"I have more than once briefed Thresk myself. He's a man of the highest reputation at the Bar, straightforward, honest; he enjoys a great practice, he is in Parliament with a great future in Parliament. In a word he is a man with everything to lose if he

218

lied as a witness in a trial. And yet—I am not satisfied."

Mr. Pettifer's voice sank to a low murmur. He sat
at his desk staring out in front of him through the
window.

"Why?" asked Hazlewood. But Pettifer did not
answer him. He seemed not to hear the question. He
went on in the low quiet voice he had used before, rather
like one talking to himself than to a companion.

"I should very much like to put a question or two
to Mr. Thresk."

"Then why don't you?" exclaimed Mrs. Pettifer.
"You know him."

"Yes." Mr. Hazlewood eagerly seconded his sister.
"Since you know him you are the very man."

Pettifer shook his head.

"It would be an impertinence. For although I look
upon Dick as a son I am not his father. You are,
Hazlewood, you are. He wouldn't answer me."

"Would he answer me?" asked Hazlewood. "I
don't know him at all. I can't go to him and ask if he
told the truth."

"No, no, you can't do that," Pettifer answered, "nor
do I mean you to. I want to put my questions myself
in my own way and I thought that you might get him
down to Little Beeding."

"But I have no excuse," cried Hazlewood, and Mrs.
Pettifer at last understood the plan which was in her

husband's mind, which had been growing to completion since the night when he had dined at Little Beeding.

"Yes, you have an excuse," she cried, and Pettifer explained what it was.

"You collect miniatures. Some time ago you bought one of Marie Antoinette at Lord Mirliton's sale. You asked a question as to its authenticity in *Notes and Queries*. It was answered——"

Mr. Hazlewood broke in excitedly:

"By a man called Thresk. That is why the name was familiar to me. But I could not remember." He turned upon his sister. "It is your fault, Margaret. You took my copy of *Notes and Queries* away with you. Dick noticed it and told me."

"Dick!" Pettifer exclaimed in alarm. But the alarm passed. "He cannot have guessed why."

Mrs. Pettifer was clear upon the point.

"No. I took the magazine because of a remark which Robert made to you. Dick did not hear it. No, he cannot have guessed why."

"For it's important he should have no suspicion whatever of what I propose that you should do, Hazlewood," Pettifer said gravely. "I propose that we should take a lesson from the legal processes of another country. It may work, it may not, but to my mind it is our only chance."

"Let me hear!" said Hazlewood.

"Thresk is an authority on old silver and miniatures.

220

He has a valuable collection himself. His advice is sought by people in the trade. You know what collectors are. Get him down to see your collection. It wouldn't be the first time that you have invited a stranger to pass a night in your house for that purpose, would it?"

"No."

"And the invitation has often been accepted?"

"Well—sometimes."

"We must hope that it will be this time. Get Thresk down to Little Beeding upon that excuse. Then confront him unexpectedly with Mrs. Ballantyne. And let me be there."

Such was the plan which Pettifer suggested. A period of silence followed upon his words. Even Mr. Hazlewood, in the extremity of his distress, recoiled from it.

"It would look like a trap."

Mr. Pettifer thumped his table impatiently.

"Let's be frank, for Heaven's sake. It wouldn't merely look like a trap, it would be one. It wouldn't be at all a pretty thing to do, but there's this marriage!"

"No, I couldn't do it," said Hazlewood.

"Very well. There's no more to be said."

Pettifer himself had no liking for the plan. It had been his intention originally to let Hazlewood know that if he wished to get into communication with Thresk there was a means by which he could do it. But the fact of Dick's engagement had carried him still further, and now that he had read the evidence of the trial carefully there was a real anxiety in his mind. Pettifer sealed up the cuttings in a fresh envelope and gave them to Hazlewood and went out with him to the door.

"Of course," said the old man, "if your legal experience, Robert, leads you to think that we should be justified——"

"But it doesn't," Pettifer was quick to interpose. He recognised his brother-in-law's intention to throw the discredit of the trick upon his shoulders but he would have none of it. "No, Hazlewood," he said cheerfully: "it's not a plan which a high-class lawyer would be likely to commend to a client."

"Then I am afraid that I couldn't do it."

"All right," said Pettifer with his hand upon the latch of the front door. "Thresk's chambers are in King's Bench Walk." He added the number.

"I simply couldn't think of it," Hazlewood repeated as he crossed the pavement to his car.

"Perhaps not," said Pettifer. "You have the envelope? Yes. Choose an evening towards the end of the week, a Friday will be your best chance of getting him."

"I will do nothing of the kind, Pettifer."

"And let me know when he is coming. Goodbye."

The car carried Mr. Hazlewood away still protesting that he really couldn't think of it for an instant. But he thought a good deal of it during the next week and his temper did not improve. "Pettifer has rubbed off the finer edges of his nature," he said to himself. "It is a pity—a great pity. But thirty years of life in a lawyer's office must no doubt have that effect. I regret very much that Pettifer should have imagined that I would condescend to such a scheme."

CHAPTER XX

They went up by the steep chalk road which skirts the park wall to the top of the conical hill above the race-course. An escarpment of grass banks guards a hollow like a shallow crater on the very summit. They rode round it upon the rim, now facing the black slope of Charlton Forest across the valley to the north, now looking out over the plain and Chichester. Thirty miles away above the sea the chalk cliffs of the Isle of Wight gleamed under their thatch of dark turf. It was not yet nine in the morning. Later the day would climb dustily to noon; now it had the wonder and the stillness of great beginnings. A faint haze like a veil at the edges of the sky and a freshness of the air made the world magical to these two who rode high above weald and sea. Stella looked downwards to the silver flash of the broad water west of Chichester spire.

"That way they came, perhaps on a day like this," she said slowly, "those old centurions."

"Your thoughts go back," said Dick Hazlewood with a laugh.

"Not so far as you think," cried Stella, and suddenly

224

her cheeks took fire and a smile dimpled them. "Oh, I dare to think of many things to-day."

She rode down the steep grass slope towards the race-course with Dick at her side. It was the first morning they had ridden together since the night of the dinner-party at Little Beeding. Mr. Hazlewood was at this moment ordering his car so that he might drive in to the town and learn what Pettifer had discovered in the cuttings from the newspapers. But they were quite unaware of the plot which was being hatched against them. They went forward under the high beech-trees watching for the great roots which stretched across their path, and talking little. An open way between wooden posts led them now on to turf and gave them the free-dom of the downs. They saw no one. With the larks and the field-fares they had the world to themselves; and in the shade beneath the hedges the dew still sparkled on the grass. They left the long arm of Hal-naker Down upon their right, its old mill standing up on the edge like some lighthouse on a bluff of the sea, and crossing the high road from Up-Waltham rode along a narrow glade amongst beeches and nut-trees and small oaks and bushes of wild roses. Open spaces came again; below them were the woods and the green country of Slindon and the deep grass of Dale Park. And so they drew near to Gumber Corner where Stane Street climbs over Bignor Hill. Here Dick Hazlewood halted.

225

THE WITNESS FOR THE DEFENCE

"I suppose we turn."

"Not to-day," said Stella, and Dick turned to her with surprise. Always before they had stopped at this point and always by Stella's wish. Either she was tired or was needed at home or had letters to write—always there had been some excuse and no reason. Dick Hazlewood had come to believe that she would not pass this point, that the down land beyond was a sort of Tom Tiddler's ground on which she would not trespass. He had wondered why, but his instinct had warned him from questions. He had always turned at this spot immediately, as if he believed the excuse which she had ready.

Stella noticed the surprise upon his face; and the blushes rose again in her cheeks.

"You knew that I would not go beyond," she said.

"Yes."

"But you did not know why?" There was a note of urgency in her voice.

"I guessed," he said. "I mean I played with guesses—oh not seriously," and he laughed. "There runs Stane Street from Chichester to London and through London to the great North Wall. Up that road the Romans marched and back by that road they returned to their galleys in the water there by Chichester. I pictured you living in those days, a Boadicea of the Weald who had set her heart, against her will, on some dashing captain of old Rome camped here on

226

the top of Bignor Hill. You crept from your own people at night to meet him in the lane at the bottom.
Then came week after week when the street rang with
the tramp of soldiers returning from London and Lich-
field and the North to embark in their boats for Gaul
and Rome."

"They took my captain with them?" cried Stella,
laughing with him at the conceit.

"Yes, so my fable ran. He pined for the circus and
the theatre and the painted ladies, so he went willingly."

"The brute," cried Stella. "And so I broke my
heart over a decadent philanderer in a suit of bright
brass clothes and remember it thirteen hundred years
afterwards in another life! Thank you, Captain
Hazlewood!"

"No, you don't actually remember it, Stella, but
you have a feeling that round about Stane Street you
once suffered great humiliation and unhappiness."
And suddenly Stella rode swiftly past him, but in a moment she waited for him and showed him a face of
smiles.

"You see I have crossed Stane Street to-day, Dick,"
she said. "We'll ride on to Arundel."

"Yes," answered Dick, "my story won't do," and
he remembered a sentence of hers spoken an hour and
a half ago: "My thoughts do not go back as far as you
think."

At all events she was emancipated to-day, for they rode on until at the end of a long gentle slope the great arch of the gate into Arundel Park gleamed white in a line of tall dark trees.

CHAPTER XXI

But Stella's confidence did not live long. Mr. Hazlewood was a child at deceptions; and day by day his anxieties increased. His friends argued with him— his folly and weakness were the themes—and he must needs repel the argument though his thoughts echoed every word they used. Never was a man brought to such a piteous depth of misery by the practice of his own theories. He sat by the hour at his desk, burying his face amongst his papers if Dick came into the room, with a great show of occupation. He could hardly bear to contemplate the marriage of his son, yet day and night he must think of it and search for expedients which might put an end to the trouble and let him walk free again with his head raised high. But there were only the two expedients. He must speak out his fears that justice had miscarried, and that device his vanity forbade; or he must adopt Pettifer's suggestion, and from that he shrank almost as much. He began to resent the presence of Stella Ballantyne and he showed it. Sometimes a friendliness, so excessive that it was almost hysterical, betrayed him; more usually a discom-

229

fort and constraint. He avoided her if by any means
he could; if he could not quite avoid her an excuse of
business was always on his lips.

"Your father hates me, Dick," she said. "He was
my friend until I touched his own life. Then I was in
the black books in a second."

Dick would not hear of it.

"You were never in the black books at all, Stella,"
he said, comforting her as well as he could. "We knew
that there would be a little struggle, didn't we? But
the worst of that's over. You make friends daily."

"Not with your father, Dick. I go back with him.
Ever since that night—it's three weeks ago now—when
you took me home from Little Beeding."

"No," cried Dick, but Stella nodded her head
gloomily.

"Mr. Pettifer dined here that night. He's an enemy
of mine."

"Stella," young Hazlewood remonstrated, "you see
enemies everywhere," and upon that Stella broke out
with a quivering troubled face.

"Is it wonderful? Oh, Dick, I couldn't lose you!
A month ago—before that night—yes. Nothing had
been said. But now! I couldn't, I couldn't! I have
often thought it would be better for me to go right away
and never see you again. And—and I have tried to tell
you something, Dick, ever so many times."

"Yes?" said Dick. He slipped his arm through hers

and held her close to him, as though to give her courage
and security. "Yes, Stella?" and he stood very still.

"I mean," she said, looking down upon the ground,
"that I have tried to tell you that I wouldn't suffer so
very much if we did part, but I never could do it. My
lips shook so, I never could speak the words." Then
her voice ran up into a laugh. "To think of your living
in a house with somebody else! Oh no!"

"You need have no fear of that, Stella."

They were in the garden of Little Beeding and they
walked across the meadow towards her cottage, talking
very earnestly. Mr. Hazlewood was watching them
secretly from the window of the library. He saw that
Dick was pleading and she hanging in doubt; and a
great wave of anger surged over him that Dick should
have to plead to her at all, he who was giving everything—even his own future.

"King's Bench Walk," he muttered to himself, taking
from the drawer of his writing-table a slip of paper on
which he had written the address lest he should forget
it. "Yes, that's the address," and he looked at it for
a long time very doubtfully. Suppose that his suspicions were correct! His heart sank at the supposition.
Surely he would be justified in setting any trap. But
he shut the drawer violently and turned away from
his writing-table. Even his pamphlets had become
trivial in his eyes. He was brought face to face with
real passions and real facts, he had been fetched out

from his cloister and was blinking miserably in a full measure of daylight. How long could he endure it, he wondered?

The question was settled for him that very evening. He and his son were taking their coffee on a paved terrace by the lawn after dinner. It was a dark quiet night, with a clear sky of golden stars. Across the meadow the lights shone in the windows of Stella's cottage.

"Father," said Dick, after they had sat in a constrained silence for a little while, "why don't you like Stella any longer?"

The old man blustered in reply:

"A lawyer's question, Richard. I object to it very strongly. You assume that I have ceased to like her."

"It's extremely evident," said Dick drily. "Stella has noticed it."

"And complained to you of course," cried Mr. Hazlewood resentfully.

"Stella doesn't complain," and then Dick leaned over and spoke in the full quiet voice which his father had grown to dread. There rang in it so much of true feeling and resolution.

"There can be no backing down now. We are both agreed upon that, aren't we? Imagine for an instant that I were first to blazon my trust in a woman whom others suspected by becoming engaged to her and then

232

endorsed their suspicions by breaking off the engagement! Suppose that I were to do that!"

Mr. Hazlewood allowed his longings to lead him astray. For a moment he hoped.

"Well?" he asked eagerly.

"You wouldn't think very much of me, would you? Not you nor any man. A cur—that would be the word, the only word, wouldn't it?"

But Mr. Hazlewood refused to answer that question. He looked behind him to make sure that none of the servants were within hearing. Then he lowered his voice to a whisper.

"What if Stella has deceived you, Dick?"

It was too dark for him to see the smile upon his son's face, but he heard the reply, and the confidence of it stung him to exasperation.

"She hasn't done that," said Dick. "If you are sure of nothing else, sir, you may be quite certain of what I am telling you now. She hasn't done that."

He remained silent for a few moments waiting for any rejoinder, and getting none he continued:

"There's something else I wanted to speak to you about."

"Yes?"

"The date of our marriage."

The old man moved sharply in his chair.

"There's no hurry, Richard. You must find out how it will affect your career. You have been so long at

233

THE WITNESS FOR THE DEFENCE

Little Beeding where we hear very little from the outer
world. You must consult your Colonel."

Dick Hazlewood would not listen to the argument.

"My marriage is my affair, sir, not my Colonel's.
I cannot take advice, for we both of us know what it
would be. And we both of us value it at its proper
price, don't we?"

Mr. Hazlewood could not reply. How often had he
inveighed against the opinions of the sleek worldly people who would add up advantages in a column and leave
out of their consideration the merits of the higher life.

"It would not be fair to Stella were we to ask her to
wait," Dick resumed. "Any delay—think what will
be made of it! A month or six weeks from now, that
gives us time enough."

The old man rose abruptly from his chair with a
vague word that he would think of it and went into the
house. He saw again the lovers as he had seen them
this afternoon walking side by side slowly towards Stella
Ballantyne's cottage; and the picture even in the retro-
spect was intolerable. The marriage must not take
place—yet it was so near. A month or six weeks! Mr.
Hazlewood took up his pen and wrote the letter to
Henry Thresk at last, as Robert Pettifer had always
been sure that he would do. It was the simplest kind
of letter and took but a minute in the writing. It mentioned only his miniatures and invited Henry Thresk
to Little Beeding to see them, as more than one stranger

234

had been asked before. The answers which Thresk had given to the questions in *Notes and Queries* were pleaded as an introduction and Thresk was invited to choose his own day and remain at Little Beeding for the night. The reply came by return of post. Thresk would come to Little Beeding on the Friday afternoon of the next week. He was in town, for Parliament was sitting late that year. He would reach Little Beeding soon after five so that he might have an opportunity of seeing the miniatures by daylight. Mr. Hazlewood hurried over with the news to Robert Pettifer. His spirits had risen at a bound. Already he saw the neighbourhood freed from the disturbing presence of Stella Ballantyne and himself cheerfully resuming his multifarious occupations.

Robert Pettifer, however, spoke in quite another strain.

"I am not so sure as you, Hazlewood. The points which trouble me are very possibly capable of quite simple explanations. I hope for my part that they will be so explained."

"You hope it?" cried Mr. Hazlewood.

"Yes. I want Dick to marry," said Robert Pettifer.

Mr. Hazlewood was not, however, to be discouraged. He drove back to his house counting the days which must pass before Thresk's arrival and wondering how he should manage to conceal his elation from the keen eyes of his son. But he found that there was no need for him to trouble himself on that point, for this very morning at luncheon Dick said to him:

"I think that I'll run up to town this afternoon, father. I might be there for a day or two."

Mr. Hazlewood was delighted. No other proposal could have fitted in so well with his scheme. The mere fact that Dick was away would start people at the pleasant business of conjecturing mishaps and quarrels. Perhaps indeed the lovers *had* quarrelled. Perhaps Richard had taken his advice and was off to consult his superiors. Mr. Hazlewood scanned his son's face eagerly but learnt nothing from it; and he was too wary to ask any questions.

"By all means, Richard," he said carelessly, "go to London! You will be back by next Friday, I suppose."

"Oh yes, before that. I shall stay at my own rooms, so if you want me you can send me a telegram."

Dick Hazlewood had a small flat of his own in some Mansions at Westminster which had seen very little of him that summer.

"Thank you, Richard," said the old man. "But I shall get on very well, and a few days change will no doubt do you good."

Dick grinned at his father and went off that afternoon without a word of farewell to Stella Ballantyne. Mr. Hazlewood stood in the hall and saw him go with a great relief at his heart. Everything at last seemed to be working out to advantage. He could not but remember how so very few weeks ago he had been urgent that Richard should spend his summer at Little Beeding and lend a hand in the noble work of defending Stella Ballantyne against ignorance and unreason. But the twinge only lasted a moment. He had made a mistake, as all men occasionally do—yes, even sagacious and thoughtful people like himself. And the mistake was already being repaired. He looked across the meadow that night at the lighted blinds of Stella's windows and anticipated an evening when those windows would be dark and the cottage without an inhabitant.

"Very soon," he murmured to himself, "very soon." He had not one single throb of pity for her now, not a single speculation whither she would go or what she would make of her life. His own defence of her had now become a fault of hers. He wished her no harm, he argued, but in a week's time there must be no light shining behind those blinds.

CHAPTER XXII

Mr. Hazlewood was very glad that Richard was away in London during this week. Excitement kept him feverish and the fever grew as the number of days before Thresk was to come diminished. He would never have been able to keep his secret had every meal placed him under his son's eyes. He was free too from Stella herself. He met her but once on the Monday and then it was in the deep lane leading towards the town. It was about five o'clock in the evening and she was driving homewards in an open fly. Mr. Hazlewood stopped it and went to the side.

"Richard is away, Stella, until Wednesday, as no doubt you knew," he said. "But I want you to come over to tea when he comes back. Will Friday suit you?"

She had looked a little frightened when Mr. Hazlewood had called to the driver and stopped the carriage; but at his words the blood rushed into her cheeks and her eyes shone and she pushed out her hand impulsively.

"Oh, thank you," she cried. "Of course I will come."

238

A WAY OUT OF THE TRAP

Not for a long time had he spoken to her with so kind a voice and a face so unclouded. She rejoiced at the change in him and showed him such gratitude as is given only to those who render great service, so intense was her longing not to estrange Dick from his father.

But she had become a shrewd observer under the stress of her evil destiny; and the moment of rejoicing once past she began to wonder what had brought about the change. She judged Mr. Hazlewood to be one of those weak and effervescing characters who can grow more obstinate in resentment than any others if their pride and self-esteem receive an injury. She had followed of late the windings of his thoughts. She put the result frankly to herself.

"He hates me. He holds me in horror."

Why then the sudden change? She was in the mood to start at shadows and when a little note was brought over to her on the Friday morning in Mr. Hazlewood's handwriting reminding her of her engagement she was filled with a vague apprehension. The note was kindly in its terms yet to her it had a menacing and sinister look. Had some stroke been planned against her? Was it to be delivered this afternoon?

Dick came at half-past four from a village cricket match to fetch her.

"You are ready, Stella? Right! For we can't spare very much time. I have a surprise for you."

Stella asked him what it was and he answered:

"There's a house for sale in Great Beeding. I think that you would like it."

Stella's face softened with a smile.

"Anywhere, Dick," she said, "anywhere on earth."

"But here best of all," he answered. "Not to run away—that's our policy. We'll make our home in our own south country. I arranged to take you over the house between half-past five and six this evening."

They walked across to Little Beeding and were made welcome by Mr. Hazlewood. He came out to meet them in the garden and nervousness made him kittenish and arch.

"How are you, Stella?" he inquired. "But there's no need to ask. You look charming and upon my word you grow younger every day. What a pretty hat! Yes, yes! Will you make tea while I telephone to the Pettifers? They seem to be late."

He skipped off with an alacrity which was rather ridiculous. But Stella watched him go without any amusement.

"I am taken again into favour," she said doubtfully.

"That shouldn't distress you, Stella," replied Dick.

"Yet it does, for I ask myself why. And I don't understand this tea-party. Mr. Hazlewood was so urgent that I should not forget it. Perhaps, however, I am inventing trouble."

She shook herself free from her apprehensions and followed Dick into the drawing-room, where the kettle

240

was boiling and the tea-service spread out. Stella went to the table and opened the little mahogany caddy.

"How many are coming, Dick?" she asked.

"The Pettifers."

"My enemies," said Stella, laughing lightly.

"And you and my father and myself."

"Five altogether," said Stella. She began to measure out the tea into the tea-pot but stopped suddenly in the middle of her work.

"But there are six cups," she said. She counted them again to make sure, and at once her fears were reawakened. She turned to Dick, her face quite pale and her big eyes dark with forebodings. So little now was needed to disquiet her. "Who is the sixth?"

Dick came closer to her and put his arm about her waist.

"I don't know," he said gently; "but what can it matter to us, Stella? Think, my dear!"

"No, of course," she replied, "it can't make any difference," and she dipped her teaspoon once more into the caddy. "But it's a little curious, isn't it?—that your father didn't mention to you that there was another guest?"

"Oh, wait a moment," said Dick. "He did tell me there would be some visitor here to-day but I forgot all about it. He told me at luncheon. There's a man from London coming down to have a look at his miniatures."

"His miniatures?" Stella was pouring the hot water into the tea-pot. She replaced the kettle on its stand and shut the tea-caddy. "And Mr. Hazlewood didn't tell you the man's name," she said.

"I didn't ask him," answered Dick. "He often has collectors down."

"I see." Her head was bent over the tea-table; she was busy with her brew of tea. "And I was specially asked to come this afternoon. I had a note this morning to remind me." She looked at the clock. "Dick, if we are to see that house this afternoon you had better change now before the visitors come."

"That's true. I will."

Dick started towards the door, and he heard Stella come swiftly after him. He turned. There was so much trouble in her face. He caught her in his arms.

"Dick," she whispered, "look at me. Kiss me! Yes, I am sure of you," and she clung to him. Dick Hazlewood laughed.

"I think we ought to be fairly happy in that house," and she let him go with a smile, repeating her own words, "Anywhere, Dick, anywhere on earth."

She waited, watching him tenderly until the door was closed. Then she covered her face with her hands and a sob burst from her lips. But the next moment she tore her hands away and looked wildly about the room. She ran to the writing-table and scribbled a note; she

242

thrust it into an envelope and gummed the flap securely down. Then she rang the bell and waited impatiently with a leaping heart until Hubbard came to the door.

"Did you ring, madam?" he asked.

"Yes. Has Mr. Thresk arrived yet?"

She tried to control her face, to speak in a careless and indifferent voice, but she was giddy and the room whirled before her eyes.

"Yes, madam," the butler answered; and it seemed to Stella Ballantyne that once more she stood in the dock and heard the verdict spoken. Only this time it had gone against her. That queer old shuffling butler became a figure of doom, his thin and piping voice uttered her condemnation. For here without her knowledge was Henry Thresk and she was bidden to meet him with the Pettifers for witnesses. But it was Henry Thresk who had saved her before. She clung to that fact now.

"Mr. Thresk arrived a few minutes ago."

Just before old Hazlewood had come forward out of the house to welcome her! No wonder he was in such high spirits! Very likely all that great show of kindliness and welcome was made only to keep her in the garden for a few necessary moments.

"Where is Mr. Thresk now?" she asked.

"In his room, madam."

"You are quite sure?"

"Quite."

"Will you take this note to him, Hubbard?" and she held it out to the butler.

"Certainly, madam."

"Will you take it at once? Give it into his hands, please."

Hubbard took the note and went out of the room. Never had he seemed to her so dilatory and slow. She stared at the door as though her sight could pierce the panels. She imagined him climbing the stairs with feet which loitered more at each fresh step. Some one would surely stop him and ask for whom the letter was intended. She went to the door which led into the hall, opened it and listened. No one was descending the staircase and she heard no voices. Then above her Hubbard knocked upon a door, a latch clicked as the door was opened, a hollow jarring sound followed as the door was sharply closed. Stella went back into the room. The letter had been delivered; at this moment Henry Thresk was reading it; and with a sinking heart she began to speculate in what spirit he would receive its message. Henry Thresk! The unhappy woman bestirred herself to remember him. He had grown dim to her of late. How much did she know of him? she asked herself. Once years ago there had been a month during which she had met him daily. She had given her heart to him, yet she had learned little or nothing of the man within the man's frame. She had not even made his acquaintance. That had been proved to her

244

one memorable morning upon the top of Bignor Hill, when humiliation had so deeply seared her soul that only during this last month had it been healed. In the great extremities of her life Henry Thresk had decided, not she, and he was a stranger to her. She beat her poor wings in vain against that ironic fact. Never had he done what she had expected. On Bignor Hill, in the Law Court at Bombay, he had equally surprised her. Now once more he held her destinies in his hand. What would he decide? What had he decided?

"Yes, he will have decided now," said Stella to herself; and a certain calm fell upon her troubled soul. Whatever was to be was now determined. She went back to the tea-table and waited.

Henry Thresk had not much of the romantic in his character. He was a busy man making the best and the most of the rewards which the years brought to him, and slamming the door each day upon the day which had gone before. He made his life in the intellectual exercise of his profession and his membership of the House of Commons. Upon the deeps of the emotions he had closed a lid. Yet he had set out with a vague reluctance to Little Beeding; and once his motor-car had passed Hindhead and dipped to the weald of Sussex the reluctance had grown to a definite regret that he should once more have come into this country. His recollections were of a dim far-off time, so dim that he could hardly believe that he had any very close relation with the young struggling man who had spent his first real holiday there. But the young man had been himself and he had missed his opportunity high up on the downs by Arundel. Words which Jane Repton had spoken to him in Bombay came back to him on this summer afternoon like a refrain to the steady hum of his car. "You can get what you want, so long as you want it enough, but you cannot control the price you will have to pay."

He had reached Little Beeding only a few moments before Dick and Stella had crossed into the garden. He had been led by Hubbard into the library, where Mr. Hazlewood was sitting. From the windows he had even seen the thatched cottage where Stella Ballantyne dwelt and its tiny garden bright with flowers.

"It is most kind of you to come," Mr. Hazlewood had said. "Ever since we had our little correspondence I have been anxious to take your opinion on my collection. Though how in the world you manage to find time to have an opinion at all upon the subject is most perplexing. I never open the *Times* but I see your name figuring in some important case."

"And I, Mr. Hazlewood," Thresk replied with a smile, "never open my mail without receiving a pamphlet from you. I am not the only active man in the world."

Even at that moment Mr. Hazlewood flushed with pleasure at the flattery.

"Little reflections," he cried with a modest deprecation, "worked out more or less to completeness—may I

246

say that?—in the quiet of a rural life, sparks from the tiny flame of my midnight oil." He picked up one pamphlet from a stack by his writing-table. "You might perhaps care to look at *The Prison Walls.*"

Thresk drew back.

"I have got mine, Mr. Hazlewood," he said firmly. "Every man in England should have one. No man in England has a right to two."

Mr. Hazlewood fairly twittered with satisfaction. Here was a notable man from the outside world of affairs who knew his work and held it in esteem. Obviously then he was right to take these few disagreeable twists and turns which would ensure to him a mind free to pursue his labours. He looked down at the pamphlet however, and his satisfaction was a trifle impaired.

"I am not sure that this is quite my best work," he said timidly—"a little hazardous perhaps."

"Would you say that?" asked Thresk.

"Yes, indeed I should." Mr. Hazlewood had the air of one making a considerable concession. "The very title is inaccurate. *The Prison Walls must Cast no Shadow.*" He repeated the sentence with a certain unction. "The rhythm is perhaps not amiss but the metaphor is untrue. My son pointed it out to me. As he says, all walls cast shadows."

"Yes," said Thresk. "The trouble is to know where and on whom the shadow is going to fall."

247

THE WITNESS FOR THE DEFENCE

Mr. Hazlewood was startled by the careless words. He came to earth heavily. All was not as yet quite ready for the little trick which had been devised. The Pettifers had not arrived.

"Perhaps you would like to see your room, Mr. Thresk," he said. "Your bag has been taken up, no doubt. We will look at my miniatures after tea."

"I shall be delighted," said Thresk as he followed Hazlewood to the door. "But you must not expect too much knowledge from me."

"Oh!" cried his host with a laugh. "Pettifer tells me that you are a great authority."

"Then Pettifer's wrong," said Thresk and so stopped. "Pettifer? Pettifer? Isn't he a solicitor?"

"Yes, he told me that he knew you. He married my sister. They are both coming to tea."

With that he led Thresk to his room and left him there. The room was over the porch of the house and looked down the short level drive to the iron gates and the lane. It was all familiar ground to Thresk or rather to that other man with whom Thresk's only connection was a dull throb at his heart, a queer uneasiness and discomfort. He leaned out of the window. He could hear the river singing between the grass banks at the bottom of the garden behind him. He would hear it through the night. Then came a knocking upon his door, and he did not notice it at once. It was repeated and he turned and said:

248

A WAY OUT OF THE TRAP

"Come in!"

Hubbard advanced with a note upon a salver.

"Mrs. Ballantyne asked me to give you this at once, sir."

Thresk stared at the butler. The name was so apposite to his thoughts that he could not believe it had been uttered. But the salver was held out to him and the handwriting upon the envelope removed his doubts. He took it up, said "Thank you" in an absent voice and waited until the door was closed again and he was alone. The last time he had seen that writing was eighteen months ago. A little note of thanks, blurred with tears and scribbled hastily and marked with no address, had been handed to him in Bombay. Stella Ballantyne had disappeared then. She was here now at Little Beeding and his relationship with the young struggling barrister of ten years back suddenly became actual and near. He tore open the envelope and read.

"Be prepared to see me. Be prepared to hear news of me. I will have a talk with you afterwards if you like. This is a trap. Be kind."

He stood for a while with the letter in his hand, speculating upon its meaning, until the wheels of a car grated on the gravel beneath his window. The Pettifers had come. But Thresk was in no hurry to descend. He read the note through many times before he hid it away in his letter-case and went down the stairs.

249

CHAPTER XXIII

METHODS FROM FRANCE

Meanwhile Stella Ballantyne waited below. She heard Mr. Hazlewood in the hall greeting the Pettifers with the false joviality which sat so ill upon him; she imagined the shy nods and glances which told them that the trap was properly set. Mr. Hazlewood led them into the room.

"Is tea ready, Stella? We won't wait for Dick," he said, and Stella took her place at the table. She had her back to the door by which Thresk would enter. She had not a doubt that thus her chair had been deliberately placed. He would be in the room and near to the table before he saw her. He would not have a moment to prepare himself against the surprise of her presence. Stella listened for the sound of his footsteps in the hall; she could not think of a single topic to talk about except the presence of that extra sixth cup; and that she must not mention if the tables were really to be turned upon her antagonists. Surprise must be visible upon her side when Thresk did come in. But she was not alone in finding conversation difficult. Embarrassment and expectancy weighed down the whole party, so that they began suddenly to speak at

250

once and simultaneously to stop. Robert Pettifer however asked if Dick was playing cricket, and so gave Harold Hazlewood an opportunity.

"No, the match was over early," said the old man, and he settled himself in his arm-chair. "I have given some study to the subject of cricket," he said.

"You?" asked Stella with a smile of surprise. Was he merely playing for time, she wondered? But he had the air of contentment with which he usually embarked upon his disquisitions.

"Yes. I do not consider our national pastime beneath a philosopher's attention. I have formed two theories about the game."

"I am sure you have," Robert Pettifer interposed.

"And I have invented two improvements, though I admit at once that they will have to wait until a more enlightened age than ours adopts them. In the first place"—and Mr. Hazlewood flourished a forefinger in the air—"the game ought to be played with a soft ball. There is at present a suggestion of violence about it which the use of a soft ball would entirely remove."

"Entirely," Mr. Pettifer agreed and his wife exclaimed impatiently:

"Rubbish, Harold, rubbish!"

Stella broke nervously into the conversation.

"Violence? Why even women play cricket, Mr. Hazlewood."

"I cannot, Stella," he returned, "accept the view

251

that whatever women do must necessarily be right. There are instances to the contrary."

"Yes. I come across a few of them in my office," Robert Pettifer said grimly; and once more embarrassment threatened to descend upon the party. But Mr. Hazlewood was off upon a favourite theme. His eyes glistened and the object of the gathering vanished for the moment from his thoughts.

"And in the second place," he resumed, "the losers should be accounted to have won the game."

"Yes, that must be right," said Pettifer. "Upon my word you are in form, Hazlewood."

"But why?" asked Mrs. Pettifer.

Harold Hazlewood smiled upon her as upon a child and explained:

"Because by adopting that system you would do something to eradicate the spirit of rivalry, the desire to win, the ambition to beat somebody else which is at the bottom of half our national troubles."

"And all our national success," said Pettifer.

Hazlewood patted his brother-in-law upon the shoulder. He looked at him indulgently. "You are a Tory, Robert," he said, and implied that argument with such an one was mere futility.

He had still his hand upon Pettifer's shoulder when the door opened. Stella saw by the change in his face that it was Thresk who was entering. But she did not move.

"Ah," said Mr. Hazlewood. "Come over here and take a cup of tea."

Thresk came forward to the table. He seemed altogether unconscious that the eyes of the two men were upon him.

"Thank you. I should like one," he said, and at the sound of his voice Stella Ballantyne turned around in her chair.

"You!" she cried and the cry was pitched in a tone of pleasure and welcome.

"Of course you know Mrs. Ballantyne," said Hazlewood. He saw Stella rise from her chair and hold out her hand to Thresk with the colour aflame in her cheeks.

"You are surprised to see me again," she said.

Thresk took her hand cordially. "I am delighted to see you again," he replied.

"And I to see you," said Stella, "for I have never yet had a chance of thanking you"; and she spoke with so much frankness that even Pettifer was shaken in his suspicions. She turned upon Mr. Hazlewood with a mimicry of indignation. "Do you know, Mr. Hazlewood, that you have done a very cruel thing?"

Mr. Hazlewood was utterly discomfited by the failure of his plot, and when Stella attacked him so directly he had not a doubt but that she had divined his treachery.

"I?" he gasped. "Cruel? How?"

253

"In not telling me beforehand that I was to meet so good a friend of mine." Her face relaxed to a smile as she added: "I would have put on my best frock in his honour."

Undoubtedly Stella carried off the honour of that encounter. She had at once driven the battle with spirit onto Hazlewood's own ground and left him worsted and confused. But the end was not yet. Mr. Hazlewood waited for his son Richard, and when Richard appeared he exclaimed:

"Ah, here's my son. Let me present him to you, Mr. Thresk. And there's the family."

He leaned back, with a smile in his eyes, watching Henry Thresk. Robert Pettifer watched too.

"The family?" Thresk asked. "Is Mrs. Ballantyne a relation then?"

"She is going to be," said Dick.

"Yes," Mr. Hazlewood explained, still beaming and still watchful. "Richard and Stella are going to be married."

A pause followed which was just perceptible before Thresk spoke again. But he had his face under control. He took the stroke without flinching. He turned to Dick with a smile.

"Some men have all the luck," he said, and Dick, who had been looking at him in bewilderment, cried:

"Mr. Thresk? Not the Mr. Thresk to whom I owe so much?"

"The very man," said Thresk, and Dick held out his hand to him gravely.

"Thank you," he said. "When I think of the horrible net of doubt and assumption in which Stella was coiled, I tell you I feel cold down my spine even now. If you hadn't come forward with your facts——"

"Yes," Thresk interposed. "If I hadn't come forward with my facts. But I couldn't well keep them to myself, could I?" A few more words were said and then Dick rose from his chair.

"Time's up, Stella," and he explained to Henry Thresk: "We have to look over a house this afternoon."

"A house? Yes, I see," said Thresk, but he spoke slowly and there was just audible a little inflection of doubt in his voice. Stella was listening for it; she heard it when her two antagonists noticed nothing.

"But, Dick," she said quickly, "we can put the inspection off."

"Not on my account," Thresk returned. "There's no need for that." He was not looking at Stella whilst he spoke and she longed to see his face. She must know exactly how she stood with him, what he thought of her. She turned impulsively to Mr. Hazlewood.

"I haven't been asked, but may I come to dinner? You see I owe a good deal to Mr. Thresk."

Mr. Hazlewood was for the moment at a loss. He had not lost hope that between now and dinner-time explanations would be given which would banish Stella

Ballantyne altogether from Little Beeding. But he had no excuse ready and he stammered out:

"Of course, my dear. Didn't I ask you? I must have forgotten. I certainly expect you to dine with us to-night. Margaret will no doubt be here."

Margaret Pettifer had taken little part in the conversation about the tea-table. She sat in frigid hostility, speaking only when politeness commanded. She accepted her brother's invitation with a monosyllable.

"Thank you," said Stella, and she faced Henry Thresk, looking him straight in the eyes but not daring to lay any special stress upon the words: "Then I shall see you to-night."

Thresk read in her face a prayer that he should hold his hand until she had a chance to speak with him. She turned away and went from the room with Dick Hazlewood.

The old man rose as soon as the door was closed.

"Now we might have a look at the miniatures, Mr. Thresk. You will excuse us, Margaret, won't you?"

"Of course," she answered upon a nod from her husband. The two men passed through the doors into the great library whilst Thresk took a more ceremonious leave of Mrs. Pettifer; and as Hazlewood opened the drawers of his cabinets Robert Pettifer said in a whisper:

"That was a pretty good failure, I must say. And it was my idea too."

"Yes," replied Hazlewood in a voice as low. "What do you think?"

"That they share no secret."

"You are satisfied then?"

"I didn't say that"; and Thresk himself appeared in the doorway and went across to the writing-table upon which Hazlewood had just laid a drawer in which miniatures were ranged.

"I haven't met you," said Pettifer, "since you led for us in the great Birmingham will-suit."

"No," answered Thresk as he took his seat at the table. "It wasn't quite such a tough fight as I expected. You see there wasn't one really reliable witness for the defence."

"No," said Pettifer grimly. "If there had been we should have been beaten."

Mr. Hazlewood began to point out this and that miniature of his collection, bending over Thresk as he did so. It seemed that the two collectors were quite lost in their common hobby until Robert Pettifer gave the signal.

Then Mr. Hazlewood began:

"I am very glad to meet you, Mr. Thresk, for reasons quite outside these miniatures of mine."

He spoke with a noticeable awkwardness, yet Henry Thresk disregarded it altogether.

"Oh?" he said carelessly.

"Yes. Being Richard's father I am naturally concerned in everything which affects him nearly—the trial of Stella Ballantyne for instance."

Thresk bent his head down over the tray.

"Quite so," he said. He pointed to a miniature. "I saw that at Christie's and coveted it myself."

"Did you?" Mr. Hazlewood asked and he almost offered it as a bribe. "Now you gave evidence, Mr. Thresk."

Thresk never lifted his head.

"You have no doubt read the evidence I gave," he said, peering fom this delicate jewel of the painter's art to that.

"To be sure."

"And since your son is engaged to Mrs. Ballantyne, I suppose that you were satisfied with it"—and he paused to give a trifle of significance to his next words —"as the jury was."

"Yes, of course," Mr. Hazlewood stammered, "but a witness, I think, only answers the questions put to him."

"That is so," said Thresk, "if he is a wise witness." He took one of the miniatures out of the drawer and held it to the light. But Mr. Hazlewood was not to be deterred.

"And subsequent reflection," he continued obstinately, "might suggest that all the questions which could throw light upon the trial had not been put."

Thresk replaced the miniature in the drawer in front

of him and leaned back in his chair. He looked now straight at Mr. Hazlewood.

"It was not, I take it, in order to put those questions to me that you were kind enough, Mr. Hazlewood, to ask me to give my opinion on your miniatures. For that would have been setting a trap for me, wouldn't it?"

Hazlewood stared at Thresk with the bland innocence of a child. "Oh no, no," he declared, and then an insinuating smile beamed upon his long thin face. "Only since you *are* here and since so much is at stake for me —my son's happiness—I hoped that you might perhaps give us an answer or two which would disperse the doubts of some suspicious people."

"Who are they?" asked Thresk.

"Neighbours of ours," replied Hazlewood, and thereupon Robert Pettifer stepped forward. He had remained aloof and silent until this moment. Now he spoke shortly, but he spoke to the point:

"I for one."

Thresk turned with a smile upon Pettifer.

"I thought so. I recognised Mr. Pettifer's hand in all this. But he ought to know that the sudden confrontation of a suspected person with unexpected witnesses takes place, in those countries where the method is practised, before the trial; not, as you so ingeniously arranged it this afternoon, two years after the verdict has been given."

Robert Pettifer turned red. Then he looked whimsically across the table at his brother-in-law.

"We had better make a clean breast of it, Hazlewood."

"I think so," said Thresk gently.

Pettifer came a step nearer. "We are in the wrong," he said bluntly. "But we have an excuse. Our trouble is very great. Here's my brother-in-law to begin with, whose whole creed of life has been to deride the authority of conventional man—to tilt against established opinion. Mrs. Ballantyne comes back from her trial in Bombay to make her home again at Little Beeding. Hazlewood champions her—not for her sake, but for the sake of his theories. It pleases his vanity. Now he can prove that he is not as others are."

Mr. Hazlewood did not relish this merciless analysis of his character. He twisted in his chair, he uttered a murmur of protest. But Robert Pettifer waved him down and continued:

"So he brings her to his house. He canvasses for her. He throws his son in her way. She has beauty —she has something more than beauty—she stands apart as a woman who has walked through fire. She has suffered very much. Look at it how one will, she has suffered beyond her deserts. She has pretty deferential ways which make their inevitable appeal to women as to men. In a word, Hazlewood sets the ball rolling and it gets beyond his reach."

METHODS FROM FRANCE

Thresk nodded.

"Yes, I understand that."

"Finally, Hazlewood's son falls in love with her—not a boy mind, but a man claiming a man's right to marry where he loves. And at once in Hazlewood conventional man awakes."

"Dear me, no," interposed Harold Hazlewood.

"But I say yes," Pettifer continued imperturbably. "Conventional man awakes in him and cries loudly against the marriage. Then there's myself. I am fond of Dick. I have no child. He will be my heir and I am not poor. He is doing well in his profession. To be an Instructor of the Staff Corps at his age means hard work, keenness, ability. I look forward to a great career. I am very fond of him. And—understand me, Mr. Thresk"—he checked his speech and weighed his words very carefully—"I wouldn't say that he shouldn't marry Stella Ballantyne just because Stella Ballantyne has lain under a grave charge of which she has been acquitted. No, I may be as formal as my brother-in-law thinks, but I hold a wider faith than that. But I am not satisfied. That is the truth, Mr. Thresk. I am not sure of what happened in that tent in far-away Chitipur after you had ridden away to catch the night mail to Bombay."

Robert Pettifer had made his confession simply and with some dignity. Thresk looked at him for a few moments. Was he wondering whether he could answer

261

the questions? Was he hesitating through anger at the trick which had been played upon him? Pettifer could not tell. He waited in suspense. Thresk pushed his chair back suddenly and came forward from behind the table.

"Ask your questions," he said.

"You consent to answer them?" Mr. Hazlewood cried joyously, and Thresk replied with coldness:

"I must. For if I don't consent your suspicions at once are double what they were. But I am not pleased."

"Oh, we practised a little diplomacy," said Hazlewood, making light of his offence.

"Diplomacy!" For the first time a gleam of anger shone in Thresk's eyes. "You have got me to your house by a trick. You have abused your position as my host. And but that I should injure a woman whom life has done nothing but injure I should go out of your door this instant."

He turned his back upon Harold Hazlewood and sat down in a chair opposite to Robert Pettifer. A little round table separated them. Pettifer, seated upon a couch, took from his pocket the envelope with the press-cuttings and spread them on the table in front of him. Thresk lolled back in his chair. It was plain that he was in no terror of Pettifer's examination.

"I am at your service," he said.

CHAPTER XXIV

THE WITNESS

The afternoon sunlight poured into the room golden and clear. Outside the open windows the garden was noisy with birds and the river babbled between its banks. Henry Thresk shut his ears against the music. For all his appearance of ease he dreaded the encounter which was now begun. Pettifer he knew to be a shrewd man. He watched him methodically arranging his press-cuttings in front of him. Pettifer might well find some weak point in his story which he himself had not discovered; and whatever course he was minded afterwards to take, here and now he was determined once more to fight Stella's battle.

"I need not go back on the facts of the trial," said Pettifer. "They are fresh enough in your memory, no doubt. Your theory as I understand it ran as follows: While you were mounting your camel on the edge of the camp to return to the station and Ballantyne was at your side, the thief whose arm you had both seen under the tent wall, not knowing that now you had the photograph of Bahadur Salak which he wished to steal, slipped into the tent unperceived, took up the rook-rifle——"

263

THE WITNESS FOR THE DEFENCE

"Which was standing by Mrs. Ballantyne's writing-table," Thresk interposed.

"Loaded it,——"

"The cartridges were lying open in a drawer."

"And shot Ballantyne on his return."

"Yes," Thresk agreed. "In addition you must remember that when Captain Ballantyne was found an hour or so later Mrs. Ballantyne was in bed and asleep."

"Quite so," said Pettifer. "In brief, Mr. Thresk, you supplied a reasonable motive for the crime and some evidence of a criminal. And I admit that on your testimony the jury returned the only verdict which it was possible to give."

"What troubles you then?" Henry Thresk asked, and Pettifer replied drily:

"Various points. Here's one—a minor one. If Captain Ballantyne was shot by a thief detected in the act of thieving why should that thief risk capture and death by dragging Captain Ballantyne's body out into the open? It seems to me the last thing which he would naturally do."

Thresk shrugged his shoulders.

"I can't explain that. It is perhaps possible that not finding the photograph he fell into a blind rage and satisfied it by violence towards the dead man."

"Dead or dying," Mr. Pettifer corrected. "There seems to have been some little doubt upon that point.

But your theory's a little weak, isn't it? To get away unseen would be that thief's first preoccupation, surely?"

"Reasoning as you and I are doing here quietly, at our ease, in this room, no doubt you are right, Mr. Pettifer. But criminals are caught because they don't reason quietly when they have just committed a crime. The behaviour of a man whose mind is influenced by that condition cannot be explained always by any laws of psychology. He may be in a wild panic. He may act as madmen act, or like a child in a rage. And if my explanation is weak it's no weaker than the only other hypothesis: that Mrs. Ballantyne herself dragged him into the open."

Mr. Pettifer shook his head.

"I am not so sure. I can conceive a condition of horror in the wife, horror at what she had done, which would make that act not merely possible but almost inevitable. I make no claims to being an imaginative man, Mr. Thresk, but I try to put myself into the position of the wife"; and he described with a vividness for which Thresk was not prepared the scene as he saw it.

"She goes to bed, she undresses and goes to bed—she must do that if she is to escape—she puts out her light, she lies in the dark awake, and under the same roof, close to her, in the dark too, is lying the man she has killed. Just a short passage separates her from

265

him. There are no doors—mind that, Mr. Thresk—
no doors to lock and bolt, merely a grass screen which
you could lift with your forefinger. Wouldn't any and
every one of the little cracks and sounds and breathings,
of which the quietest and stillest night is full, sound to
her like the approach of the dead man? The faintest
breath of air would seem a draught made by the swinging of the grass-curtain as it was stealthily lifted—lifted
by the dead man. No, Mr. Thresk. The wife is just
the one person I could imagine who would do that
needless barbarous violence of dragging the body into
the open—and she would do it, not out of cruelty, but
because she must or go mad."

Thresk listened without a movement until Robert
Pettifer had finished. Then he said:

"You know Mrs. Ballantyne. Has she the strength
which she must have had to drag a heavy man across
the carpet of a tent and fling him outside?"

"Not now, not before. But just at the moment?
You argued, Mr. Thresk, that it is impossible to foresee
what people will do under the immediate knowledge
that they have committed a capital crime. I agree.
But I go a little further. I say that they will also ex-
hibit a physical strength with which it would be other-
wise impossible to credit them. Fear lends it to them."

"Yes," Thresk interrupted quickly, "but don't you
see, Mr. Pettifer, that you are implying the existence
of an emotion in Mrs. Ballantyne which the facts prove

266

THE WITNESS

her to have been without—fear, panic? She was found quietly asleep in her bed by the ayah when she came to call her in the morning. There's no doubt of that. The ayah was never for a moment shaken upon that point. The pyschology of crime is a curious and surprising study, Mr. Pettifer, but I know of no case where terror has acted as a sleeping-draught."

Mr. Pettifer smiled and turned altogether away from the question.

"It is, as I said, a minor point, and perhaps one from which any sort of inference would be unsafe. It interested me. I lay no great stress upon it."

He dismissed the point carelessly, to the momentary amusement of Henry Thresk. The art of slipping away from defeat had been practised with greater skill. Thresk lost some part of his apprehension but none of his watchfulness.

"Now, however, we come to something very different," said Pettifer, hitching himself a little closer to his table and fixing his eyes upon Thresk. "The case for the prosecution ran like this: Stephen Ballantyne was, though a man of great ability, a secret drunkard who humiliated his wife in public and beat her in private. She went in terror of him. She bore on more than one occasion the marks of his violence; and upon that night in Chitipur, perhaps in a panic and very likely under extreme provocation, she snatched up her rook-rifle and put an end to the whole bad business."

267

THE WITNESS FOR THE DEFENCE

"Yes," Thresk agreed, "that was the case for the Crown."

"Yes, and throughout the sitting at the Stipendiary's inquiry before you came upon the scene that theory was clearly developed."

"Yes."

Thresk's confidence vanished as quickly as it had come. He realised whither Pettifer's questions were leading. There was a definitely weak link in his story and Pettifer had noticed it and was testing it.

"Now," the solicitor continued—"and this is the important point—what was the answer to that charge foreshadowed by the defence during those days before you appeared?"

Thresk answered the question quickly, if answer it could be called.

"The defence had not formulated any answer. I came forward before the case for the Crown finished."

"Quite so. But Mrs. Ballantyne's counsel did cross-examine the witnesses for the prosecution—we must not forget that, Mr. Thresk—and from the cross-examination it is quite clear what answer he was going to make. He was going—not to deny that Mrs. Ballantyne shot her husband—but to plead that she shot him in self-defence."

"Oh?" said Thresk, "and where do you find that?"

He had no doubt himself in what portion of the report of the trial a proof of Pettifer's statement was to be

268

discovered, but he made a creditable show of surprise that any one should hold that opinion at all.

Pettifer selected a column of newspaper from his cuttings.

"Listen," he said. "Mr. Repton, a friend of Mrs. Ballantyne, was called upon a subpœna by the Crown and he testified that while he was a Collector at Agra he went up with his wife from the plains to the hill-station of Moussourie during a hot weather. The Ballantynes went up at the same time and occupied a bungalow next to Repton's. One night Repton's house was broken into. He went across to Ballantyne the next morning and advised him in the presence of his wife to sleep with a revolver under his pillow."

"Yes, I remember that," said Thresk. He had indeed cause to remember it very well, for it was just this evidence given by Repton with its clear implication of the line which the defence meant to take that had sent him in a hurry to Mrs. Ballantyne's solicitor. Pettifer continued by reading Repton's words slowly and with emphasis.

"'Mrs. Ballantyne then turned very pale, and running after me down the garden like a distracted woman cried: "Why did you tell him to do that? It will some night mean my death."' This statement, Mr. Thresk, was elicited in cross-examination by Mrs. Ballantyne's counsel, and it could only mean that he intended to

THE WITNESS FOR THE DEFENCE

set up a plea of self-defence. I find it a little difficult to reconcile that intention with the story you subsequently told."

Henry Thresk for his part knew that it was not merely difficult, it was, in fact, impossible. Mr. Pettifer had read the evidence with an accurate discrimination. The plea of self-defence was here foreshadowed and it was just the certainty that the defence was going to rely upon it for a verdict which had brought Henry Thresk himself into the witness-box at Bombay. Given all that was known of Stephen Ballantyne and of the life he had led his unhappy wife, the defence would have been a good one, but for a single fact—the discovery of Ballantyne's body outside the tent. No plea of self-defence could safely be left to cover that. Thresk himself wondered at it. It struck at public sympathy, it seemed the act of a person insensate and vindictive. Therefore he had come forward with his story. But Mr. Pettifer was not to know it.

"There are three things for you to remember," said Thresk. "In the first place it is too early to assume that self-defence was going to be the plea. Assumptions in a case of this kind are very dangerous, Mr. Pettifer. They may lead to an irreparable injustice. We must keep to the fact that no plea of self-defence was ever formulated. In the second place Mrs. Ballantyne was brought down to Bombay in a state of complete collapse. Her married life had been a torture

270

to her. She broke down at the end of it. She was indifferent to anything that might happen."

Pettifer nodded. "Yes, I can understand that."

"It followed that her advisers had to act upon their own initiative."

"And the third point?" Pettifer asked.

"Well, it's not so much a point as an opinion of mine. But I hold it strongly. Her counsel mishandled the case."

Pettifer pursed up his lips and grunted. He tapped a finger once or twice on the table in front of him. He looked towards Thresk as if all was not quite said. Harold Hazlewood, to whom the position of a neglected listener was rare and unpalatable, saw an opportunity for intervention.

"The three points are perhaps not very conclusive," he said.

Thresk turned towards him coldly:

"I promised to answer such questions as Mr. Pettifer put to me. I am doing that. I did not undertake to discuss the value of my answers afterwards."

"No, no, quite so," murmured Mr. Hazlewood. "We are very grateful, I am sure," and he left once more the argument to Pettifer.

"Then I come to the next question, Mr. Thresk. At some moment in this inquiry you of your own account put yourself into communication with Mrs. Ballantyne's advisers and volunteered your evidence?"

271

"Yes."

"Isn't it strange that the defence did not at the very outset get into communication with you?"

"No," replied Thresk. Here he was at his ease. He had laid his plans well in Bombay. Mr. Pettifer might go on asking questions until midnight upon this point. Thresk could meet him. "It was not at all strange. It was not known that I could throw any light upon the affair at all. All that passed between Ballantyne and myself passed when we were alone; and Ballantyne was now dead."

"Yes, but you had dined with the Ballantynes on that night. Surely it's strange that since you were in Bombay Mrs. Ballantyne's advisers did not seek you out."

"Yes, yes," added Mr. Hazlewood, "very strange indeed, Mr. Thresk—since you were in Bombay"; and he looked up at the ceiling and joined the tips of his fingers, his whole attitude a confident question: "Answer that if you can."

Thresk turned patiently round.

"Hasn't it occurred to you, Mr. Hazlewood, that it is still more strange that the prosecution did not at once approach me?"

"Yes," said Pettifer suddenly. "That question too has troubled me"; and Thresk turned back again.

"You see," he explained, "I was not known to be in Bombay at all. On the contrary I was supposed to be somewhere in the Red Sea or the Mediterranean on my way back to England."

Mr. Pettifer looked up in surprise. The statement was news to him and if true provided a natural explanation of some of his chief perplexities. "Let me understand that!" and there was a change in his voice which Thresk was quick to detect. There was less hostility.

"Certainly," Thresk answered. "I left the tent just before eleven to catch the Bombay mail. I was returning direct to England. The reason why Ballantyne asked me to take the photograph of Bahadur Salak was that since I was going on board straight from the train it could be no danger to me."

"Then why didn't you go straight on board?" asked Pettifer.

"I'll tell you," Thresk replied. "I thought the matter over on the journey down to Bombay, and I came to the conclusion that since the photograph might be wanted at Salak's trial I had better take it to the Governor's house at Bombay. But Government House is out at Malabar Point, four miles from the quays. I took the photograph out myself and so I missed the boat. But there was an announcement in the papers that I had sailed, and in fact the consul at Marseilles came on board at that port to inquire for me on instructions from the Indian Government."

Mr. Pettifer leaned back.

"Yes, I see," he said thoughtfully. "That makes a

273

difference—a big difference." Then he sat upright again and said sharply:

"You were in Bombay then when Mrs. Ballantyne was brought down from Chitipur?"

"Yes."

"And when the case for the Crown was started?"

"Yes."

"And when the Crown's witnesses were cross-examined?"

"Yes."

"Why did you wait then all that time before you came forward?" Pettifer put the question with an air of triumph. "Why, Mr. Thresk, did you wait till the very moment when Mrs. Ballantyne was going to be definitely committed to a particular line of defence before you announced that you could clear up the mystery? Doesn't it rather look as if you had remained hidden on the chance of the prosecution breaking down, and had only come forward when you realised that tomorrow self-defence would be pleaded, the firing of that rook-rifle admitted and a terrible risk of a verdict of guilty run?"

Thresk agreed without a moment's hesitation.

"But that's the truth, Mr. Pettifer," he said, and Mr. Pettifer sprang up.

"What?"

"Consider my position"—Thresk drew up his chair close to the table—"a barrister who was beginning to have one of the large practices, the Courts opening in London, briefs awaiting me, cases on which I had already advised coming on. I had already lost a fortnight. That was bad enough, but if I came forward with my story I must wait in Bombay not merely for a fortnight but until the whole trial was completed, as in the end I had to do. Of course I hoped that the prosecution would break down. Of course I didn't intervene until it was absolutely necessary in the interests of justice that I should."

He spoke so calmly, there was so much reason in what he said, that Pettifer could not but be convinced.

"I see," he said. "I see. Yes. That's not to be disputed." He remained silent for a few moments. Then he shuffled his papers together and replaced them in the envelope. It seemed that his examination was over. Thresk rose from his chair.

"You have no more questions to ask me?" he inquired.

"One more."

Pettifer came round the table and stood in front of Henry Thresk.

"Did you know Mrs. Ballantyne before you went to Chitipur?"

"Yes," Thresk replied.

"Had you seen her lately?"

"No."

"When had you last seen her?"

275

"Eight years before, in this neighbourhood. I spent a holiday close by. Her father and mother were then alive. I had not seen her since. I did not even know that she was in India and married until I was told so in Bombay."

Thresk was prepared for that question. He had the truth ready and he spoke it frankly. Mr. Pettifer turned away to Hazlewood, who was watching him expectantly.

"We have nothing more to do, Hazlewood, but to thank Mr. Thresk for answering our questions and to apologise to him for having put them."

Mr. Hazlewood was utterly disconcerted. After all, then, the marriage must take place; the plot had ignominiously failed, the great questions which were to banish Stella Ballantyne from Little Beeding had been put and answered. He sat like a man stricken by calamity. He stammered out reluctantly a few words to which Thresk paid little heed.

"You are satisfied then?" he asked of Pettifer; and Pettifer showed him unexpectedly a cordial and good-humoured face.

"Yes. Let me say to you, Mr. Thresk, that ever since I began to study this case I have wished less and less to bear hardly upon Mrs. Ballantyne. As I read those columns of evidence the heavy figure of Stephen Ballantyne took life again, but a very sinister life; and when I look at Stella and think of what she went through

276

during the years of her married life while we were comfortably here at home I cannot but feel a shiver of discomfort. Yes, I am satisfied and I am glad that I am satisfied"; and with a smile which suddenly illumined his dry parched face he held out his hand to Henry Thresk.

It was perhaps as well that the questions were over, for even while Pettifer was speaking Stella's voice was heard in the hall. Pettifer had just time to thrust away the envelope with the cuttings into a drawer before she came into the room with Dick. She had been forced to leave the three men together, but she had dreaded it. During that one hour of absence she had lived through a lifetime of terror and anxiety. What would Thresk tell them? What was he now telling them? She was like one waiting downstairs while a surgical operation is being performed in the theatre above. She had hurried Dick back to Little Beeding, and when she came into the room her eyes roamed round in suspense from Thresk to Hazlewood, from Hazlewood to Pettifer. She saw the tray of miniatures upon the table.

"You admire the collection?" she said to Thresk.

"Very much," he answered, and Pettifer took her by the arm and in a voice of kindness which she had never heard him use before he said:

"Now tell me about your house. That's much more interesting."

Stella looked at him in doubt.

"You want really to know?"

"Yes, I do," he answered. "Will it suit you when you are married?"

There was no longer any possibility of doubt. By some miracle this hour of suspense had transformed her enemy into her friend. Her troubles then were really over? She could sleep without waking up every hour in terror lest this wonderful happiness which had come to her should be no more than a dream, a wreath of smoke? She felt weak. For a moment it seemed to her that she must fall; and she would have fallen but that Pettifer's arm steadied and supported her.

"Sit down," he said gently and he placed her on the couch beside him. "I know. You have had a time of anxiety, Stella. You must not blame us too much. Look up and talk to me! You are going to be my neighbour. Tell me about your house!"

Stella looked up at him with shining eyes, and in her cheeks which had grown pale slowly the rose bloomed again.

"There's a high garden looking right across Hinksey Park," she said, "where once ages ago I lived. There are a couple of bath-rooms—isn't that splendid in a small house?" And then across the room she heard the scratch of a lucifer and words were spoken which brought her fears in an overmastering legion back to her.

278

THE WITNESS

"So you smoke a pipe?" Dick Hazlewood was saying to Thresk, and Thresk, as he set the match to the tobacco in the bowl, remarked:

"Ah! You didn't know that, Captain Hazlewood? I am lost without my pipe. Before now when I have left it behind me I have come back for it under all sorts of circumstances, even at the risk of losing a train. But you didn't know that, Captain Hazlewood?"

The words were aimed at her, were spoken so that she might hear them. She sat and trembled. Mr. Pettifer was satisfied; yes, but there was another here who sent her a warning across the room which she had yet to reckon with.

CHAPTER XXV

Henry Thresk took Mrs. Pettifer in to dinner that night and she found him poor company. He tried indeed by fits and starts to entertain her, but his thoughts were elsewhere. He was in a great pother and trouble about Stella Ballantyne, who sat over against him on the other side of the table. She wore no traces of the consternation which his words had caused her a couple of hours before. She had come dressed in a slim gown of shimmering blue with her small head erect, a smile upon her lips and a bright colour in her cheeks. Thresk hardly knew her, he had to tell himself again and again that this was the Stella Ballantyne whom he had known here and in India. She was not the girl who had ridden with him upon the downs and made one month of his life very memorable and one day a shameful recollection. Nor was she the stricken creature of the tent in Chitipur. She was a woman sure of her resources, radiant in her beauty, confident that what she wore was her colour and gave her her value. Yet her trouble was greater than Thresk's, and many a time during the course of that dinner, when she felt his eyes

280

resting upon her, her heart sank in fear. She sought his company after dinner, but she had no chance of a private word with him. Old Mr. Hazlewood took care of that. One moment Stella must sing; at another she must play a rubber of bridge. He at all events had not laid aside his enmity and suspected some understanding between her and his guest. At eleven Mrs. Pettifer took her leave. She came across the room to Henry Thresk.

"Are you staying over to-morrow?" she asked, and Thresk with a laugh answered:

"I wish that I could. But I have to catch an early train to London. Even to-night my day's work's not over. I must sit up for an hour or two over a brief."

Stella rose at the same time as Mrs. Pettifer.

"I was hoping that you would be able to come across and see my little cottage to-morrow morning," she said. Thresk hesitated as he took her hand.

"I should very much like to see it," he said. He was in a very great difficulty, and was not sure that a letter was not the better if the more cowardly way out of it. "If I could find the time."

"Try," said she. She could say no more for Mr. Hazlewood was at her elbow and Dick was waiting to take her home.

It was a dark clear night; a sky of stars overarched the earth, but there was no moon, and though lights shone brightly even at a great distance there was no

281

glimmer from the road beneath their feet. Dick held her close in his arms at the door of her cottage. She was very still and passive.

"You are tired?" he asked.

"I think so."

"Well, to-night has seen the last of our troubles, Stella."

She did not answer him at once. Her hands clung about his shoulders and with her face smothered in his coat she whispered:

"Dick, I couldn't go on without you now. I couldn't. I wouldn't."

There was a note of passionate despair in her voice which made her words suddenly terrible to him. He took her and held her a little away from him, peering into her face.

"What are you saying, Stella?" he asked sternly. "You know that nothing can come between us. You break my heart when you talk like that." He drew her again into his arms. "Is your maid waiting up for you?"

"No."

"Call her then, while I wait here. Let me see the light in her room. I want her to sleep with you to-night."

"There's no need, Dick," she answered. "I am unstrung to-night. I said more than I meant. I swear to you there's no need."

282

IN THE LIBRARY

He raised her head and kissed her on the lips.

"I trust you, Stella," he said gently; and she answered him in a low trembling voice of so much tenderness and love that he was reassured. "Oh, you may, my dear, you may."

She went up to her room and turned on the light, and sat down in her chair just as she had done after her first dinner at Little Beeding. She had foreseen then all the troubles which had since beset her, but she had seemed to have passed through them—until this afternoon. Over there in the library of the big house was Henry Thresk—the stranger. Very likely he was at this moment writing to her. If he had only consented to come over in the morning and give her the chance of pleading with him! She went to the window and, drawing up the blind, leaned her head out and looked across the meadow. In the library one of the long windows stood open and the curtain was not drawn. The room was full of light. Henry Thresk was there. He had befriended her this afternoon as he had befriended her at Bombay, for the second time he had won the victory for her; but the very next moment he had warned her that the end was not yet. He would send her a letter, she had not a doubt of it. She had not a doubt either of the message which the letter would bring.

A sound rose to her ears from the gravel path below her window—the sound of a slight involuntary move-

ment. Stella drew sharply back. Then she leaned
out again and called softly:

"Dick."

He was standing a little to the left of the window
out of reach of the light which streamed out upon the
darkness from the room behind her. He moved forward now.

"Oh, Dick, why are you waiting?"

"I wanted to be sure that all was right, Stella."

"I gave you my word, Dick," she whispered and she
wished him good-night again and waited till the sound
of his footsteps had altogether died away. He went
back to the house and found Thresk still at work in the
library.

"I don't want to interrupt you," he said, "but I
must thank you again. I can't tell you what I owe
you. She's pretty wonderful, isn't she? I feel coarse
beside her, I tell you. I couldn't talk like this to any
one else, but you're so sympathetic."

Henry Thresk had responded with nothing more than
a grunt. He sat slashing at his brief with a blue pen-
cil, all the while that Dick Hazlewood was speaking,
and wishing that he would go to bed. Dick however
was unabashed.

"Did you ever see a woman look so well in a blue
frock? Or in a black one either? There's a sort of
painted thing she wears sometimes too. Well, perhaps
I had better go to bed."

IN THE LIBRARY

"I think it would be wise," said Thresk.

Young Hazlewood went over to the table in the corner and lit his candle.

"You'll shut that window before you go to bed, won't you?"

"Yes."

Hazlewood filled for himself a glass of barley-water and drank it, contemplating Henry Thresk over the rim. Then he went back to him, carrying his candle in his hand.

"Why don't you get married, Mr. Thresk?" he asked. "You ought to, you know. Men run to seed so if they don't."

"Thank you," said Thresk.

The tone was not cordial, but mere words were an invitation to Dick Hazlewood at this moment. He sat down and placed his lighted candle on the table between Thresk and himself.

"I am thirty-four years old," he said, and Thresk interposed without glancing up from his foolscap:

"From your style of conversation I find that very difficult to believe, Captain Hazlewood."

"I have wasted thirty-four complete years of twelve months each," continued the ecstatic Captain, who appeared to think that on the very day of his birth he would have recognised his soul's mate. "Just jogging along with the world, a miracle about one and not half an eye to perceive it. You know."

285

"No, I don't," Thresk observed. He lifted the candle and held it out to Dick. Dick got up and took it.

"Thank you," he said. "That was very kind of you. I told you—didn't I?—how sympathetic I thought you."

Thresk was not proof against his companion's pertinacity. He broke into a laugh. "Are you going to bed?" he pleaded, and Dick Hazlewood replied, "Yes, I am." Suddenly his tone changed.

"Stella had a very good friend in you, Mr. Thresk. I am sure she still has one," and without waiting for any answer he went upstairs. His bedroom was near to the front in the side of the house. It commanded a view of the meadow and the cottage and he rejoiced to see that all Stella's windows were dark. The library was out of sight round the corner at the back, but a glare of light from the open door spread out over the lawn. Hazlewood looked at his watch. It was just midnight. He went to bed and slept.

In the library Thresk strove to concentrate his thoughts upon his brief. But he could not, and he threw it aside at last. There was a letter to be written, and until it was written and done with his thoughts would not be free. He went over to the writing-table and wrote it. But it took a long while in the composition and the clock upon the top of the stable was striking one when at last he had finished and sealed it up.

IN THE LIBRARY

"I'll post it in the morning at the station," he resolved, and he went to the window to close it. But as
he touched it a slight figure wrapped in a dark cloak
came out of the darkness at the side and stepped
past him into the room. He swung round and saw
Stella Ballantyne.

"You!" he exclaimed. "You must be mad."

"I had to come," she said, standing well away from
the window in the centre of the room as though she
thought he would drive her out. "I heard you say you
would be sitting late here."

"How long have you been waiting out there?"

"A little while . . . I don't know. . . . Not very
long. I wasn't sure that you were alone."

Thresk closed the window and drew the curtain
across it. Then he crossed the room and locked the
doors leading into the dining-room and hall.

"There was no need for you to come," he said in a
low voice. "I have written to you."

"Yes." She nodded her head. "That's why I had
to come. This afternoon you spoke of leaving your
pipe behind. I understood," and as he drew the letter
from his pocket she recoiled from it. "No, it has never
been written. I came in time to prevent its being
written. You only had an idea of writing. Say that!
You are my friend." She took the letter from him now
and tore it across and again across. "See! It has
never been written at all."

But Thresk only shook his head. "I am very sorry. I see to-night the stricken woman of the tent in Chitipur. I am very sorry," and Stella caught at the commiseration in his voice. She dropped the cloak from her shoulders; she was dressed as she had been at the dinner some hours before, but all her radiance had gone, her cheeks trembled, her eyes pleaded desperately.

"Sorry! I knew you would be. You are not hard. You couldn't be. You must come close day by day in your life to so much that is pitiful. One can talk to you and you'll understand. This is my first chance, the first real chance I have ever had, Henry, the very first."

Thresk looked backwards over the years of Stella Ballantyne's unhappy life. It came upon him with a shock that what she said was the bare truth; and remorse followed hard upon the heels of the shock. This was her first real chance and he himself was to blame that it had come no earlier. The first chance of a life worth the living—it had been in his hands to give her and he had refused to give it years ago on Bignor Hill.

"It's quite true," he admitted. "But I don't ask you to give it up, Stella." She looked at him eagerly. "No! You would have understood that if you had read my letter instead of tearing it up. I only ask you to tell your lover the truth."

"He knows it," she said sullenly.

288

IN THE LIBRARY

"No!"

"He does! He does!" she protested, her voice rising to a low cry.

"Hush! You'll be heard," said Thresk, and she listened for a moment anxiously. But there was no sound of any one stirring in the house.

"We are safe here," she said. "No one sleeps above us. Henry, he knows the truth."

"Would you be here now if he did?"

"I came because this afternoon you seemed to be threatening me. I didn't understand. I couldn't sleep. I saw the light in this room. I came to ask you what you meant—that's all."

"I'll tell you what I meant," said Thresk, and Stella with her eyes fixed upon him sank down upon a chair. "I left my pipe behind me in the tent on the night I dined with you. Your lover, Stella, doesn't know that. I came back to fetch it. He doesn't know that. You were standing by the table——" and Stella Ballantyne broke in upon him to silence the words upon his lips.

"There was no reason why he should know," she exclaimed. "It had nothing to do with what happened. We know what happened. There was a thief"—and Thresk turned to her then with such a look of sheer amazement upon his face that she faltered and her voice died to a murmur of words—"a lean brown arm—a hand delicate as a woman's."

"There was no thief," he said quietly. "There was

289

a man delirious with drink who imagined one. There was you with the bruises on your throat and the unutterable misery in your eyes and a little rifle in your hands. There was no one else."

She ceased to argue; she sat looking straight in front of her with a stubborn face and a resolution to cling at all costs to her chance of happiness.

"Come, Stella," Thresk pleaded. "I don't say tell every one. I do say tell him. For unless you do I must."

Stella stared at him.

"You?" she said. "You would tell him that you came back into the tent and saw me?"

"Oh, much more—that I lied at the trial, that the story which secured your acquittal was false, that I made it up to save you. That I told it again this afternoon to give you a chance of slipping out from an impossible position."

She looked at Thresk for a moment in terror. Then her expression changed. A wave of relief swept over her; she laughed in Thresk's face.

"You are trying to frighten me," she said. "Only I know you. Do you realise what it would mean to you if it were ever really known that you had lied at the trial?"

"Yes."

"Your ruin. Your absolute ruin."

"Worse than that."

IN THE LIBRARY

"Prison!"

"Perhaps. Yes."

Stella laughed again.

"And you would run the risk of the truth becoming known by telling it to so much as one person. No, no! Another, perhaps—not you! You have had one dream all your life—to rise out of obscurity, to get on in the world, to hold the high positions. Everything and every one has been sacrificed to its fulfilment. Oh, who should know better than I?" and she struck her hands together sharply as she uttered that bitter cry. "You have lain down late and risen early, and you have got on. Well, are you the man to throw away all this work and success now that they touch fulfilment? You are in the chariot. Will you step down and run tied to the wheels? Will you stand up and say, 'There was a trial. I perjured myself'? No. Another, perhaps. Not you, Henry."

Thresk had no answer to that indictment. All of it was true except its inference, and it was no news to him. He made no effort to defend himself.

"You are not very generous, Stella," he replied gently. "For if I lied, I saved you by the lie."

Stella was softened by the words. Her voice lost its hardness, she reached out her hand in an apology and laid it on his arm.

"Oh, I know. I sent you a little word of thanks when you gave me my freedom. But it won't be of

291

much value to me if I lose—what I am fighting for now."

"So you use every weapon?"

"Yes."

"But this one breaks in your hand," he said firmly. "The thing you think it incredible that I should do I shall do none the less."

Stella looked at him in despair. She could no longer doubt that he really meant his words. He was really resolved to make this sacrifice of himself and her. And why? Why should he interfere?

"You save me one day to destroy me the next," she said.

"No," he replied. "I don't think I shall do that, Stella," and he explained to her what drove him on. "I had no idea why Hazlewood asked me here. Had I suspected it I say frankly that I should have refused to come. But I am here. The trouble's once more at my door but in a new shape. There's this man, young Hazlewood. I can't forget him. You will be marrying him by the help of a lie I told."

"He loves me," she cried.

"Then he can bear the truth," answered Thresk. He pulled up a chair opposite to that in which Stella sat. "I want you to understand me, if you will. I don't want you to think me harsh or cruel. I told a lie upon my oath in the witness-box. I violated my traditions, I struck at my belief in the value of my own

292

profession, and such beliefs mean a good deal to any man." Stella stirred impatiently. What words were these? Traditions! The value of a profession!

"I am not laying stress upon them, Stella, but they count," Thresk continued. "And I am telling you that they count because I am going to add that I should tell that lie again to-morrow, were the trial to-morrow and you a prisoner. I should tell it again to save you again. Yes, to save you. But when you go and—let me put it very plainly—use that lie to your advantage, why then I am bound to cry 'stop.' Don't you see that? You are using the lie to marry a man and keep him in ignorance of the truth. You can't do that, Stella! You would be miserable yourself if you did all your life. You would never feel safe for a moment. You would be haunted by a fear that some day he would learn the truth and not from you. Oh, I am sure of it." He caught her hands and pressed them earnestly. "Tell him, Stella, tell him!"

Stella Ballantyne rose to her feet with a strange look upon her face. Her eyes half closed as though to shut out a vision of past horrors. She turned to Thresk with a white face and her hands tightly clenched.

"You don't know what happened on that night, after you rode away to catch your train?"

"No."

"I think you ought to know—before you sit in judgment"; and so at last in that quiet library under the

293

Sussex Downs the tragic story of that night was told. For Thresk as he listened and watched, its terrors lived again in the eyes and the hushed voice of Stella Ballantyne, the dark walls seemed to fall back and dissolve. The moonlit plain of far-away Chitipur stretched away in front of him to the dim hill where the old silent palaces crumbled; and midway between them and the green signal-lights of the railway the encampment blazed like the clustered lights of a small town. But Thresk learnt more than the facts. The springs of conduct were disclosed to him; the woman revealed herself, dark places were made light; and he bowed himself beneath a new burden of remorse.

CHAPTER XXVI

"You came back to the tent," she began, "and ever since then you have misunderstood what you saw. For this is the truth: I was going to kill myself."

Thresk was startled as he had not expected to be; and a great wave of relief swept over him and uplifted his soul. Here was the simplest explanation, yet it had never occurred to him. Always he had been besieged by the vision of Stella standing quietly by the table, deliberately preparing her rifle for use, always he had linked up that vision with the death of Stephen Ballantyne in a dreadful connection. He did not doubt that she spoke the truth now. Looking at her and noticing the anguish of her face, he could not doubt it. So definite a premeditation as he had imagined there had not been, and relief carried him to pity.

"So it had come to that?" he said.

"Yes," replied Stella. "And you had your share in bringing it to that—you who sit in judgment."

"I!" Thresk exclaimed.

"Yes, you who sit in judgment. I am not alone. No, I am not alone. A crime was committed? Then you must shoulder your portion of the blame."

Thresk asked himself in vain what was his share. He had done a cowardly thing years ago a few miles from this spot. He had never ceased to reproach himself for the cowardice. But that it had lived and worked like some secret malady until in the end it had made him an all-unconscious accomplice in that midnight tragedy, a sharer in its guilt, if guilt there were—here again was news for him. But the knowledge which her first words had given to him, that all these years he had never got the truth of her, kept him humble now. He ceased to be judge. He became pupil and as pupil he answered her.

"I am ready to shoulder it."

He was seated on a cushioned bench which stood behind the writing-table and Stella sat down at his side.

"When we parted—that morning—it was in the drawing-room over there in my cottage. We parted, you to your work of getting on, Henry, I to think of you getting on without me at your side. There was a letter lying on the table, a letter from India. Jane Repton had written it and she asked me to go out to her for the cold weather. I went. I was a young girl, lonely and very unhappy, and as young girls often do who are lonely and very unhappy I drifted into marriage."

"I see," said Thresk in a hushed voice. The terrible conviction grew upon him now, lurid as the breaking of a day of storm, that the cowardice he had shown on Bignor Hill ruined her altogether and hurt him not at all. "Yes, I see. There my share begins."

"Oh no. Not yet," she answered. "Then I spoke when I should have kept silence. I let my heart go out when I should have guarded it. No, I cannot blame you."

"You have the right none the less."

But Stella would not excuse herself now and to him by any subtlety or artifice.

"No: I married. That was my affair. I was beaten—despised—ridiculed—terrified by a husband who drank secretly and kept all his drunkenness for me. That, too, was my affair. But I might have gone on. For seven years it had lasted. I was settling into a dull habit of misery. I might have gone on being bullied and tortured had not one little thing happened to push me over the precipice."

"And what was that?" asked Thresk.

"Your visit to me at Chitipur," she replied, and the words took his breath away. Why, he had travelled to Chitipur merely to save her. He leaned forward eagerly but she anticipated him. She smiled at him with an indulgent forgiveness. "Oh, why did you come? But I know."

"Do you?" Thresk asked. Here at all events she was wrong.

"Yes. You came because of that one weak soft spot of sentimentalism there is in all of you, the strongest,

297

the hardest. You are strong for years. You live alone for years. Then comes the sentimental moment and it's we who suffer, not you."

And deep in Thresk's mind was the terror of the mistakes people make in ignorance of each other, and of the mortal hurt the mistakes inflict. He had misread Stella. Here was she misreading him and misreading him in some strange way to her peril and ruin.

"You are sure of that?" he asked. She had no doubt—no more doubt than he had had of the reason why she stood preparing her rifle.

"Quite," she answered. "You had heard of me in Bombay and it came over you that you would like to see how the woman you had loved looked after all these years: whether she retained her pretty way, whether she missed you—ah, above all, whether she missed you. You wanted to fan up into a mild harmless flame the ashes of an old romance, warm your hands at it for half an hour, recapture a savour of dim and pleasant memories and then go back to your own place and your own work, untouched and unhurt."

Thresk laughed aloud with bitterness at the mistake she had made. Yet he could not blame her. There was a certain shrewd insight which though it had led her astray in this case might well have been true in any other case, might well have been true of him. He remembered her disbelief in all that he had said to her in that tent at Chitipur; and he was appalled by the irony of things and the blind and feeble helplessness of men to combat it.

"So that's why I came to Chitipur?" he cried.

"Yes," Stella answered without a second of hesitation. "But I couldn't be left untouched and unhurt. You came and all that I had lost came with you, came in a vivid rush of bright intolerable memories." She clasped her hands over her eyes and Thresk lived over again that evening in the tent upon the desert, but with a new understanding. His mind was illumined. He saw the world as a prison in which each living being is shut off from his neighbour by the impenetrable wall of an inability to understand.

"Memories of summers here," she resumed, "of women friends, of dainty and comfortable things, and days of great happiness when it was good—oh so very good!—to be alive and young. And you were going back to it all, straight by the night-mail to Bombay, straight from the station on board your ship. Oh, how it hurt to hear you speak of it, with a casual pleasant word about exile and next-door neighbours!" She clasped her hands together in front of her, her fingers worked and twisted. "No, I couldn't endure it," she whispered. "The blows, the ridicule, the contempt, I determined, should come to an end that night, and when you saw me with the rifle in my hand I was going to end it."

"Yes?"

"And then the stupidest thing happened. I couldn't find the little box of cartridges."

Stella described to him how she had run hither and thither about the tent, opening drawers, looking into bags and growing more nervous and more flurried with every second that passed. She had so little time. Ballantyne was not going as far as the station with Thresk. He merely intended to see his visitor off beyond the edge of the camp. And it must all be over and done with before he came back. She heard Ballantyne call to Thresk to sit firm while the camel rose; and still she had not found them. She heard Thresk's voice saying good-night.

"The last words, Henry, I wanted to hear in the world. I thought that I would wait for them and the moment they had died away—then. But I hadn't found the cartridges and so the search began again."

Thresk, watching her as she lived through again those desperate minutes, was carried back to Chitipur and seemed to be looking into that tent. He had a dreadful picture before his eyes of a hunted woman rushing wildly from table to table, with a white, quivering face and lips which babbled incoherently and feverish hands which darted out nervously, over-setting books and ornaments—in a vain search for a box of cartridges wherewith to kill herself. She found them at last behind the whisky bottle, and clutched at them with a great sigh of relief. She carried them over to the table on which

300

she had laid her rifle, and as she pushed one into the breech, Stephen Ballantyne stood in the doorway of the tent.

"He swore at me," Stella continued. "I had taken the necklace off. I had shown you the bruises on my throat. He cursed me for it, and he asked me roughly why I didn't shoot myself and rid him of a fool. I stood without answering him. That always maddened him. I didn't do it on purpose. I had become dull and slow. I just stood and looked at him stupidly, and in a fury he ran at me with his fist raised. I recoiled, he frightened me, and then before he reached me—yes." Her voice died away in a whisper. Thresk did not interrupt. There was more for her to tell and one dreadful incident to explain. Stella went on in a moment, looking straight in front of her and with all the passion of fear gone from her voice.

"I remember that he stood and stared at me foolishly for a little while. I had time to believe that nothing had happened, and to be glad that nothing had happened and to be terrified of what he would do to me. And then he fell and lay quite still."

It seemed that she had no more to say, that she meant to leave unexplained the inexplicable thing; and even Thresk put it out of his thoughts.

"It was an accident then," he cried. "After all, Stella, it was an accident."

But Stella sat mutely at his side. Some struggle was

taking place in her and was reflected in her countenance. Thresk's eager joy was damped.

"No, my friend," she said at length, slowly and very deliberately. "It was not an accident."

"But you fired in fear." Thresk caught now at that alternative. "You shot in self-defence. Stella, I blundered at Bombay." He moved away from her in his agitation. "I am sorry. Oh, I am very sorry. I should never have come forward at all. I should have lain quiet and let your counsel develop his case, as he was doing, on the line of self-defence. You would have been acquitted—and rightly acquitted. You would have had the sympathy of every one. But I didn't know your story. I was afraid that the discovery of Ballantyne outside the tent would ruin you. I knew that my story could not fail to save you. So I told it. But I was wrong, Stella. I blundered. I did you a great harm."

He was standing before her now and so poignant an anguish rang in his voice that Stella was moved by it to discard her plans. Thus she had meant to tell the story if ever she was driven to it. Thus she had told it. But now she put out a timid hand and took him by the arm.

"I said I would tell you the truth. But I have not told it all. It's so hard not to keep one little last thing back. Listen to me"; and with a bowed head and her hand still clinging desperately to his arm she made the final revelation.

TWO STRANGERS

"It's true I was crazy with fear. But there was just one little moment when I knew what I was going to do, when it came upon me that the way I had chosen before was the wrong one, and this new way the right one. No, no," she cried as Thresk moved. "Even that's not all. That moment—you could hardly measure it in time, yet to me it was distinct enough and is marked distinctly in my memories, for during it *he* drew back."

"What?" cried Thresk. "Don't say it, Stella!"

"Yes," she answered. "During it he drew back, knowing what I was going to do just as I suddenly knew it. It was a moment when he seemed to me to bleat—yes, that's the word—to bleat for mercy."

She had told the truth now and she dropped her hand from his sleeve.

"And you? What did you do?" asked Thresk.

"I? Oh, I went mad, I think. When I saw him lying there I lost my head. The tent was flecked with great spots of fire which whirled in front of my eyes and hurt. A strength far greater than mine possessed me. I was crazy. I dragged him out of the tent—for no reason—that's the truth—for no reason at all. Can you believe that?"

"Yes," replied Thresk readily enough. "I can well believe that."

"Then something broke," she resumed. "I felt weak and numbed. I dragged myself to my room. I went to bed. Does that sound very horrible to you?

I had one clear thought only. It was over. It was all over. I slept." She leaned back in her chair, her hands dropped to her side, her eyes closed. "Yes, I did actually sleep."

A clock ticking upon the mantelshelf seemed to grow louder and louder in the silence of the library. The sound of it forced itself upon Thresk. It roused Stella. She opened her eyes. In front of her Thresk was standing, his face grave and very pitiful.

"Now answer me truly," said Stella, and leaning forward she fixed her eyes upon him. "If you still loved me, would you, knowing this story, refuse to marry me?"

Thresk looked back across the years of her unhappy life and saw her as the sport of a malicious destiny.

"No," he said, "I should not."

"Then why shouldn't Dick marry me?"

"Because he doesn't know this story."

Stella nodded her head.

"Yes. There's the flaw in my appeal to you, I know. You are quite right. I should have told him. I should tell him now," and suddenly she dropped on her knees before Thresk, the tears burst from her eyes, and in a voice broken with passion she cried:

"But I daren't—not yet. I have tried to—oh, more than once. Believe that, Henry! You must believe it! But I couldn't. I hadn't the courage. You will give me a little time, won't you? Oh, not long. I will tell him of my own free will—very soon, Henry. But not now—not now."

The sound of her sobbing and the sight of her distress wrung Thresk's heart. He lifted her from the ground and held her.

"There's another way, Stella," he said gently.

"Oh, I know," she answered. She was thinking of the little bottle with the tablets of veronal which stood by her bed, not for the first time that night. She did not stop to consider whether Thresk, too, had that way in his mind. It came to her so naturally; it was so easy, so simple a way. She never thought that she misunderstood. She had come to the end of the struggle; the battle had gone against her; she recognised it; and now, without complaint, she bowed her head for the final blow. The inherited habit of submission taught her that the moment had come for compliance and gave her the dignity of patience. "Yes, I suppose that I must take that way," she said, and she walked towards the chair over which she had thrown her wrap. "Goodnight, Henry."

But before she had thrown the cloak about her shoulders Thresk stood between her and the window. He took the cloak from her hands.

"There have been too many mistakes, Stella, between you and me. There must be no more. Here are we—until to-night strangers, and because we were strangers, and never knew it, spoiling each other's lives."

305

Stella looked at him in bewilderment. She had taught Thresk that night unimagined truths about herself. She was now to learn something of the inner secret man which the outward trappings of success concealed. He led her to a sofa and placed her at his side.

"You have said a good many hard things to me, Stella," he said with a smile—"most of them true, but some untrue. And the untrue things you wouldn't have said if you had ever chanced to ask yourself one question: why I really missed my steamer at Bombay."

Stella Ballantyne was startled. She made a guess but faltered in the utterance of it, so ill it fitted with her estimate of him.

"You missed it on purpose?"

"Yes. I didn't come to Chitipur on any sentimental journey"; and he told how he had seen her portrait in Jane Repton's drawing-room and learnt of the misery of her marriage.

"I came to fetch you away."

And again Stella stared at him.

"You? You pitied me so much? Oh, Henry!"

"No. I wanted you so much. It's quite true that I sacrificed everything for success. I don't deny that it is well worth having. But Jane Repton said something to me in Bombay so true—you can get whatever you want if you want it enough, but you cannot control

306

the price you will have to pay. I know, my dear, that I paid too big a price. I trampled down something better worth having."

Stella rose suddenly to her feet.

"Oh, if I had known that on the night in Chitipur! What a difference it would have made!" She turned swiftly to him. "Couldn't you have told me?"

"I hadn't a chance. I hadn't five minutes with you alone. And you wouldn't have believed me if I had had the chance. I left my pipe behind me in order to come back and tell you. I had only the time then to tell you that I would write."

"Yes, yes," she answered, and again the cry burst from her: "What a difference it would have made! Merely to have known that you really wanted me!"

She would never have taken that rifle from the corner and searched for the cartridges, that she might kill herself! Whether she had consented or not to go away and ruin Thresk's future she would have had a little faith wherewith to go on and face the world. If she had only known! But up on the top of Bignor Hill a blow had been struck under which her faith had reeled and it had never had a chance of recovery. She laughed harshly. The heart of her tragedy was now revealed to her. She saw herself the sport of gods who sat about like cruel louts torturing a helpless animal and laughing stupidly at its sufferings. She turned again to Thresk and held out her hand.

"Thank you. You would have ruined yourself for me."

"Ruin's a large word," he answered, and still holding her hand he drew her down again. She yielded reluctantly. She might misread his character, but when the feelings and emotions were aroused she had the unerring insight of her sex. She was warned by it now. She looked at Thresk with startled eyes.

"Why have you told me all this?" she asked in suspense, ready for flight.

"I want to prepare you. There's a way out of the trouble—the honest way for both of us: to make a clean breast of it together and together take what follows."

She was on her feet and away from him in a second.

"No, no," she cried in alarm, and Thresk mistook the cause of the alarm.

"You can't be tried again, Stella. That's over. You have been acquitted."

She temporised.

"But you?"

"I?" and he shrugged his shoulders. "I take the consequences. I doubt if they would be so very heavy. There would be some sympathy. And afterwards— it would be as though you had slipped down from Chitipur to Bombay and joined me as I had planned. We can make the best of our lives together."

There was so much sincerity in his manner, so much

308

simplicity she could not doubt him; and the immensity of the sacrifice he was prepared to make overwhelmed her. It was not merely scandal and the Divorce Court which he was ready to brave now. He had gone beyond the plan contemplated at Bombay. He was willing to go hand in hand with her into the outer darkness, laying down all that he had laboured for unsparingly.

"You would do that for me?" she said. "Oh, you put me to shame!" and she covered her face with her hands.

"You give up your struggle for a footing in the world—that's what you want, isn't it?" He pleaded, and she drew her hands away from her face. He believed that? He imagined that she was fighting just for a name, a position in the world? She stared at him in amazement, and forced herself to understand. Since he himself had cared for her enough to remain unmarried, since the knowledge of the mistake which he had made had grown more bitter with each year, he had fallen easily into that other error that she had never ceased to care too.

"We'll make something of our lives, never fear," he was saying. "But to marry this man for his position, and he not knowing—oh, my dear, I know how you are driven—but it won't do! It won't do!"

She stood in silence for a little while. One by one he had torn her defences down. She could hardly bear the gentleness upon his face and she turned away from him and sat down upon a chair a little way off.

"Stand there, Henry," she said. A strange composure had succeeded her agitation. "I must tell you something more which I had meant to hide from you —the last thing which I have kept back. It will hurt you, I am afraid."

There came a change upon Thresk's face. He was steeling himself to meet a blow.

"Go on."

"It isn't because of his position that I cling to Dick. I want him to keep that—yes—for his sake. I don't want him to lose more by marrying me than he needs must"; and comprehension burst upon Henry Thresk.

"You care for him then! You really care for him?"

"So much," she answered, "that if I lost him now I should lose all the world. You and I can't go back to where we stood nine years ago. You had your chance then, Henry, if you had wished to take it. But you didn't wish it, and that sort of chance doesn't often come again. Others like it—yes. But not quite the same one. I am sorry. But you must believe me. If I lost Dick I should lose all the world."

So far she had spoken very deliberately, but now her voice faltered.

"That is my one poor excuse."

The unexpected word roused Thresk to inquiry.

"Excuse?" he asked, and with her eyes fixed in fear upon him she continued:

"Yes. I meant Dick to marry me publicly. But I saw that his father shrank from the marriage. I grew afraid. I told Dick of my fears. He banished them. I let him banish them."

"What do you mean?" Thresk asked.

"We were married privately in London five days ago."

Thresk uttered a low cry and in a moment Stella was at his side, all her composure gone.

"Oh, I know that it was wrong. But I was being hunted. They were all like a pack of wolves after me. Mr. Hazlewood had joined them. I was driven into a corner. I loved Dick. They meant to tear him from me without any pity. I clung. Yes, I clung."

But Thresk thrust her aside.

"You tricked him," he cried.

"I didn't dare to tell him," Stella pleaded, wringing her hands. "I didn't dare to lose him."

"You tricked him," Thresk repeated; and at the note of anger in his voice Stella found herself again.

"You accuse and condemn me?" she asked quietly.

"Yes. A thousand times, yes," he exclaimed hotly, and she answered with another question winged on a note of irony:

"Because I tricked him? Or because I—married him?"

311

Thresk was silenced. He recognised the truth implied in the distinction, he turned to her with a smile.

"Yes," he answered. "You are right, Stella. It's because you married him."

He stood for a moment in thought. Then with a gesture of helplessness he picked up her cloak. She watched his action and as he came towards her she cried:

"But I'll tell him now, Henry." In a way she owed it to this man who cared for her so much, who was so prepared for sacrifice, if sacrifice could help. That morning on the downs was swept from her memory now. "Yes, I'll tell him now," she said eagerly. Since Henry Thresk set such store upon that confession, why, so very likely would Dick, her husband, too.

But Thresk shook his head.

"What's the use now? You give him no chance. You can't set him free"; and Stella was as one turned to stone. All argument seemed sooner or later to turn to that one dread alternative which had already twice that night forced itself on her acceptance.

"Yes, I can, Henry, and I will, I promise you, if he wishes to be free. I can do it quite easily, quite naturally. Any woman could. So many of us take things to make us sleep."

There was no boastfulness in her voice or manner, but rather a despairing recognition of facts.

TWO STRANGERS

"Good God, you mustn't think of it!" said Thresk eagerly. "That's too big a price to pay."

Stella shook her head wistfully.

"You hear it said, Henry," she answered with an indescribable wistfulness, "that women will do anything to keep the men they love. They'll do a great deal—I am an example—but not always everything. Sometimes love runs just a little stronger. And then it craves that the loved one shall get all he wants to have. If Dick wants his freedom I too, then, shall want him to have it."

And while Thresk stood with no words to answer her there came a knocking upon the door. It was gentle, almost furtive, but it startled them both like a clap of thunder. For a moment they stood rigid. Then Thresk silently handed Stella her cloak and pointed towards the window. He began to speak aloud. A word or two revealed his plan to Stella Ballantyne. He was rehearsing a speech which he was to make in the Courts before a jury. But the handle of the door rattled and now old Mr. Hazlewood's voice was heard.

"Thresk! Are you there?"

Once more Thresk pointed to the window. But Stella did not move.

"Let him in," she said quietly, and with a glance at her he unlocked the door.

Mr. Hazlewood stood outside. He had not gone to

313

bed that night. He had taken off his coat and now wore a smoking-jacket.

"I knew that I should not sleep to-night, so I sat up," he began, "and I thought that I heard voices here."

Over Thresk's shoulder he saw Stella Ballantyne standing erect in the middle of the room, her shining gown the one bright patch of colour. "You here?" he cried to her, and Thresk made way for him to enter. He advanced to her with a look of triumph in his eyes.

"You here—at this house—with Thresk? You were persuading him to continue to hold his tongue."

Stella met his gaze steadily.

"No," she replied. "He was persuading me to tell the truth, and he has succeeded."

Mr. Hazlewood smiled and nodded. There was no magnanimity in his triumph. A schoolboy would have shown more chivalry to the opponent who was down.

"You confess then? Good! Richard must be told."

"Yes," answered Stella. "I claim the right to tell him."

But Mr. Hazlewood scoffed at the proposal.

"Oh dear no!" he cried. "I refuse the claim. I shall go straight to Richard now."

He had actually taken a couple of steps towards the door before Stella's voice rang out suddenly loud and imperative.

314

TWO STRANGERS

"Take care, Mr. Hazlewood. After you have told him he will come to me. Take care!"

Hazlewood stopped. Certainly that was true.

"I'll tell Dick to-morrow, here, in your presence," she said. "And if he wishes it I'll set him free and never trouble either of you again."

Hazlewood looked at Thresk and was persuaded to consent. Reflection showed him that it was the better plan. He himself would be present when Stella spoke. He would see that the truth was told without embroidery.

"Very well, to-morrow," he said.

Stella flung the cloak over her shoulders and went up to the window. Thresk opened it for her.

"I'll see you to your door," he said.

The moon had risen now. It hung low with the branches of a tree like a lattice across its face; and on the garden and the meadow lay that unearthly light which falls when a moonlit night begins to drown in the onrush of the dawn.

"No," she said. "I would rather go alone. But do something for me, will you? Stay to-morrow. Be here when I tell him." She choked down a sob. "Oh, I shall want a friend and you are so kind."

"So kind!" he repeated with a note of bitterness. Could there be praise from a woman's lips more deadly? You are kind; you are put in your place in the ruck of men; you are extinguished.

315

"Oh yes, I'll stay."

She stood for a moment on the stone flags outside the window.

"Will he forgive?" she asked. "You would. And he is not so very young, is he? It's the young who don't forgive. Good-night."

She went along the path and across the meadow. Thresk watched her go and saw the light spring up in her room. Then he closed the window and drew the curtain. Mr. Hazlewood had gone. Thresk wondered what the morrow would bring. After all, Stella was right. Youth was a graceful thing of high-sounding words and impetuous thoughts, but like many other graceful things it could be hard and cruel. Its generosity did not come from any wide outlook on a world where there is a good deal to be said for everything. It was rather a matter of physical health than judgment. Yes, he was glad Dick Hazlewood was half his way through the thirties. For himself—well, he knew his business. It was to be kind. He turned off the lights and went to bed.

CHAPTER XXVII

"Six, seven, eight," said Mr. Hazlewood, counting the letters which he had already written since breakfast and placing them on the salver which Hubbard was holding out to him. He was a very different man this morning from the Mr. Hazlewood of yesterday. He shone, complacent and serene. He leaned back in his chair and gazed mildly at the butler. "There must be an answer to the problem which I put to you, Hubbard."

Hubbard wrinkled his brows in thought and succeeded only in looking a hundred and ten years old. He had the melancholy look of a moulting bird. He shook his head and drooped.

"No doubt, sir," he said.

"But as far as you are concerned," Mr. Hazlewood continued briskly, "you can throw no light upon it?"

"Not a glimmer, sir."

Mr. Hazlewood was disappointed and with him disappointment was petulance.

"That is unlike you, Hubbard," he said, "for sometimes after I have been deliberating for days over some curious and perplexing conundrum, you have solved it the moment it has been put to you."

Hubbard drooped still lower. He began the droop as a bow of acknowledgment but forgot to raise his head again.

"It is very good of you, sir," he said. He seemed oppressed by the goodness of Mr. Hazlewood.

"Yet you are not clever, Hubbard! Not at all clever."

"No, sir. I know my place," returned the butler, and Mr. Hazlewood continued with a little envy.

"You must have some wonderful gift of insight which guides you straight to the inner meaning of things."

"It's just common-sense, sir," said Hubbard.

"But I haven't got it," cried Mr. Hazlewood. "How's that?"

"You don't need it, sir. You are a gentleman," Hubbard replied, and carried the letters to the door. There, however, he stopped. "I beg your pardon, sir," he said, "but a new parcel of *The Prison Walls* has arrived this morning. Shall I unpack it?"

Mr. Hazlewood frowned and scratched his ear.

"Well—er—no, Hubbard—no," he said with a trifle of discomfort. "I am not sure indeed that *The Prison Walls* is not almost one of my mistakes. We all make mistakes, Hubbard. I think you shall burn that parcel, Hubbard—somewhere where it won't be noticed."

"Certainly, sir," said Hubbard. "I'll burn it under the shadow of the south wall."

Mr. Hazlewood looked up with a start. Was it possible that Hubbard was poking fun at him? The mere notion was incredible and indeed Hubbard shuffled with so much meekness from the room that Mr. Hazlewood dismissed it. He went across the hall to the dining-room, where he found Henry Thresk trifling with his breakfast. No embarrassment weighed upon Mr. Hazlewood this morning. He effervesced with good-humour.

"I do not blame you, Mr. Thresk," he said, "for the side you took yesterday afternoon. You were a stranger to us in this house. I understand your position."

"I am not quite so sure, Mr. Hazlewood," said Thresk drily, "that I understand yours. For my part I have not closed my eyes all night. You, on the other hand, seem to have slept well."

"I did indeed," said Hazlewood. "I was relieved from a strain of suspense under which I have be n labouring for a month past. To have refused my consent to Richard's marriage with Stella Ballantyne on no other grounds than that social prejudice forbade it would have seemed a complete, a stupendous reversal of my whole theory and conduct of life. I should have become an object of ridicule. People would have laughed at the philosopher of Little Beeding. I have heard their laughter all this month. Now, however, once the truth is known no one will be able to say——"

Henry Thresk looked up from his plate aghast.

"Do you mean to say, Mr. Hazlewood, that after Mrs. Ballantyne has told her story you mean to make that story public?"

Mr. Hazlewood stared in amazement at Henry Thresk.

"But of course," he said.

"Oh, you can't be thinking of it!"

"But I am. I must do it. There is so much at stake," replied Hazlewood.

"What?"

"The whole consistency of my life. I must make it clear that I am not acting upon prejudice or suspicion or fear of what the world will say or for any of the conventional reasons which might guide other men."

To Thresk this point of view was horrible; and there was no arguing against it. It was inspired by the dreadful vanity of a narrow, shallow nature, and Thresk's experience had never shown him anything more difficult to combat and overcome.

"So for the sake of your reputation for consistency you will make a very unhappy woman bear shame and obloquy which she might easily be spared? You could find a thousand excuses for breaking off the marriage."

"You put the case very harshly, Mr. Thresk," said Hazlewood. "But you have not considered my position," and he went indignantly back to the library.

Thresk shrugged his shoulders. After all if Dick Hazlewood turned his back upon Stella she would not hear the abuse or suffer the shame. That she would take the dark journey as she declared he could not doubt. And no one could prevent her—not even he himself, though his heart might break at her taking it. All depended upon Dick.

He appeared a few minutes afterwards fresh from his ride, glowing with good-humour and contentment. But the sight of Thresk surprised him.

"Hulloa," he cried. "Good-morning. I thought you were going to catch the eight forty-five."

"I felt lazy," answered Thresk. "I sent off some telegrams to put off my engagements."

"Good," said Dick, and he sat down at the breakfast-table. As he poured out a cup of tea, Thresk said:

"I think I heard you were over thirty."

"Yes."

"Thirty's a good age," said Thresk.

"It looks back on youth," answered Dick.

"That's just what I mean," remarked Thresk. "Do you mind a cigarette?"

"Not at all."

Thresk smoked and while he smoked he talked, not carelessly yet careful not to emphasize his case. "Youth is a graceful thing of high-sounding words and impetuous thoughts, but like many other graceful things it can be very hard and very cruel."

Dick Hazlewood looked closely and quickly at his companion. But he answered casually:

321

THE WITNESS FOR THE DEFENCE

"It is supposed to be generous."

"And it is—to itself," replied Thresk. "Generous when its sympathies are enlisted, generous so long as all goes well with it: generous because it is confident of triumph. But its generosity is not a matter of judgment. It does not come from any wide outlook upon a world where there is a good deal to be said for everything. It is a matter of physical health."

"Yes?" said Dick.

"And once affronted, once hurt, youth finds it difficult to forgive."

So far both men had been debating on an abstract topic without any immediate application to themselves. But now Dick leaned across the table with a smile upon his face which Thresk did not understand.

"And why do you say this to me this morning, Mr. Thresk?" he asked pointedly.

"Yes, it's rather an impertinence, isn't it?" Thresk agreed. "But I was looking into a case late last night in which irrevocable and terrible things are going to happen if there is not forgiveness."

Dick took his cigarette-case from his pocket.

"I see," he remarked, and struck a match. Both men rose from the table and at the door Dick turned.

"Your case, of course, has not yet come on," he said.

"No," answered Thresk, "but it will very soon."

They went into the library, and Mr. Hazlewood

322

greeted his son with a vivacity which for weeks had been absent from his demeanour.

"Did you ride this morning?" he asked.

"Yes, but Stella didn't. She sent word over that she was tired. I must go across and see how she is."

Mr. Hazlewood interposed quickly:

"There is no need of that, my boy; she is coming here this morning."

"Oh!"

Dick looked at his father in astonishment.

"She said no word of it to me last night—and I saw her home. I suppose she sent word over about that too?"

He looked from one to the other of his companions, but neither answered him. Some uneasiness indeed was apparent in them both.

"Oho!" he said with a smile. "Stella's coming over and I know nothing of it. Mr. Thresk's lazy, so remains at Little Beeding and delivers a lecture to me over breakfast. And you, father, seem in remarkable spirits."

Mr. Hazlewood seized upon the opportunity to interrupt his son's reflections.

"I am, my boy," he cried. "I walked in the fields this morning and——" But he got no further with his explanations, for the sound of Mrs. Pettifer's voice rang high in the hall and she burst into the room.

"Harold, I have only a moment. Good morning,

Mr. Thresk," she cried in a breath. "I have something to say to you."

Thresk was disturbed. Suppose that Stella came while Mrs. Pettifer was here! She must not speak in Mrs. Pettifer's presence. Somehow Mrs. Pettifer must be dismissed. No such anxiety, however, harassed Mr. Hazlewood.

"Say it, Margaret," he said, smiling benignantly upon her. "You cannot annoy me this morning. I am myself again," and Dick's eyes turned sharply upon him. "All my old powers of observation have returned, my old interest in the great dark riddle of human life has re-awakened. The brain, the sedulous, active brain, resumes its work to-day asking questions, probing problems. I rose early, Margaret," he flourished his hands like one making a speech, "and walking in the fields amongst the cows a most curious speculation forced itself upon my mind. How is it, I asked myself——"

It seemed that Mr. Hazlewood was destined never to complete a sentence that morning, for Margaret Pettifer at this point banged her umbrella upon the floor.

"Stop talking, Harold, and listen to me! I have been speaking with Robert and we withdraw all opposition to Dick's marriage."

Mr. Hazlewood was dumfoundered.

"You, Margaret—you of all people!" he stammered.

"Yes," she replied decisively. "Robert likes her

and Robert is a good judge of a woman. That's one thing. Then I believe Dick is going to take St. Quentins; isn't that so, Dick?"

"Yes," answered Dick. "That's the house we looked over yesterday."

"Well, it's not a couple of a hundred yards from us, and it would not be comfortable for any of us if Dick and Dick's wife were strangers. So I give in. There, Dick!" She went across the room and held out her hand to him. "I am going to call on Stella this afternoon."

Dick flushed with pleasure.

"That's splendid, Aunt Margaret. I knew you were all right, you know. You put on a few frills at first, of course, but you are forgiven."

Mr. Hazlewood made so complete a picture of dismay that Dick could not but pity him. He went across to his father.

"Now, sir," he said, "let us hear this problem."

The old man was not proof against the invitation.

"You shall, Richard," he exclaimed. "You are the very man to hear it. Your aunt, Richard, is of too practical a mind for such speculations. It's a most curious problem. Hubbard quite failed to throw any light upon it. I myself am, I confess, bewildered. And I wonder if a fresh young mind can help us to a solution." He patted his son on the shoulder and then took him by the arm.

"The fresh young mind will have a go, father," said Dick. "Fire away."

"I was walking in the fields, my boy."

"Yes, sir, among the cows."

"Exactly, you put your finger on the very point. How is it, I asked myself——"

"That's quite your old style, father."

"Now isn't it, Richard, isn't it?" Mr. Hazlewood dropped Dick's arm. He warmed to his theme. He caught fire. He assumed the attitude of the orator. "How is it that with the advancement of science and the progress of civilization a cow gives no more milk to-day than she did at the beginning of the Christian era?"

With outspread arms he asked for an answer and the answer came.

"A fresh young mind can solve that problem in two shakes. It is because the laws of nature forbid. That's your trouble, father. That's the great drawback to sentimental enthusiasm. It's always up against the laws of nature."

"Dick," said Mrs. Pettifer, "by some extraordinary miracle you are gifted with common-sense. I am off." She went away in a hurricane as she had come, and it was time that she did go, for even while she was closing the door Stella Ballantyne came out from her cottage to cross the meadow. Dick was the first to hear the gate click as she unlatched it and passed into the

326

garden. He took a step towards the window, but his father interposed and for once with a real authority.

"No, Richard," he said, "Wait with us here. Mrs. Ballantyne has something to tell us."

"I thought so," said Dick quietly, and he came back to the other two men. "Let me understand." His face was grave but without anger or any confusion. "Stella returned here last night after I had taken her home?"

"Yes," said Thresk.

"To see you?"

"Yes."

"And my father came down and found you together?"

"Yes."

"I heard voices," Mr. Hazlewood hurriedly interposed, "and so naturally I came down."

Dick turned to his father.

"That's all right, father. I didn't think you were listening at the keyhole. I am not blaming anybody. I want to know exactly where we are—that's all."

Stella found the little group awaiting her, and standing up before them she told her story as she had told it last night to Thresk. She omitted nothing nor did she falter. She had trembled and cried for a great part of the night over the ordeal which lay before her, but now that she had come to it she was brave. Her composure indeed astonished Thresk and filled him with compassion. He knew that the very roots of her heart were bleeding. Only once or twice did she give any sign of what these few minutes were costing her. Her eyes strayed towards Dick Hazlewood's face in spite of herself, but she turned them away again with a wrench of her head and closed her eyelids lest she should hesitate and fail. All listened to her in silence, and it was strange to Thresk that the one man who seemed least concerned of the three was Dick Hazlewood himself. He watched Stella all the while she was speaking, but his face was a mask, not a gesture or movement gave a clue to his thoughts. When Stella had finished he asked composedly:

"Why didn't you tell me all this at the beginning, Stella?"

And now she turned to him in a burst of passion and remorse.

"Oh, Dick, I tried to tell you. I made up my mind so often that I would, but I never had the courage. I am terribly to blame. I hid it all from you—yes. But oh! you meant so much to me—you yourself, Dick. It wasn't your position. It wasn't what you brought with you, other people's friendship, other people's esteem. It was just you—you—you! I longed for you to want me, as I wanted you." Then she recovered herself and stopped. She was doing the very thing she had resolved not to do. She was pleading, she was

328

making excuses. She drew herself up and with a dignity which was quite pitiful she now pleaded against herself.

"But I don't ask for your pity. You mustn't be merciful. I don't *want* mercy, Dick. That's of no use to me. I want to know what you think—just what you really and truthfully think—that's all. I can stand alone—if I must. Oh yes, I can stand alone." And as Thresk stirred and moved, knowing well in what way she meant to stand alone, Stella turned her eyes full upon him in warning, nay, in menace. "I can stand alone quite easily, Dick. You mustn't think that I should suffer so very much. I shouldn't! I shouldn't——"

In spite of her control a sob broke from her throat and her bosom heaved; and then Dick Hazlewood went quietly to her side and took her hand.

"I didn't interrupt you, Stella. I wanted you to tell everything now, once for all, so that no one of us three need ever mention a word of it again."

Stella looked at Dick Hazlewood in wonder, and then a light broke over her face like the morning. His arm slipped about her waist and she leaned against him suddenly weak, almost to swooning. Mr. Hazlewood started up from his chair in consternation.

"But you heard her, Richard!"

"Yes, father, I heard her," he answered. "But you see Stella is my wife."

"Your——" Mr. Hazlewood's lips refused to speak

the word. He fell back again in his chair and dropped his face in his hands. "Oh, no!"

"It's true," said Dick. "I have rooms in London, you know. I went to London last week. Stella came up on Monday. It was my doing, my wish. Stella is my wife."

Mr. Hazlewood groaned aloud.

"But she has tricked you, Richard," and Stella agreed.

"Yes, I tricked you, Dick. I did," she said miserably, and she drew herself from his arm. But he caught her hand.

"No, you didn't." He led her over to his father. "That's where you both make your mistake. Stella tried to tell me something on the very night when we walked back from this house to her cottage and I asked her to marry me. She has tried again often during the last weeks. I knew very well what it was—before you turned against her, before I married her. She didn't trick me."

Mr. Hazlewood turned in despair to Henry Thresk. "What do you say?" he asked.

"That I am very glad you asked me here to give my advice on your collection," Thresk answered. "I was inclined yesterday to take a different view of your invitation. But I did what perhaps I may suggest that you should do: I accepted the situation."

He went across to Stella and took her hands.

THE VERDICT

"Oh, thank you," she cried, "thank you."

"And now"—Thresk turned to Dick—"if I might look at a *Bradshaw* I could find out the next train to London."

"Certainly," said Dick, and he went over to the writing-table. Stella and Henry Thresk were left alone for a moment.

"We shall see you again," she said. "Please!"

Thresk laughed.

"No doubt. I am not going out into the night. You know my address. If you don't ask Mr. Hazlewood. It's in King's Bench Walk, isn't it?" And he took the time-table from Dick Hazlewood's hand.

THE END